Mar

Marooned

S A Pavli

Copyright 2021 by S.A.Pavli
The rights of S A Pavli, identified as author, have been asserted by him in accordance with the Copyright, Design and Patents Act 1988.

All rights reserved. No part of this book may be used or reproduced by any means, graphic, electronic or mechanical, including photocopying, recording, taping or by any information retrieval system without the written permission of the author, except in the case of brief quotations embodied in articles or reviews.

To my good friend Chris Michael for all that he has done for us over the years S A Pavli

Other Books by the author

Space Scout

Sequels to 'Space Scout'

The Peacekeepers
The Makers

Others:

Worlds Apart
Virtual
The Inheritors
Alien Mind
Fantasy Universe
Sentinel
The Lost Colony
Stagecoach
Future Human
Interstellar Odyssey
Sirens
3001
The Dream Machine

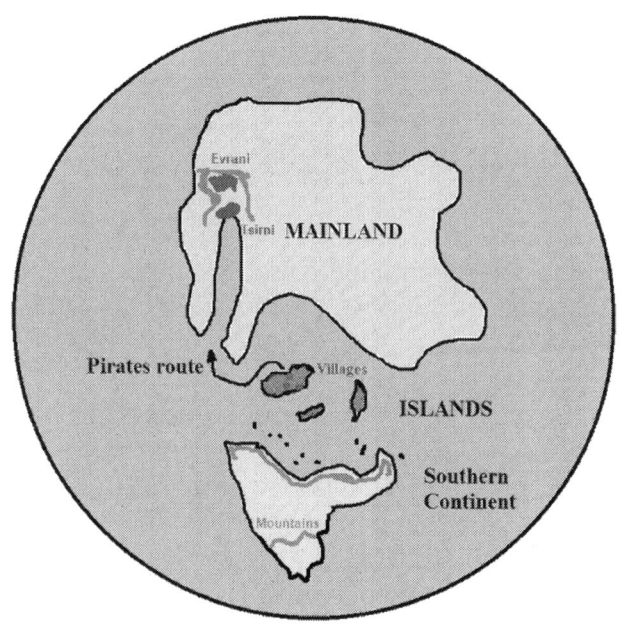

MAP OF ENLAI WORLD

Part 1
MAROONED

Chapter 1

"Capacitors fully charged, Hyperspace exit in ten seconds," my ship's AI announced in her velvety aristocratic English accent.

"Check, all systems green," I agreed. Flying a star ship is a totally automatic process under the control of the ship's AI. But we humans are allowed the face saving duty of 'double checking' the AI with our own separate instruments.

As the only human on board the Space Exploration Service scout ship *Aegina* I was the Captain and backup pilot, chief engineer, computer specialist, navigator and general dogs body. But I had no illusions; Gina, the ship's AI, short for *Aegina*, could quite happily do all those jobs!

Our destination was a 'G' type star six hundred light years from Earth. Giant planets had been detected orbiting the star with a trio of small rocky planets but I was not optimistic that we would hit the 'jackpot'. Habitable planets were incredibly rare; in four hundred years of interstellar exploring only two other habitable planets had been discovered. As a result, one 'man' Scout ships like *Aegina* were used to do the preliminary exploration of new star systems. This was cheaper and more effective than sending huge fully manned ships.

The countdown proceeded and on 'zero' I felt the ship shudder as the capacitors discharged their megawatts of energy into the HS switch. I felt the gut churning shock of the switch operating and then the main screen cleared to show the blaze of stars that was the physical universe.

"We are back baby," I said with relief. It did not matter how many times I made the trip, there was always tension when it came to the return back into the physical universe. My relief turned to shock when my control panel lit up with red and orange lights.

"Fuck, what's happened Gina?" I pressed buttons and examined my displays, desperately looking for the cause. Gina was silent, which was definitely a bad sign.

The indicators for the fusion generator were green and we were still on main power, which was a good start. The red and orange lights concerned the navigation computer. I brought up the status displays and examined them. The first line stated bluntly that the navigation computer did not know where we were.

"You are the navigation computer mate. You are not allowed to be lost," I protested punching buttons. "Gina, where are you girl?"

"One second Theo, I am investigating."

"I'll stay here then," I suggested. My examination of the navigation computers status displays was not encouraging. It was not just lost. In addition to not knowing where it was, it had no idea where it had come from or where it was supposed to be going to.

"You are a pathetic excuse for a navcomp," I told it. "Gina, perhaps we should re-boot the navcomp?"

"Theo, I do not wish to delete the history log. I am backing it up for examination before I re-boot the navcomp," replied Gina.

"Gina, the history log is backed up," I pointed out. "A copy is automatically taken."

"That has also failed," Gina replied.

"Ah. Good thing you checked." I knew that we had a replacement navcomp so for the time being I was not overly concerned. If we had arrived at the wrong place we should be able to determine where we were and either continue our journey or reluctantly return to Earth.

"While you are doing that I will go grab the backup navcomp in case it is needed." I unbuckled and floated out of the ship's flight deck and down the central corridor towards the store on deck five. *Aegina* consisted of a central spindle with six decks. Deck one was the Flight Deck. This contained all the controls and displays. A large wrap around screen displayed the exterior view, any comms transmissions and status displays. There was the Captain's seat and a co-pilot seat, currently unoccupied.

Decks two and three were engineering, for replacement parts and special machinery. It was also the home of a number of specialized engineering robots. Deck four was the home of the Captain. It had two rooms, the bedroom with its washing facilities and the mess and lounge area. Decks five was for stores. Deck six held the three specialized exploration robots.

The exterior of *Aegina* was bracketed by huge water cylinders and the atmosphere shuttle used to land on planets suitable for exploration.

I knew that the backup navcomp was in the engineering store on deck two. When I arrived I asked Gina for the exact location which she specified as row 'B' location 12.

Location B12 was empty.

"Gina, location B12 is empty." There was a pause, which meant Gina executed a few million instructions doing something or other before replying.

"That is the only location I have for the replacement navcomp."

"I will look around the store in case it has been misplaced," I suggested.

My 'look around' became an extended search

through the whole store on deck two then deck three with no result.

"This is not looking good Gina. How is the re-boot going?"

"Nearly complete Theo, coming on line now."

I was still not particularly worried. If the re-boot did not fix the navcomp Gina could take sightings and fix our position in the galaxy. She knew exactly where Sol was in relation to the galaxy hub and a number of 'landmarks'. We could head there with a series of jumps until we had a precise fix.

"Meanwhile, are we near any system Gina?" I was heading back to the Flight Deck.

"Unfortunately we have not arrived at our destination," replied Gina, "But fortunately," she added quickly, "Yes, there is a sun within a few minutes jump. I am taking sightings."

"If we can't explore our official destination we can take a look at that, if it looks interesting," I suggested.

"Let's see where we are first. Navcomp is on line."

I took my seat and examined the display. It did not look promising.

"Not telling us much." I prodded a few buttons and entered an enquiry. The navcomp stubbornly refused to answer.

I began to worry. Suddenly Space seemed a very big place. The magic of Hyperspace made it seem a few days trip from one star to another, masking the actual mind numbing distances. The Earth was not even a needle in a haystack; it was a needle in a million haystacks!

Gina confirmed that our navcomp was terminally faulty and we had a discussion to decide what to do. I learned that it would take Gina some hours to make the scans and calculations that would confirm where we were and calculate a series of jumps to allow us to return to Earth. Meanwhile I suggested that I attempt a repair of the navcomp.

I had a snack and a coffee in my quarters before testing the navcomp. My bedroom was a cell barely three yards by three. The kitchen was a cubbyhole with a giant freezer, a water dispenser, microwave heater and coffee machine. The relaxation area had a small table and two chairs bolted to the floor with a big screen on one wall.

It was hardly cozy. My current girlfriend Tanya had contributed a small potted plant, the name of which I had forgotten. Secured in the centre of the table it contributed a splash of color against the ubiquitous white, pale grey and pastel beige of the walls and floor.

After my snack I returned to the Flight Deck and after powering off the navcomp I removed the main processor board and took it to the engineering deck. I connected it to the test rig and selected the appropriate test program. It took a few minutes to inform me that just about nothing worked on the board. A close examination revealed a hairline crack from one end of the printed circuit to the other. How it had ever worked was a mystery. It was beyond repair.

It remained for us to decide whether to begin our return home or take a few days to investigate the nearby system.

"Gina, what say we have a look and see if there are any interesting planets," I suggested. "If they are all barren we won't bother to go and look."

"I have made some preliminary scans of the system," she said. "There is a rocky planet in the habitable zone, a little smaller than Earth."

"That's promising. Let's go take a look."

Preparations for the jump took a few minutes. Gina would carry out the jump 'manually' by setting up the destination parameters into the Hyperspace Switch instead of using the defunct navcomp.

We were in and out of Hyperspace in a few minutes and the screen showed the planet as a small blue dot. Gina increased magnification.

"Very Earth like," I remarked.

"Instruments are showing Earth like atmosphere with low carbon dioxide and twenty three percent oxygen. There are also profuse signs of life."

"Whoa! Profuse signs of life?"

"Thick vegetation and seas."

"Right." I knew that signs of animal life on the planet would not be visible at this distance, but if there was vegetation there would almost certainly be animal life.

"Let's take a closer look."

We would have to 'motor' the last few million miles by rocket; using the hyperspace switch close to the planet's gravity well was not possible. Which meant, ironically, the last million miles would take ten times as long as the previous one hundred million.

Time for a nap I told myself.

Chapter 2

My nap became a good sleep. I awoke and had breakfast then floated up to the Flight Deck to see what was happening. Gina anticipated me and lit up the screen with a view of the planet. It was a blue and white orb almost identical to Earth, except for the shape of the continents. Ratio of sea to land looked greater, the land mass being restricted to a couple of continents around the equator. One continent was a long strip horizontal to the equator and the other was horseshoe shaped but mostly in the southern half of the planet. The middle of the horseshoe was dotted with islands.

"Beautiful looking planet, looks like it is eighty percent ocean."

"You are correct Theo. Eighty-six percent ocean. The equatorial landmass is temperate. The southern land mass is sub tropical. The islands have a Mediterranean climate."

"Animal life?" I asked.

"Very rich in animal life. And there are signs of intelligent life."

"Intelligent life?" I jerked up in disbelief. We had not yet encountered any intelligent life in the cosmos. Our only Earth like planet had lots of vegetation but very primitive animal life, insects and 'creepy crawlies'.

"How intelligent?"

"There are many primitive villages on the northern continent as well as on the islands and the coasts."

"Villages? Fuck me, this will shock everyone back home. Can I see the pics?"

"They are very fuzzy for now," said Gina. The screen

changed to show twenty or so grey and white blobs surrounded by green forest. They were in a rough circle with a square grey patch in the centre.

"Blimey, a village with a village green," I remarked. "Well, a village square. It's not very green."

As we got closer the pictures became clearer. The 'horseshoe' continent was well populated with villages particularly in the islands and around the inside the horseshoe. But I was waiting to see what the inhabitants looked like.

Aegina slipped into a high orbit and then gradually descended lower. The village houses became real instead of abstract blobs. They were made of tree trunks bound together and then sealed with mud. It was very primitive, I guessed Iron Age human. The inhabitants turned from pale blobs into pale insects and then two legged creatures.

Gina enhanced the images and displayed them. They were amazingly human; two arms and two legs and a head with two eyes a nose and a mouth. Gina calculated their height to be very close to ours. A close up of the face revealed pointy elf like ears, a furry covering instead of hair, big round eyes and fleshy lips with high cheekbones. Otherwise their bodies looked totally human. They wore simple clothing, fur garments belted or with a broad waistband.

"That's amazing. How can they be so similar to us?" I asked.

"Perhaps because their planet is so similar to Earth?" she suggested.

"This is going to cause a sensation back home."

There was no question of us landing of course, our orders were clear; collect the evidence and return. It would be up to the powers that be to determine what happened after that. I suspected that there would be great reluctance to contact the natives. Their stage of development was such that they would not be able to understand who or what we were or where we had come from. The danger was that we could interfere with the development of their civilization causing massive culture shock.

The ship was in a synchronous orbit over the horseshoe continent and we gradually acquired more and more detailed pictures and video of the natives.

We spent the next few hours collecting evidence. I would have loved to land and have a swim in the blue waters of the horseshoe bay. This was a planet without any industry; un-spoilt virgin forests and crystal clear oceans.

It seemed appropriate to briefly explore the other planets of the system before heading home. I waved goodbye to the beautiful world and strapped myself into my Captain's chair while Gina started the countdown.

There was one more rocky planet very close to the sun but we decided to ignore that. It seemed to be a copy of Mercury. There were also three giant planets, again copies of our own giant planets. But they had many moons and they were more interesting than the planets, often having oceans of water and even aquatic life.

"Engaging Hyperdrive," announced Gina.

There was a thud which shook the ship and the lights went out.

"Jesus what now!" My guts clenched with fear. I fought to ignore that and focus on my console displays which were still active. The displays for the Hyperdrive were red or blinking. The emergency lights came on making it easier to see what I was doing. The screen was still showing the planet; we had not jumped into Hyperspace.

The Hyperspace Drive coils were all showing an

overload except for two, which were black. That meant they were dead or shorted. *Must be shorted* I thought. That would explain the overload. If that was the case then, without the HS switch, we were going nowhere.

"Theo, the HS switch has overloaded and the main circuit breakers have dropped out," announced Gina. "I am resetting them now."

At least we still had power I thought. The SES would send a rescue ship to our destination if we did not return in time. *But we would not be there.*

The ship's power would last forever, but not the food or water. Could I land on the planet and gather food and water? I would not want to spend the rest of my days inside the claustrophobic environment of my star ship.

I groaned and collapsed forward, my head in my arms. Visions and memories of my parents, my brother and sister and my friends passed before my minds eye. And the beautiful Tanya with her happy personality and dimpled smile.

Stop feeling sorry for yourself Theo I told myself *you are still alive, for now!*

"Gina, there is no chance of fixing the HS switch I suppose?"

"No Theo. The windings are sealed inside a non-conducting medium. They cannot be repaired."

"Has this happened before?" I asked.

"Yes. One ship failed to return but was found at the correct location. Like us its HS coil had burnt out. Other ships have been lost and never found. It is possible they were marooned in Hyperspace."

"I guess I should consider myself lucky then. I could have been marooned in Hyperspace. Instead I have a beautiful planet to explore."

"Captain, it is forbidden to make contact with an intelligent species."

"When we return you can report me to the SES authorities," I said, then I felt sorry for my rudeness. "It's okay Gina, we will find a nice spot somewhere private where we can avoid all contact with the natives. Just you and me. Okay?"

"I am not sure I can trust you. The native females look very human."

I could not help laughing at her quip. "Gina, you malign me. Inter-species sex is not my thing." Then I could not help thinking how right Gina was. They *did* look very human.

"That is exactly my point," said Gina, as if reading my mind.

"Seriously Gina, I can't spend the rest of my days stuck here in this star ship. I will go stir crazy, even with your delightful company."

"I understand Theo. Let us consider about how best to solve the problem. Examine the geography of the planet and pick a place to live. Also consider what you need to take with you to survive."

"I have no desire to be Robinson Crusoe," I said. "How am I going to feed myself?"

"You can use the ship's exploration robots to help you."

"Can they be re-programmed to do that? I mean, dig the ground and plant crops?"

"Yes, they have a mode that allows them to learn new tasks. It should not be beyond them to master digging, planting and watering."

"Right. From star ship Captain to dirt farmer. What about you Gina?"

"I will be busy gathering and classifying information about the planet and advising you. Also remember that if you get into any trouble you will have the shuttle and the ship's robots to help you."

"It's a shame you do not have a beautiful android body," I said wistfully. "You can join me on the planet and keep me company."

"I am a star ship AI, not a sex droid."

"Just thinking of the company," I said. *Mostly,* I thought.

Chapter 3

It took us some days to explore the planet more thoroughly and make a decision about my new home. Eventually I decided on a small island in the horseshoe gulf. It was occupied; there were two villages on one side of the island and one village on the other side. There was a range of low mountains in between the east and west of the island which would provide some isolation although access was still possible by sea.

There was also a location hidden from the sea that we could hide the shuttle. It seemed sensible for me to live in the shuttle at first, eating my stock of food from the ship until my farming, hunting or fishing efforts achieved success. I was more inclined towards fishing than hunting; cleaning a fish seemed a much simpler and agreeable process than butchering a dead animal. I was beginning to realize that despite being an explorer I was not cut out to be the survival type.

The ship contained a small motorized plastic dinghy to be used for field trips over water. It was an item of equipment I had never used but could be useful now for fishing trips.

Self defense was another issue. On field trips I always carried a small pistol which fired tiny explosive bullets. It was quite deadly and could kill a dinosaur, if I ever met a dinosaur. My two exploration robots, who I called Tweedledee and Tweedledum, or Dee and Dum for short, were also armed. Those two fearsome insect like individuals were designed to collect samples of the environment and could operate quite happily in vacuum or poisonous atmospheres.

I began to move tools, equipment and supplies into the shuttle, including the dinghy. But I was in no rush to begin my life as Robinson Crusoe. I was hoping for some kind of miracle, for the HS switch to magically fix itself. I am a self contained individual, happy with my own company and the restricted environment of the ship. I had a limitless supply of entertainment but not a limitless supply of food. And eventually even I would become bored and restless, particularly with a beautiful world to explore beneath my feet.

On the ground and living in the shuttle, I would be in continuous contact with Gina as well as safe from any predators or poisonous snakes. A luxury the original Robinson Crusoe never had!

After a couple of weeks the shuttle was loaded with everything I could think of. It could return at any time to collect more food from the ship when I ran out. There was no reason to delay my departure but I was oddly reluctant to leave the comfort, safety and familiarity of my ship. It was my womb, my home from Earth, my link to my family and friends. For the first time I felt distress, real pain and misery.

But staying in the ship and drowning in my self pity seemed a pointless and pathetic way to behave. I decided it was time to go.

Aegina's shuttle was attached to the exterior of the ship and entered via a common air lock. The shuttle was tiny, but was designed to accommodate the lone explorer on the ground. It had a cubicle for sleeping and toilet/bathroom facilities as well as a kitchen/relaxation area.

I entered the small cockpit and took the pilot's seat. I had already checked out the shuttle's systems so it was just a case of going through the power up sequence. This took a few minutes with all indicators green.

"Ready to detach Gina."

"Stand by, clamps released in three, two one."

I felt the thump as the clamps released and then the lurch as the shuttle floated free. I used the maneuvering jets to push the shuttle clear of *Aegina* and then waited for the fusion rockets to warm up. That took a few minutes, then, using the maneuvering jets I moved the shuttle well clear of Aegina. Before re-entering the atmosphere I had to do a full check of the engines.

"So long Gina. Look after yourself while I am away."

"Do stay in touch Theo."

"Very funny." I grinned. Gina did have an understanding of humor and sometimes managed the odd amusing quip.

I applied power and accelerated away from *Aegina*. The engines responded normally but I gave them a good blast just to make sure. I had become a little nervous recently.

Once I was confident that the engines were operating normally I eased off the power and used the maneuvering rockets again to turn the shuttle around until she was facing backwards.

"See you downstairs Gina." I switched to automatic and Gina took over. I could have continued to fly the shuttle and bring it in to land but Gina would do it more efficiently. The rockets came on to slow the craft and *Aegina* rapidly disappeared from the view screen.

At the right point she throttled back the main engines and then turned the shuttle to face forward. Soon the first sound of atmosphere on the wings began as we were transformed from a Space ship to an aircraft.

Our destination was still three thousand miles away but the shuttle's speed was twice that. Speed scrubbed off until we were subsonic and I took the controls back. Beneath me the sea was a shining azure. I was reminded of Homer's description of the 'wine dark sea'. An odd expression since the sea was never the color of wine. But somehow, the phrase resonates in the imagination. Perhaps it was the quality, not the color I told myself, particularly after one had drunk half the bottle!

But this was an alien sea, one that Homer could never have seen or imagined. Islands appeared beneath like jewels scattered by a careless God into the foamy seas. My island was not far from the mainland. The autopilot was set so I let it do its work. We were now flying very low and slow with the engines switching from horizontal to vertical thrust. Beneath was a sandy coast. The aircraft ran parallel with the coast until we arrived at a range of low mountains. It maneuvered over a low hill and then settled behind it, hidden from the sea. With a gentle thump we were down and the hum of the engines subsided.

"Welcome to your new home Theo Pallas," I muttered. "Hope the neighbors are nice."

I peered out of the cockpit window at a green and rugged scene. The shuttle had landed in the lee of a grassy knoll. A small stream wound through low hills from the low mountains and down towards the sea. Gnarled bushes dotted the landscape on the lower slopes and gave way to low chunky trees climbing up into the hills. It was very pretty and very Earth like.

But before I could enjoy my new habitat I had to go through the tedium of acclimatization. This involved taking samples of the local biology, isolating bacteria and viruses and checking that they did not want to kill me and my own viruses/bacteria did not want to kill them. If so then my magic medical machinery would develop vaccinations against them. That was the theory. Unless my viruses or bacteria were inimical to the local biology; in which case I would not be able to live on the planet. I could not risk starting a pandemic and wiping out all living things on the planet. As a rule, if the planet was safe for me then I would be safe for the planet.

I left the cockpit and went to the equipment room next to the airlock. There I found the protective suit, white with a glass bubble helmet, and struggled into it. I collected the box for the samples and accompanied by my two exploration robots entered the airlock.

Dum and Dee were a scary pair at first acquaintance. Waist high to a man they were like giant insects with arms. Their large heads contained shiny red orbs and a black speaker grill. Their job was to collect and store samples of the environment and to defend me against any predators we may find. So far, that had been totally academic but may now be needed for the first time.

Dum had a big 'U' on his side and Dee had a big 'E'. The airlock was crowded with the three of us. We exited onto green grass.

"Dum, take a sample of the grass," I ordered.

"Yes Captain," it replied in its deep artificial voice.

"With a bit of luck it may be edible. I can become a herbivore. Mooo."

I strolled down the hill towards the stream, giving the robots time to collect their samples. It was a substantial stream, fifteen or so feet in width and four or five feet in depth at the centre. The flow of water was strong and the water looked clear. I even spotted some fish.

"Lunch," I muttered.

Dee took a few samples of the water. The robot then waded into the stream and quick as a flash grabbed a fish and stored it.

"With you guys around I definitely won't starve," I remarked.

We made our way slowly around the hill towards the sea. The stream opened out and became shallower before joining the sea. It was a very pretty sandy beach, twenty or thirty yards wide and stretching into the distance in both directions.

"Holiday hotel there and there, swimming pools there and there and a row of cafes and bars over there," I said pointing out the locations. "Quality resort of course, no common layabouts allowed."

Having sorted out my future plans to become a holiday entrepreneur I ordered the robots to take samples of the sea water and some seaweed and other plants. A crab like creature scuttled in front of me and I grabbed it, giving it to Dum to store.

I strolled along the beach admiring the beauty of the scene while my robots gathered seaweed, insects and any plants on the edges of the sand. I was looking forward to discarding my protective clothing and going in for a swim.

"Good start guys, let's head back," I said to the robots. "Tomorrow we can head up the hill towards the mountains."

We returned to the shuttle and stored our samples. I loaded up my analyzing instruments and put them under Gina's control to begin the chemical and biological analysis of our samples before preparing my evening meal and relaxing.

I could watch a movie from the ship's library or read a book but I was physically tired from the hours of physical activity. And in any case, how could I be distracted by fantasy I asked myself when I was experiencing something no other Human had experienced; the exploration of a new inhabited world.

The Human species was expanding exponentially into Space. There was surely a good possibility of rescue in the future I told myself. I retired to sleep with that positive thought.

The next day we headed in the other direction, up into the hills and the lower slopes of the mountains. It was rich with vegetation and trees. We also spotted flocks of birds and the odd rabbit like creature. Dum and Dee loaded up with lots of samples.

Late in the afternoon we were high up in the mountains and the trees began to get sparser. The going also became more difficult and I decided to call it a day. I was no mountain climber and had no desire to become one. The view was spectacular and I took out my binoculars and scanned the area. As my view wandered over the sea I spotted something moving. I adjusted the power to reveal a small wooden boat. It had oars and a primitive sail and I could see three individuals leaning over the side. They were clearly fishing, one with a spear and the other two with nets.

"Bugger, there goes my privacy. Gina do you see that?" Gina was permanently connected in one way or another, usually through the robots but also through my comms unit which was permanently attached to my belt. The binoculars also had a comms feed.

"I see them Theo. Three individuals fishing in a small boat."

"Looks like I have to careful when going swimming or fishing."

"We can install some surveillance cameras on the beach," she suggested.

"If they decide to stop off on the beach for a fish barbecue I will have to join them," I remarked.

"You can't resist food and drink in general," responded Gina.

"I have a very fast metabolism."

Gina made no response to that.

I watched the fishing boat for a while until it

disappeared around the bay. It was late and we made our way back to the shuttle. It appeared that my privacy was not going to be so secure after all. On the one hand I was concerned about interfering in the affairs of an alien civilization, but on the other hand I was secretly pleased at the possibility of having company.

It took a few days to carry out our analysis of all the samples and test them for possible harm. It appeared that the local bugs were totally baffled by Earth organisms and avoided all contact, and the opposite also applied. It would therefore be safe for me to go unprotected. The plant growths and animals also contained the same proteins and carbohydrates as Earth so they would be safe and nourishing for me to eat.

The same results had been obtained in the other habitable planet discovered and settled by Humans. It appeared that nature in our universe had only one way of creating life. The same elements made the same living structures everywhere. Very convenient, thank you God!

I installed a number of surveillance cameras on the rocks above the beach as suggested by Gina before venturing out into the sea.

Going out without the protective clothing was a pleasure but I was careful in the sea, staying in the shallows at first. Being eaten by the planet's equivalent of a shark would be a humiliating failure for an explorer. I wanted to go out in the dinghy and explore the ocean first before swimming unprotected into the deep.

It is remarkable how the new and incredible soon becomes everyday. After a few weeks I had settled into a routine. I became brown and fit from swimming and tramping the hills and lower mountains with my two trusty robot friends. They were not much for conversation but if I wanted that I could wake up Gina for a chat.

I augmented my food supply with fish and a few fruit and vegetables that we gathered from the hills. It appeared I may not need to take up farming after all. I could not resist building a barbecue to cook my fish; it was a bit makeshift but did the job. Gina was concerned that smoke from my fire would be smelled by the locals but I chose to ignore her warning.

I also constructed a three sided shelter with no roof so that I could sleep out under the stars occasionally. I was never much into open air stuff; you have to be a bit of a studious type to become a scout for the SES. There are usually not many opportunities to camp out on alien planets! But sleeping under the stars was in no way onerous. As marooned sailors go I had a very comfortable life.

The shock came after about twelve weeks. After going fishing in my dinghy in the morning and getting a good catch I decided to light my BBQ. I had constructed a rough table and moved out one of the shuttle's chairs. Fish nicely cooked I settled down to enjoy my food. I was thinking that a glass of white wine would go well with my fish and I should try my hand at wine making, when I heard a falling rock. I looked up the hill to see three natives peering at me from the top of the hill. They had clearly come in from the sea and smelling my BBQ had come to investigate. I should have been checking my surveillance cameras I belatedly told myself.

Their eyes took in the aircraft and their mouths dropped open. Then my two robots leapt up and bounded between me and the intruders. One sight of the robots was more than enough and with screams of terror they fled down the hill and disappeared.

"Fuck, that's torn it." I expected Gina to say *'I told*

you so' but she was too polite. I opened my tablet and dialed up the displays from my surveillance cameras. Camera 3 showed the natives galloping down the hill towards the sea throwing terrified looks behind them. Camera 2 showed their wooden fishing boat floating some yards out with an anchor over the side.

"Oh well, they are so terrified they will keep well away from here in future," I said.

Chapter 4

When the fishermen came back with the story about the god who had landed on the shore on a giant silver bird, Salny was incredulous and amused. She had little respect for Yovna the Mahik, who lit his fire and rattled his twigs and rocks and chanted his incantations. When he then declared that it was a visit from the Sky God Vulious and they must send a gift to placate the god she thought he was being ridiculous.

"Let's take the boat around the shore and find this so called god," she suggested to her brother Lons. He was her oldest brother and was held in esteem as a promising warrior and hunter although he preferred fishing.

"Salny, why must you always be the odd one out," he said. "Why must you always show contempt for our customs?"

"It's not our customs that I am contemptuous of, it is the people who use them to make us do what they want. Like Yovna, who is a parasite and wants us all to feed him while he does nothing. And every time he comes near me he tries to touch my bottom."

Lons grunted and made a face.

"He is a disgusting individual. But he is the holy man and has the ear of the chief and the elders."

"Why are gods always bad? If we don't do what they say they always do bad things to us. Why not reward us to do good?"

"Salny, you always ask difficult questions. You are a woman, it is not your place to question everything. You are already in trouble with the elders. They found you a husband and you rejected him. You are the most difficult female in the village."

"Tarsik is ugly and he smells."

"He is Panstrosh's brother so you have made an enemy of the village chief and his family. But he is ugly and you are the best looking female in the village, even if you are my sister."

"I take after you big brother."

He grinned and punched her on the shoulder.

"You take after mother. She was also the best looking female in the village. And the most difficult."

"Yes. I miss her." The loss of her mother had devastated Salny. She had died when giving birth to her third child when Salny was thirteen. It was six years ago now but the memory of that loss had not faded and never would. Her mother had not just been her mother but also her friend and confident. It had been a relationship no other girls in the village had with their mothers.

"So we all have to give gifts to this god? Probably Panstrosh and his friends will steal all the gifts." Salny looked contemptuous.

"No I think they are serious about this god. The three fishermen were terrified and they all give the same story. The silver bird was huge, as big as four huts with giant wings."

"Did they see the god himself?"

"Yes, he was like us. But he had two giant creatures guarding him. Insects bigger than a srenich."

"The god was like us?"

"Yes. When gods come down to the world they assume any shape they like. Sometimes the shape of animals, sometimes of mortals."

"Why do they do that?"

"To fool us. They like to mate with females. Usually the best looking virgin they can find." He was smirking at her.

"Shut up Lons, that's not funny!" Salny said pushing him away.

"It's okay, they won't send you. Tarsik wants you for himself."

"He can whistle."

They were sitting outside the family home and Salny was preparing the evening meal. Lons and his brother had gone hunting and bagged two fat birds which Salny was plucking and cleaning.

Salny often went hunting with her brothers and was proud of her skill with the bow. But she particularly enjoyed fishing. Her uncle owned a small canoe and she would fight with her brothers to go fishing with him. She was also a strong swimmer, which was unheard of for females. Women never went swimming and she would create gossip when she did. But she cared less for their gossip.

She finished the birds and washed them with water from the stream then wrapped them in two layers of the thick leaves from the lamnan tree. They would cook on the coals without burning and the leaves would keep the meat moist.

She was finishing when she saw Tarsik with three other men coming from the path that led to the sea. They came over to their hut.

"You are wanted by the elders down on the beach." Tarsik scowled at her.

"Me? Why do they want me?" Salny felt a surge of fear.

"They will tell you when you get there," Tarsik said. The other three spread out to surround her. Lons pushed forward and faced Tarsik.

"What is this Tarsik? You can't just take my sister."

The three men pulled out their swords threateningly.

"She is wanted on the beach where they are preparing the gifts for the god. I do not know why."

Tarsik looked surly and hostile.

"I will come with you," said Lons.

"Please yourself." Tarsik turned to leave and one of the three guards pushed Salny forward. She glared at him before reluctantly following Tarsik.

As she followed Tarsik, Salny began to have an increasing feeling of dread. Her brother's words uttered in jest reverberated in her mind sending shivers of horror through her. She tried to stiffen her muscles and walk straight and with a firm stride.

I will not show any fear she said to herself, but her body was betraying her.

On the beach they were preparing one of the fishing catamarans, loading it with jugs and containers of food. Her uncle came over.

"Uncle, what is happening? What do they want me for?"

"My girl, the council has bestowed a great honor upon our family," he began.

"I do not want their honor," blurted Salny.

"You will go to meet the god. I am sure he will shower his love upon you and reward us all."

Salny was seized by a horror she could not control and found herself sobbing with terror.

"Please Uncle, do not let them do this to me," she begged between sobs.

"Do not be afraid. Vulious is a benign god. He will not harm you," he said.

"You do not know that. You cannot believe the words of this... liar and pretender." She pointed to Yovna, who stood stooped on one side, his gaze on the ground, his face fixed.

Lons stepped forward to stand next to his sister and pulled out his sword.

"Anyone who takes my sister will have to take me first," he hissed, crouching, his blade held ready.

A forest of swords were taken from their scabbards.

"No, Lons!" cried Salny. "There is no reason for you to die also. I will go quietly. Perhaps Vulious is a benign god. If so I hope he curses you all. Except for my brother."

She turned and embraced her brother.

"Wait for me, I will return," then stepped forward. "I am ready."

Chapter 5

The idea that the fishermen had been so terrified they would keep away was wishful thinking on my part, although not unreasonable. After all I asked myself, why should they return to a place that housed a giant monster and its attendant smaller monsters? I had forgotten that primitive societies are not ruled by reason but by superstition.

Five days later I was alerted by Gina that she had detected movement on the surveillance cameras. I switched them on to see an armada of small boats sailing towards our beach. They moored close to the shore and a number of individuals got out. They took out a pallet from one boat and then trays of what appeared to be fruit and vegetables and the carcass of a small animal. They placed the trays on the pallet and carried it up the beach. They left the pallet on a large flat rock at the top of the beach.

Then to my horror they manhandled a female out of one of the boats and carried her roughly up the beach. They placed a stake into the sand and tied the female to the stake. At last it dawned on me what they were doing.

"Dear god they are offering up gifts to us. They must think the shuttle is a giant bird and the robots its servants." Then an even more horrifying thought occurred to me. "Gina, they are not going to sacrifice the female are they?"

"I cannot see any knives or weapons," she replied.

"I am taking my gun and going there. I won't let them sacrifice her."

"Theo, do not reveal yourself until we know what their intentions are."

"Okay. Leave Dum and Dee here for now. We don't want to terrify them."

"I suggest that horse has bolted," she replied.

Gina *was* developing a sense of humor I decided.

I retrieved my pistol and headed around the hill towards the beach. As I turned the corner and caught sight of the natives Gina informed me that they were leaving. I waited for them to board their boats and get well out to sea before continuing down to the beach.

As I got close to the female I examined her with interest. We had only seen the natives at long range so far and got a slightly fuzzy view of their appearance. Close up I thought her appearance was remarkably human even though she obviously was not human. She was tall and slender with a warm brown skin. Her pointy ears were the most alien thing about her. Her face had an alien beauty, its proportions not quite human, with a broad high forehead, her head covered in thick fluffy auburn hair with huge dark eyes, a slim nose with full plump lips. She was wearing a long white silky gown with colorful embroidery. I could see that she had two breasts under the gown. He dress stretched across shapely hips and long well muscled thighs.

She was tied to a stake and she looked terrified, her eyes huge her mouth gaping open. As I approached she started gasping and moaning in terror.

"It is okay love, no need to be frightened." I spoke quietly and reassuringly; at least I hoped it sounded reassuring. I held my arms apart, hands open to show I was carrying no weapons. I walked past her to the pallet and examined its contents. It was food, a selection of meats vegetables and fruit. I groaned in frustration at what I had done.

"Offerings to the gods, food and a sacrificial virgin. Probably started a new religion," I muttered in disgust. I went back to the female and had a look at her bindings.

"Look, I am going to undo the ropes okay?" I pointed to the ropes and made a sign to show I was undoing them. She was shuddering with fear and crying, tears running down her cheeks. I tried to make reassuring signs and noises as I undid her bonds. When the last one came off she lurched away from me, running up the hill. But she was unable to climb it, her feet scrabbling in the sand.

I felt distress and pity for the poor girl. I went over to the food and picked up a fruit.

"Look, don't worry. You can have this. I won't hurt you." I did not know what to say so I said whatever came into my head. I squatted down next to the food and waved her over. She was sneaking around me with the hill at her back clearly thinking about making a break for it.

I took a bite of the fruit and made a face to say how tasty it was. But the fruit was disgusting and with a gasp I spat it out.

"Whoa man, this is shit!" I exclaimed throwing the fruit into the sand and spitting out the mouthful. I looked down at the pallet but there was nothing familiar on it. I looked up at the female, shook my head and spread my arms in confusion. "Anything here edible?" I asked poking at the other goods on the pallet. She was looking at me cautiously now, her face strained, her body still poised for flight.

I picked up another fruit and waved it at her questioningly.

"Uh? Yes?" I pointed to my mouth and the fruit. She still looked terrified but she nodded cautiously.

"Aha!" I gave an exaggerated smile of pleasure and took a bite out of the fruit, which looked like a large plum. It was rather good and I nodded my approval and continued to eat. I waved her over to join me but she suddenly fell to her knees, put her head down and started crying and speaking at the same time.

Probably begging not to be eaten or raped or killed I guessed.

I stood and made what I hoped were placating gestures, nodding and smiling. I backed away from the food pallet and made a gesture to show it was hers. Then I turned and started walking away, back up the beach.

I got about twenty yards up the beach before the female called to me. I stopped and turned around but remained where I was.

"Insanta. Con sa rema halny teka," she shouted. I shook my head then my hand to show I did not understand then pointed out to sea. I made waving gestures to show far, far out to sea.

"Oulana penta kan?" She was asking me something. I guessed 'where is your boat?'

I pointed up the hill and made a gesture with both hands to show something big.

She gaped at me, her face showing disbelief. She held out both arms and flapped them like a bird.

"Penta kan sa boula?"

I guessed 'your boat is a bird?" and I nodded.

"Con sa rona Insanta?"

"Yes baby, I am not a God." I grinned and nodded. "And you are one smart cookie." I waved at her and pointed up the hill. She looked awed and went down on her knees again, her head down on the sand.

Oh shit, if my boat is a bird then she must think I am definitely a god. I groaned in frustration.

I went over to her, stopped a few feet away and held out a hand. "Penta kan." I pointed up the hill and nodded amiably. She stood and when I turned and walked up the hill she followed.

"Gina, can you ask Dum and Dee to go inside the ship. I think she is not ready to meet them yet."

"Yes Theo. Good work by the way. You handled that very sensitively."

"Thanks Gina. That's me, mister sensitive." I couldn't be sure but I may have heard a snort of derision from my AI. Nevertheless I felt a stab of painful emotion at what the poor native female was going through because of my selfishness.

When we came around the hill and she caught sight of the shuttle she gave a moan of terror and froze in her tracks.

"It's okay. Penta kan, penta kan," I repeated. I continued walking confidently towards the shuttle. She held back but I continued to the aircraft and when I reached it I picked up a rock and banged it against the metal. She looked from me to the shuttle and then back again, her eyes wide with amazement.

She cautiously approached the aircraft and touched the metal, then banged it with her fist. I smiled encouragingly and she smiled back tremulously. I was pleased to see she was getting over her terror. I could imagine how the poor creature must have been feeling, being abandoned to the whims of an unknown god.

Seeing her close up she appeared very young almost juvenile. *Poor little thing.* History repeating itself across the Universe. It was depressing!

But I now had some difficult problems to solve. Firstly, what to do with the female. How was she going to react to the robots? Should I return her to her people? How do I discourage them from any further such activities?

My plan to live in isolation in order not to interfere with the indigenous population's development had failed. I must think carefully how to proceed in order to cause minimum further damage and if possible, to repair what damage I had already done. It seemed a tall order.

Firstly, how to introduce her to Dee and Dum? I had an idea. I went over to the young female and held out a hand. She looked at me then hesitantly reached out and took my hand. Her hand was slender and warm in mine. I gently led her to my external dining table and indicated that she should sit on the chair. She perched nervously on it her eyes on me. I made a sign that I would fetch food and drink and indicated the aircraft, then walked over to the airlock. I made motions to her to indicate that she should stay seated, then entered the aircraft and quickly went to my kitchen. I retrieved a glass and made her an orange juice then found a sweet granola bar.

Back outside she was still seated on the chair her eyes fixed fearfully on the airlock entrance. *Probably thinking I had been eaten by the beast* I thought. She looked relieved when I stepped out of the airlock. I carried the orange juice and granola bar to her and put them on the table. I tore open the granola bar and showed it to her then broke off a piece which I ate. I then took a sip of the orange juice. Smiling I invited her to try them.

She picked up the orange juice and took a nervous sip. To my relief she smiled and nodded her approval. She took a bite of the granola bar and her face showed her pleasure. I smiled back approvingly.

One step at a time I thought. I waited for her to finish the granola bar and the orange juice. She wolfed them down, clearly hungry.

I pulled out my tablet and switched on the screen.

"Gina, display a picture of a small village on Earth." When the picture appeared I placed the tablet in front of her. Her eyes went wide when she saw the picture and she looked at me in amazement.

I thumped my chest and pointed to the picture.

"Gina, zoom in and show a street with traffic moving around. Then show airplanes taking off and landing with people getting in and out."

Gina obliged and I allowed the girl to get used to what she was seeing.

When she had seen a good selection of Earth scenes I again asked Gina to change the view.

"Gina, show some video of our two robots doing some normal chores. Loading and unloading stuff, and working with humans. I want her to understand that they are not animals that will attack her."

"I'll see what I can find." Gina's voice came directly into my ear implant so the girl could not hear.

The girl gasped when she saw the robots and clutched the table nervously. I patted her on the shoulder reassuringly. She watched the screen in fascination. I pointed to the robots on the screen then pointed to the aircraft, walking over and banging on the metal.

Would she understand that they were machines? Could she even understand what a machine *was*?

I walked to the aircraft air lock.

"Gina, would you direct Dum and Dee to come out, They are to go down to the beach and retrieve the food that the natives have left. But first they will stand next to me and I will pat their heads, then order them to go."

"I understand Theo."

After a few seconds the two robots exited the airlock and stood next to me. At first sight of them the girl screamed and stood as if to run.

"No, it's okay," I shouted placing a hand on each of the robots heads. They stood unmoving next to me. "They will not harm you, look." I patted their heads and then gave each of them a little cuddle.

She was moaning and shuddering and looked ready to run. But she may have thought that if she ran the 'animals' would come after her, so she stayed frozen to the spot.

"Dum and Dee, go bring the food back from the beach as instructed." I pointed in the direction of the beach and the two robots bounded off. She gave a little scream, grabbing hold of the table as if her legs were about to buckle but as the robots headed down the hill and disappeared she relaxed.

I went over and put an arm around her shoulder to calm her. Close up I had to admit that she was quite cute. And her body was remarkably human. Clearly her species were also descended from simian ancestors. Perhaps the 'Pan Spermia' idea was really true and we were all descended from an ancient species whose DNA had been spread throughout the galaxy.

She was shivering and breathing heavily and she suddenly began to wail. It was the wail of a child in distress and I felt a pang of pain myself. How could her parents allow this beautiful child to be sacrificed to an unknown God?

I made what I hoped were reassuring noises and patted her shoulders. After a few minutes and with a few very human sniffles she settled down. While we waited for the robots to return I showed her more video of my home world. That helped to take her mind of her predicament.

When the robots returned carrying the food she was more composed. She moved away from the table when they came close to place the food onto it.

"Dum and Dee you can go inside now," I said. Once they disappeared inside the shuttle the girl relaxed and began to examine the food. She picked up a ripe looking fruit and handed it to me. I bit into it and fortunately found it to be delicious. I nodded agreeably and she smiled back.

"No point throwing this food away I guess," I said to Gina.

"Avoid the meat," said Gina.

I examined the meat carefully. It did look pretty unappetizing. It appeared to be ribs cooked over a BBQ, which I would normally find very appetizing. But the meat looked discolored and uncooked in some places.

"Trying to poison your god huh?" I pointed to the meat and looked enquiringly at the alien girl. She nodded eagerly and I thought *oh oh!* I guess I can slice it up and give it a blast in the microwave I decided.

But what to now do with this female? Could I return her to her home? Or keep her here? The idea of having company, was attractive. But what if her village decided that regular 'sacrifices' were necessary? Would I get deliveries of food and virgins every month?

You could have too much of a good thing I decided!

Chapter 6

Salny had thought she would die of terror when the God appeared around the hill. Up to that point she had been convinced that it was all just superstition; the fishermen had seen something unusual and run away, then decided to make a name for themselves by inventing Gods or devils.

Nevertheless, being abandoned on a strange beach, tied to a stake was enough to terrify her; what if an animal came down to the beach and found her helpless she asked herself. She would be eaten alive by wild snarf.

The appearance of the God was a shock that immediately turned her muscles and insides to jelly. Her legs collapsed and she moaned with terror. She was prevented from falling to the floor by the bonds tying her to the stake.

It was true! The thought overwhelmed her mind. There were Gods, and she was about to meet one. As the God came closer she was confused by what she was seeing. Then she realized that it was wearing odd clothing that covered its body, with only its head and arms bare.

It was in Enlai shape! Her brothers joking words came back to her and she felt fear coursing through her body, weakening her, her bladder threatening to release its contents. *Perhaps it is a good God* she told herself desperately.

The God was smiling and making noises; was it looking forward to ravishing her she asked herself. But it passed by and went to the food. It would feed first *then* ravish her. She moaned in terror trying not to imagine what it would do to her. The God tried the food but did not seem impressed, spitting it out in disgust. *Would it get angry and destroy her and the food* she asked herself. Then it tried another fruit and seemed to like it, nodding and smiling.

The god then came over and released the ropes tying her to the stake. Close up the god looked very Enlai, but with odd differences. *He is not ugly at least* she thought. But it was no consolation and when he stepped away from her she stood and ran away from him. He did not come after her but she could not climb the sandy hill.

Where am I to go? she asked herself. The god remained by the food smilling at her and making calming motions with his hands.

She felt relief and plucked up her courage. "Where is your ship?" she asked. The god shook his head as if he did not understand. She pointed out to sea and repeated the question. He frowned then repeated "...My ship?" then pointed to the giant silver bird. She felt disbelief then resignation. *He was the Sky god and she was his gift.*

Now, some time later as she sat next to the giant silver bird eating the god's food offering and drinking the delicious golden liquid, she marveled at what had just happened to her. The god was a benign god after all, unless it was saving her for later. The thought brought a frisson of terror back but she banished it quickly.

He was after all the Sky God, who was known to be benign, despite ravishing the occasional virgin. She was sure of that when she saw his sky blue eyes. He was tall and broad shouldered with a pale face, his hair the color of the clouds in the evening with the setting sun behind them. She tried to comfort herself; *If I am to be sacrificed to a god then the Sky god at least is beautiful.* But it was no consolation. She did not want to be sacrificed to any god.

Gina and I decided that the first priority was to learn the native's language. Over the next few weeks we concentrated on that with great success. The girl's name was Salny and with the flexibility of youth she quickly accepted her new environment and settled in. Gina had a built in program to learn alien languages; somewhat speculative of course, it had never been used 'in anger'.

Gina used the tablet to communicate with Salny. The method was a 'show and tell' system; Gina would display something simple and common place and Salny was expected to pronounce its name in her language. It took a while for her to get the idea. After acquiring a good vocabulary of nouns Gina moved on to verbs, and then to the construction of sentences.

Salny's language was basic and Gina soon analyzed and tabulated structure and constructed a dictionary. I sat next to Salny and participated. I am lucky to have an excellent memory and with Gina's support I was soon able to converse with Salny.

I was quite impressed with Salny's intelligence. She picked up on ideas quickly; after all, what we were doing was incredibly new for her. And she showed patience and concentration in the task. She also became comfortable in my presence and eventually even the presence of the robots.

After the first few days she began to develop a fairly ripe odor. She would go around the hill to carry out her private functions and then wash herself in the sea, but she was clearly not doing a very thorough job.

I introduced her to the ship's shower and soap, showing her how to scrub her head and hair, and indicated she should wash her body before leaving her to it.

After three weeks Gina and I could conduct a conversation with Salny and we began to learn about her life and her tribe. They lived partly as hunter gatherers and partly as farmers and fishermen. They kept the equivalent to chickens and small animals. The ribs we had been gifted were from a large cow like animal.

Gina had a clear view of their village and she counted seventy two huts. There were two other neighboring villages of a similar size on the island. We calculated about one thousand natives living on the island which was approximately fifty by seventy miles.

Their name for their species was Enlai, their world was called Enlaiya and their village was called Faro. Salny told us that their neighboring village was the Hoshna. There was hostility between them, each side raiding the other for livestock and females. It was the usual tale of primitive conflict.

The village had a head man, an individual called Panstrosh. He was elected by the village elders, a group of ten of the oldest males. It was very much a male dominated society with the females relegated to child rearing and domestic tasks. It all seemed depressingly familiar.

On the subject of the religion it took a while to explain what we meant. The village had a Shaman who advised the elders and the village Headman. He contacted spirits of nature, the sea and sky, the earth and plants and its animals. Their religion, if it could be called a religion, was a cross between Shamanism and Naturism.

I asked Salny what had happened after the fishing party had discovered me and my aircraft. She said the fishing party were terrified in case they disturbed the giant silver bird. They returned to the village and reported to the elders. The Shaman went into a trance and consulted the spirits. He told them that the bird belonged to the God of the Sky Vulious. The God was well known as a great lover and must be placated by food and a beautiful virgin.

Salny had looked at me and asked "You are Vulious the Sky God?"

"No, I am not a god."

She lowered her eyes then looked me up and down with a questioning expression.

She is not yet convinced I decided. With no understanding of the real world. Everything she knows is imaginary. The world is driven by spirits and magic. How can she possibly understand my technology? For her it can only be magic, which means I am a god.

I had no desire to conform to the wishes of a bunch of ignorant savages, and certainly not to force myself on the young woman, for I was convinced that her age must be late teens. It was a matter of moral principle.

I also had a duty not to interfere with the evolution of this civilization. Behaving like a god could do that in ways that I could not predict.

I found some of my clothing that I adapted to replace Salny's white shift which was getting grubby. She was almost as tall as me but she was smaller across the shoulders. Some pants and a vest of mine fitted, being tight around the bottom and baggy up top. This allowed me to wash her dress and underwear and hang them out to dry. Salny watched my cleaning operations with interest and I could see that she liked her new appearance and cleanliness.

I had set up a makeshift mattress in the living area for her to sleep on. But she would not enter the shuttle if the robots were inside, which meant that at night Dum and Dee kept guard outside.

Having achieved a workable use of the native language we now had to decide what to do with our guest and how to proceed in our relations, if any, with the natives. I confess that I liked having Salny around. Once she had understood that she was not in any danger she relaxed and began to behave like an intelligent and curious adult. Since my presence on the planet was revealed I was of the view that there was no reason why I could not have closer contact with them.

Gina was not so sure. It was all right for her to be so inclined I thought sourly, she had no need for human company. Gina pointed out that Salny still considered me a god and it was almost certain that her compatriots would also maintain that view. The consequences of that were impossible to forecast.

But I argued that refusing further contact would simply confirm the natives in their belief that Vulious the Sky God was still amongst them while his giant silver bird was still on the ground. If I went amongst them I would eventually be able to persuade them that I was mortal.

"You have not had any success with Salny," Gina pointed out. "She still firmly believes that you are Vulious the Sky God."

"Well I don't blame her," I said, tongue in cheek. "But give her time."

"Theo, somebody once said that for a primitive people, advanced technology is no different from magic. From their world view, you *are* a god."

"Hmmm." I scowled. She was right of course, but I still could not face the prospect of living alone, while just around the bay there were people who were to all intents and purposes human and who would I was sure welcome me.

But would they? Welcome me that is. It occurred to me that the powers that be may not welcome a powerful god living amongst them. The shaman would no longer be the pipeline into the mystical realm while a member of that realm was amongst them. The head man and leaders of the village would also be undermined.

Unless I united with them and reinforced their power; I remembered the fate of Jesus who had turned against the establishment and what happened to him, despite his followers claiming that he was the son of God. I was not immortal. If they decided to kill me they could not doubt engineer an opportunity.

I asked Salny what she wanted to do. "Do you want to return to your people or stay here with me?"

"If I return it means you have rejected me," she replied.

"And so?"

"They will send other gifts."

"Other females?"

"Yes. More than one."

"I don't want any more females."

"Then you have to keep me."

"Can you return and tell your people that I am very happy with their gifts and do not want more."

"They will not believe me. They will think I have escaped and you are angry with them."

"If I come with you and explain that I am happy with their gifts and thank them? Will they accept that?"

"Perhaps. But they will want favors from you. And many females will want to mate with you to have children with god like powers."

"We cannot have children. You are Enlai, I am human."

"You are a god. Gods come down to us to mate with Enlai females. There are ancient tales of the children of the gods."

I sighed in frustration.

"Forget about your people and what they think or believe or want. What do *you* want?" I asked.

"You have been very kind to me and I have learned many things. But I want to see my family," she said, her eyes humbly to the ground.

Later I discussed our situation with Gina.

"I have a choice of living here in isolation or trying to have some kind of relationship with the natives."

"You will be getting into a very difficult situation if you go to live with the natives."

"Difficult is interesting. I need companionship and some kind of challenge."

"I understand Theo. What do you propose?"

Chapter 7

Salny had told Theo that she wanted to return to the village to see her family, and that was true, although the only person she was truly close to was her brother Lon. She wanted him to know that she was well.

But she also wanted to return to get one up on Pankrosh, his brother Tarsik the mate she had turned down, and the disgusting Youva the Mahik. She wanted them to know that she had the ear of the God. She did not believe what Theo was saying; that he was just a mortal like her from another world. She was sure that he was saying that just to make her feel comfortable.

Is it proper to love a God? she asked herself. Not love in the religious sense, although that was there, but love in the mortal sense. She had been told that Vulious was a promiscuous God but he had behaved with respect towards her. Perhaps he did not desire her? That was an unexpected and unusual thought for Salny; she was after all the most beautiful and desirable female in the village. All the eligible males desired her. Why would Vulious not?

But she was content with her relationship with the God. He had taught her many things, opened her mind to ideas that were revolutionary and astonishing. Every day she would talk to his wonderful servant Gina, who knew everything and could take Salny on visual trips to far flung worlds. Surely the world of the Gods was wondrous and rich.

She struggled to understand much of what she was told. The nature of the universe and what it was made from seemed against common sense; how can normal things be made of tiny particles, so small they could not be seen? How did those particles stick together to make huge things like mountains? And the same particles make the sea? And make the Enlai and animals? They were difficult questions that taxed her mind but she enjoyed the challenge and always looked forward to her talks with Gina.

Salny wanted to continue her relationship with the god. He had treated her as if she was his equal. But more than that, being around him and his magical servants had opened a new world for her. She knew that her life would never be the same again.

I had to give some thought to how we would return Salny to her village and what kind of relationship I could have with her people. I did not want to be a god but clearly the natives would continue to treat me as such. Should I then act the part, or should I insist on moving amongst them as if I was one of them. Was I prepared to give up the comforts of my shuttle home and live in a hut? I decided that would be going too far!

I tried to persuade myself that if I flew my shuttle to the outskirts of the village and took up residence there, then, over time, they could come to accept me. I knew there was an element of wishful thinking there but at the end of the day, I told myself, if it did not work out I could return to my end of the island and tell the natives to keep their distance.

Gina reminded me of the damage I could do to the native's development. I could bring about the start of a new religion. But then, I argued, they already had a primitive religion. That was not going to go away. Gina metaphorically shrugged and washed her hands of the whole thing.

I moved everything back into the shuttle, leaving my makeshift shelter and BBQ behind. Gina had studied the geography of our surroundings and from the description of her journey given by Salny Gina had determined the location of her village. She showed pictures to Salny who identified it.

We picked a landing location close to the village on a knoll above it and overlooking the sea.

"Good location for a nice bungalow," I mused. "Nice view of the sea, swimming pool just here, BBQ area over here."

"Let's get the builders in," agreed Gina.

There was no convenient stream nearby to provide a supply of fresh water, but the shuttle had the means to desalinate sea water so that was not a problem. I would miss my nice river, but I could take little trips with my motorized dinghy to do some fishing.

We were ready to go and I took Salny into the cockpit and strapped her into the co-pilot's seat. Our trip would take seconds but I decided to give her a view of her planet as an education.

After living in the shuttle for the last few weeks she had become used to it, but when the engines started and the noise built up she began to moan.

I reassured her, reaching out to pat her hand. I increased power and the aircraft lurched and lifted off the ground. She gave a scream of terror and her hands fumbled with the seat belt. Fortunately she was unable to release it.

The shuttle gained speed and the ground receded rapidly. Once Salny had realized she was not about to die she relaxed a little, looking through the cockpit at the sea and land with wide eyes and mouth agape. We climbed higher until the land and sea beneath us was a haze and the curve of the horizon began to appear.

I had already tried to explain the elements of cosmology to her with very limited success. She lacked the basic concepts to understand how a planet could float in Space, or how it could be round yet appear flat! Now, what she was seeing was equally confusing and mysterious. As we climbed higher she began gripping her seat and gasping. She appeared to be going into shock and I decided my attempt at education was not going to work.

"Gina, take us down for a landing at the village."

"Yes Theo." The engine roar lessened and we began to come down.

Salny screamed "We are falling," clutching her seat.

"We are coming down to land," I explained. "Everything is good. Gina, descend more slowly."

Gina took the aircraft on a long slow glide down until we could again sea the sea and forest beneath us. As we came over the village Salny gasped and pointed.

"My house!"

I could see figures running around the village and pointing, then disappearing rapidly into the forest.

"Everyone is running for cover."

"Understandable," said Gina. "They are seeing a giant silver bird making a thunderous noise. They think they are all about to be eaten or killed. Or both!"

As we came close for a landing I took over the controls gently maneuvering the aircraft towards the beachside knoll we had selected. There were tall trees growing up the sides but the top was rocky and bare.

Always wanted a beachside mansion I thought. *This will have to do!*

I examined the ground carefully before landing. I did not want the wheels to sink into the sand, perhaps preventing the shuttle from taking off again. The shuttle had automatic ground sensing radar which would report if it was boggy or unsuitable. The hilltop looked firm and rocky and the landing radar remained green. The ship settled with a thump. I waited for the indicators to show a stable landing then powered down.

"Right, let's go investigate our new home Gina."

Salny seemed as if she was recovering her wits but her legs were shaking as she attempted to stand.

"Take your time Salny." I helped her up.

"You are a great and powerful god," she whispered.

"Of course I am," I said in resignation. "Now, I think your fellow citizens have all run into the forest. You will have to go down and find them and explain that I am a friendly god who wishes to help them."

"We are honored that such a powerful god should want to help us." She bowed low. I straightened her and took her hand leading her out of the cockpit. I opened the airlock and with Dum and Dee following we exited. It was warm, as usual, but there was a cool breeze blowing in from the sea. I could smell the pine like smell of the trees and there was a twittering of birds and the hum of insects. I felt a stab of nostalgia.

This place is so Earthlike.

The slope to the sea was gradual with many large boulders. There was a well worn track down to the beach on one side and back towards the village in the other direction.

Salny looked around, a smile on her face. "We used to play here as children. There is a dirt slide over there which dumps you in the sea."

"That sounds like fun," I said

"It is child's play," she said. I guess she meant 'it is for children' rather than 'it is tame'.

"Gods also like to play like children," I said. "You must never lose your love for child's play."

"You are a wise god," she said with a warm glance.

You are sweet, I thought. *And easy to fool!*

"So you must now go down to your village and find your leaders. You must tell them that Vulious is a wise and friendly god who is pleased with their gifts and will stay here for a while. Your village leaders can come here to meet me and we can talk."

"Thank you Vulious." She paused for a few moments before speaking. "May I remain here with you as your servant if you wish?"

"Is that what you want Salny?"

"Yes it is." She nodded shyly, her eyes on the ground.

"Then of course you may. I will enjoy that."

She nodded and with a smile she turned and ran down the path towards the village. I watched her tall lithe form until she disappeared and then wondered what I had let myself in for.

While I waited, I carried out an examination of the aircraft and asked Dum and Dee to investigate the surroundings for any unwanted or potentially dangerous animals. Once they had finished I asked them to post themselves on either side of the airlock.

In my lounge/kitchen/dining room I made some coffee and relaxed with the wall screen showing views from the robots eyes and a couple of external cameras on the shuttle.

What to do about Salny? I asked myself. Or any of the native females for that matter, if it was the case that they would all want to be fertilized by the god. I had no reservations about having sex with them; they were human enough to be attractive, and if Salny was anything to go by even beautiful. But not on the basis that I was a god. I was not sure that I could perform at that level!

I was chuckling to myself whilst fondly reminiscing on my past romantic adventures when I spotted some figures coming up the path from the village. I counted thirteen, not unlucky I hoped. As they came closer I saw Salny in the lead, striding ahead of the others along the path.

I stood and went to the exit and stepped down between the robots. Do I look 'Godly' enough I asked myself. Perhaps I should put on a Spacesuit. That would scare the shit out of them! I was wearing my dark blue one piece overall with orange trims along the sides of the legs and shoulders and a grey belt with a holster holding my pistol. Not really very impressive as a rule, but perhaps for savages wearing animal skins it would be.

The villagers stopped at the edge of the clearing gazing with awe at the shuttle. Salny continued walking until she was close to me. She looked pleased with herself.

"I bring the village elders and the priest," she said

"Tell the leader of your village to approach me."

She walked back to the villagers, who had stopped some twenty yards away, and conversed with one of the villagers, then led him forward towards me. They stopped a few yards away with the individual looking nervously at the robots.

"This is Emla Panstrosh, our village Headman," said Salny.

"I am pleased to meet you Emla Panstrosh," I said, speaking strongly. "I thank you and the others of you village for your gifts. I have enjoyed Salny's company. She is intelligent and beautiful."

"We are all delighted that we pleased you," said Panstrosh. "Salny has informed us that you wish to remain here for a while. We are humbled by your presence. What is it that you want from us?"

"I want nothing from you other than your friendship and companionship. I am far from home and cannot return for a while. This seemed a pleasant place to pass the time."

"Forgive me but you are a god. Why cannot you return to your home?"

I had anticipated the question and answered

confidently.

"Gods, like mortals, have duties. You are fortunate to receive my attention for a while. But if you do not want it, I will go elsewhere."

"No, no!" he said hastily. "We will do all we can to make you welcome." He paused for a moment. I thought he was looking a bit shifty. "Perhaps you can help us also."

"What did you have in mind?" I asked while thinking *'Cheeky sod. Only just been introduced and he is asking favors already'*

"Our neighbors, the Hoshna, have taken to raiding our crops and animals, even stealing our women. We are preparing a raiding party to pay them back. Perhaps you can teach them a lesson?"

"As a rule gods do not take sides in mortal disputes. But preventing violence is a good cause. I will consider how best I can help," I said. "Now, introduce me to your friends." I added, indicating the others.

He nodded and waved them over. They were all fairly elderly except for one youthful fellow. Big and burly he had the appearance of a hunter or warrior. He examined me with keen interest, his eyes also taking in the robots and the shuttle. He was the only one who did not look awed, except for one other individual. That individual was obviously the Shaman. He appeared the oldest of the group and the only one dressed in a long white robe that covered his body and a white hood. He looked back at me with hooded eyes.

I had arranged a little magic trick to impress my visitors and I whispered into my comm for Gina to begin. Dum and Dee were not normally armed with flame throwers but they did have that option in the remote circumstance that I would want to clear a path in a forest. They now came to life suddenly, startling my guests who looked terrified.

"Have no fear, my soldiers have detected movement in the trees and will investigate," I said.

The robots tramped off into a copse of trees and then turned the flame throwers on to burn the ground inside the little clearing. There were cries of fear and astonishment from the natives at the sight and sound of the flames. The robots just gave a couple of blasts and then returned to their stations. The natives were looking ready to run for it and I held up a calming hand.

"My soldiers will not harm you. Whatever animals were there have run away."

Panstrosh was looking shaken.

"If your soldiers use those against the Hoshna they will never bother us again."

"Perhaps a quick visit by my soldiers to their village will be enough," I said. "No need to kill anybody."

"If you kill a few that will be better," said Panstrosh with a ferocious scowl. The other nodded and grunted their agreement except for the young warrior who remained impassive.

"Peace between your villages would be better for everyone," I said.

"We cannot trust the Hoshna," said Panstrosh. "We have fought with them for ever. If you help us we kill all the men and take their women and their land. Then there will be peace."

I tried not to show my horror.

"I can defend your village but I will not help you to kill anyone who is not attacking you," I said firmly.

There were some uneasy movements amongst the natives and sideways looks at each other. Panstrosh eventually replied.

"If that is your wish," he said with a little bow.

"It is," I said firmly. "Do any of you have any contacts within the Hoshna?"

The young warrior stepped forward.

"My woman is Hoshna. I allow her to return to her village to see her family."

"What is your name?" I asked.

"I am Kemlo."

"Kemlo, bring your woman to see me."

"Yes your highness."

"Now, I would enjoy a tour of your village. Then perhaps I can see how I can help you."

I waved Salny over. "You may walk next to me," then whispered into my comm. "Gina, instruct the robots to flank me and Salny. They are to look out for any suspicious activity from any natives nearby or in the forest."

In addition to my pistol I was also armed with an ultra-sonic repellent for animals. This generated a focused powerful ultra-sonic sound that was very effective in scaring away animals. It also had a setting for people which was also very effective at short distances.

The natives led the way down the path towards the village. It was very pretty with a variety of trees and bushes growing thickly over the hills. At the bottom the ground was clear of trees with only small stunted bushes growing on the rocky ground. Then lower there appeared a thick coating of soil and the appearance of horticulture with cleared fields, fruit trees and bushes.

The houses of the village appeared and I began to see domesticated and farm animals. It looked very much how I would have imagined an ancient Iron Age village would look, which seemed to accentuate my feelings of loneliness and alienation.

Kemlo had run ahead to warn the villagers of our arrival and they were now coming out of their houses and gathering in the village square. The sight of the robots caused a commotion with some people hiding back in their huts or running away.

I felt that I should do some kind of god-like trick; perhaps arriving on a golden chariot pulled by two dragons, or just flying in riding a unicorn.

"Gina, tell the robots to blow a blast of fire into the air."

"Becoming quite the showman Theo."

"I am supposed to be a god. Just walking on my two feet seems tame."

"Remember that you did not want to be a god."

"I seem to have no choice at the moment. Let's take that re-education gradually."

I pulled my ultra-sonic gun from my pocket and set it to the 'human' setting. As the robots lifted their flame guns I waved the gun in an arc taking in the villagers. There was a satisfyingly terrified reaction as the robots roared with flame and the intolerable ultra-sonic scream split the air. Salny and I were shielded from the noise as it was pointing away from us but we still caught a painful blast. I switched it off hastily and returned it to my pocket.

The villagers had dispersed, either running away or hiding in their houses. I stopped in the centre of the village square between my robots with Salny still bravely next to me. I felt like a charlatan but then thought *'fuck it, in for a penny...'*

"Salny, go around and tell people they are safe. Tell them to gather here so I can talk to them."

It took a while but eventually Salny, with the help of Kemlo, gathered the villagers in the square. I was beginning to develop some respect for Kemlo who seemed cool and calm and a natural leader.

"Friends," I held my arms up to gain their attention. "I am Vulious the sky god. I have taken this form to come amongst you in order to help you, my followers. I would like to bring peace between you and your enemies. I would like to help you to improve you lives by growing more food, farming more animals and better hunting. My time here is limited so use my help while you can. When I leave, you must stand on your own feet and live by your wits with the knowledge that I have given you. Do not be afraid of my servants." I paused and indicated the robots. "They are peaceful. But be warned that if you turn against them or me you will instantly be vaporized. Do you have any questions?"

Kemlo was first to put his hand up.

"Your highness, how will you help us with hunting and farming?"

"I can show you how to make new tools and weapons. That will allow you to improve your buildings and your hunting. I will show you how to grow improved crops. Also how to recognize and treat illnesses and improve your health and the health of your children. These are all things you have to learn and remember. I will not do things for you because I will not remain here. You must understand that."

I emphasized the last phrases and he nodded his understanding.

"The key to progress is knowledge," I said. "You must understand the world you live in. The world does not work with magic. It follows rules. You must learn those rules to improve your lives."

"That is an interesting idea," said Kemlo. His face was lit up with excitement. *There you go* I thought. *The keen mind awakens!*

But I also saw the Shaman scowling. *That does not suit you. Ignorance and magic are your stock in trade.*

Can there be such a thing as a rational religion? A religion that says don't expect God to do anything for you; he has given you intelligence and hands. Use them to understand and build. Your fate and future is up to you.

I could maybe believe in such a religion I told myself.

Except that the whole basis of religion is faith. Unthinking faith in the so-called word of God, handed down second and third hand through a bunch self appointed disciples.

Could I give these people a better start than humans had? A more rational approach to religious belief? Or was that a contradiction doomed to failure? I could try, although I would probably not live to see the results.

Chapter 8

When Salny returned to her village with Vulious she had mixed feelings; She felt triumphant and elated to have not just survived her ordeal, but befriend a god. She was now his handmaiden and servant. But everyone in the village, including the odious Panstrosh and disgusting Yovna the Mahik, would assume that she had mated with the god. If so, then like the god, she was now untouchable, to be treated with awe and respect.

But she was also nervous; she was aware that she was living a lie. The god appeared not to want to mate with her but treated her as a friend. He treated her with respect and taught her many new and amazing things. Nevertheless, she could not help feeling that her womanhood was not adequate for him.

Am I not beautiful compared to the females in his kingdom she asked herself. That seemed very likely. But then, if the god-like females in his kingdom were so beautiful, why would he descend to this world to ravish Erani females? It was all very puzzling but then, she asked herself, who could understand the ways of the Gods? Enjoying her revenge on Yovna and Panstrosh was adequate reward.

And also enjoying the relief and affection of her brother when she returned to their hut. He was convinced when he saw her that she was a phantom, returning from the world of the dead to terrorize him. He almost turned to run away but when she spoke and reassured him he paused, staring at her wide eyed.

"Lons it's me Salny. I have returned." She held arms

wide. "Vulious is a good god and he has come to our village to help us."

"Salny? Is it really you? I had given you up for dead." He ran to her, holding her tight then looking at her with awe and disbelief, struggling to hold back his emotions. "What are you saying? Vullious is a good god...?"

"Sit down and let's make some tea and I will explain," she said.

She explained her experience, how the god first met her and treated her gently. She told Lons about the god's wonderful servants, indestructible soldiers who could kill at a distance or create fire just by extending a hand.

Lons eventually asked. "So, did the god.... you know...?" He made vague motions with his hands.

Salny amused herself by pretending not to understand what he was trying to say.

"Are you... carrying his child?" Lons blurted out.

"No," Salny laughed although there was an underlying tone of sadness. "The god has not mated with me. He has treated me as a friend."

"Oh. Well that's good," Lons said. "It would be terrifying to be ravished by a god."

"Yes," Salny agreed, while thinking ....*not by this god!*

I had no hope of giving the natives the sort of skills and knowledge they needed to survive and prosper without Gina of course. I am not a farmer or hunter and my knowledge of electronics, computers, star ship technology and piloting would be completely useless and incomprehensible to them.

Over the next few days I became a frequent visitor to the village. I wanted to get to know the inhabitants and their problems and way of life. Salny and Kemlo, and Salny's brother Lon, became my guides. I took presents of food delicacies; my granola bars and biscuits were great favorites, particularly with the children. Fortunately I had a big stock.

I examined their farming techniques and after consulting with Gina I was able to make suggestions. We designed and made digging and trimming tools and a better plough. I spent some time on designing a simpler way to construct a wheel. They had a very primitive buggy pulled by horse like animals and Gina was able to come up with a hugely improved design.

Cleanliness and hygiene were not things the natives took much notice of, for themselves or their animals. I did not try to explain about bacteria or viruses; I felt that would be pointless and in any case would probably not be believed; Invisible tiny creatures living in the air and the soil? That's ridiculous!

I instead explained the idea that some things were 'poisonous'. They had no word in their language for 'poisonous' so I used the English word. I asked my assistants Salny and Kemlo to find a wild fruit or berry that was bad to eat and would either cause death or serious stomach pain and diarrhea. I then associated the word 'poisonous' with the berry they provided, miming stomach pain and death. I explained that the soil was also poisonous and that soil and dust got into the air, onto hands and into mouths and food.

I explained the importance of washing and thoroughly cooking food and washing hands, cleaning any wounds and scratches. Dirt must not get into the blood I explained.

It was hard work and much of it was beyond most of the older people. But the youngsters learned quickly and accepted what I was saying implicitly. The females in general were also more accepting particularly with the ideas on hygiene. They had inherited some primitive ideas on food hygiene from their mothers and grandmothers and what I said made sense to them.

I was no longer a remote god to be worshipped and feared but a friendly and caring god who disseminated help and ideas. But it soon became obvious that my power and influence was undermining the village headman and leaders. They decided to assert their authority by organizing a raiding party to attack the Hoshna village. When Kemlo came and told me I knew that this was a challenge to my authority. I asked him his opinion of the raid.

"It is not the Hoshna who raid. We do it more often and they occasionally retaliate. Panstrosh and Yovna want to be strong men to get support of the warriors."

Yovna was the Shaman who I knew was becoming more and more isolated in the new atmosphere of reason that I was instilling. He had attempted a couple of séances and ceremonies to which I had been invited, the outcome of which had been a lukewarm endorsement of my regime.

"I do not want to allow the raid," I said. "You said your wife was Hoshna. I wanted her to take me to her village so I can talk to the Hoshna. Is that possible?"

"She visited her village five days ago," said Kemlo. "She told them of you and they became frightened that you would destroy them. But Ilnira my woman told them you are a good god who does not kill for no reason. The Hoshna will not attack the Faro while you are here. There is no reason for this raid."

"Yes, I agree. I'll tell Panstrosh to stop the raid until I have spoken with the Hoshna."

"He and Yovna and the warriors will not like it. They want to raid for women."

"Tell me Kemlo, when did you capture your woman?"

"I did not capture her. I was out hunting in Hoshna territory and she was with her friends picking ruzni. She was frightened at first thinking I would kidnap her but I did not. I just smiled and greeted her. After that I would go there often and she would come. After some time I asked her to be my woman and she agreed."

"How did Panstrosh react to you finding a Hoshna woman?"

"I told him that I had captured her."

"Kemlo, you have my respect."

"Thank you Highness. That is most important to me." He bowed low. I took him by the shoulder and straightened him.

"No need to bow to me when we are alone. Only when we are with others."

"I understand."

"Now, let's go see Panstrosh. It is time he understood that the old days are gone."

"He will not be easily persuaded."

"Then he will be persuaded the hard way," I said causing a grin to spread across Kemlo's face.

With the robots in attendance we walked to the village. Panstrosh's house was the largest in the village and strategically placed at the head of the square. Most of the houses were made from crudely cut slender logs packed with mud but Panstrosh had made his from inexpertly fired bricks painted with a muddy grey 'whitewash'. Nevertheless it was much grander than any other house in the village as befitting the chief.

Panstrosh was outside his house with a group of warriors clearly preparing for the upcoming raid. The Faro warriors had wooden iron tipped spears and bows and arrows. Some had clubs or axes with iron blades. I had considered making improvements to their weapons but decided against; they were adequate for hunting and I did not want to improve their war making abilities.

The warriors used horse like steeds for riding. They were hard to catch and tame so there were few of them and they were valuable. Only the top warriors had one. There were six of them being saddled while the other twenty or so warriors would walk.

I stood back and called Panstrosh.

"I wish to talk with you."

He spent a few seconds doing up the saddle straps before turning and walking over to me.

"I told you that there would be no raids on the Hoshna until I had talked with them." I spoke loudly to make sure all the warriors heard.

"It has been a long time," he replied.

"Nothing has changed. The Hoshna know I am here and will not attack."

"How do the Hoshna know you are here?"

"Kemlo's woman told them. They are afraid I will destroy them and are keeping away."

"Then you should destroy them," he said fiercely.

"Not without talking to them first."

"But when you leave they will go back to their old ways."

"It is not just their old ways. It is also your old ways. You must both stop otherwise nothing will change."

"We may stop for a while. But then something will happen. Someone will steal a woman or a *gron.* There will be an argument, someone will be killed and then it will all begin again."

I had to concede he had a point. Without a formal agreement and law enforcement then it was the law of the jungle.

"Panstrosh, the way things are, you are correct. But if there is an agreement between you then if someone breaks that agreement he should be punished. Would you want to go to war when many people may die in order to defend a thief?"

I could see that he was struggling with the novel ideas of an agreement and law enforcement.

I pressed home the argument.

"Kemlo told me that he did not kidnap his woman. He met her when he was hunting and they talked. They liked each other and continued to meet secretly. Then, Ilnira agreed to come and be his woman. Because she wanted to, not because he forced her."

"Kemlo, is this true?" asked Panstrosh, scowling at Kemlo.

"Yes, it is as Vulious said."

"Why did you lie to me?"

"Because you and the others would think little of me. I wanted to appear a big warrior," Kemlo replied. "But I see now that it is better to win a woman's respect than to take her by force."

"Women respect a warrior," said Panstrosh.

"If anyone doubts that I am a warrior then let them speak now," said Kemlo loudly, looking defiantly at the others. "And I suggest you ask your women which they prefer," he added.

"I do not ask my woman," one of the warriors shouted. "I tell her."

There were grunts of agreement from the others.

"You are a brave warrior," said Kemlo. His sarcasm was not lost on the others. The one who spoke stepped forward and pulled out his sword.

"I will show you how much of a brave warrior I am," he said.

Kemlo quickly pulled out his sword.

Oh shit I thought. *This is getting out of control.*

"Stop!" I shouted. "There will be no fighting amongst us."

"Ha! You are very brave with your god to protect you," shouted the irate warrior.

"I am not afraid of you Toldus," said Kemlo. He

turned to me. "Vulious, allow us to settle this our way."

"If that is your wish," I said. I was seriously annoyed with what had happened but I knew that I could not stop it. Kemlo had to respond to the challenge. But if anything happened to him I knew that I would feel awful. "But there is no need to fight to the death," I added. "The first to be disarmed can stop the bout."

They both said nothing to that. I guessed they did not want to appear the wimp. *What a bloody macho culture* I thought.

The warriors formed a square and the two combatants squared up to each other. I looked carefully at Kemlo's opponent. He was older and as tall as Kemlo and bigger, more burly. But his bulk showed some flab.

The combatants' swords had crudely fashioned iron blades with wooden handles. They did not appear very sharp and the points were rough. Clearly metal working was at an early stage. But I was impressed that such a primitive culture had discovered how to smelt iron.

The two circled each other warily then Toldus rushed Kemlo his sword high. He swung at the younger man as he came in. Kemlo jumped back then swiveled, his sword arm swung in an arc and connected with the other man's sword with a clang, then the blade slid down to the hilt with a powerful thrust that almost knocked it from Toldus grip. Kemlo swung his sword back to the defense position and circled his opponent.

Toldus again rushed the younger man this time swinging his sword like a scythe. Kemlo met him with a powerful swing. The swords clanged loudly and I could see Toldus arm was jolted. Kemlo pressed his advantage, swinging his sword with great power, driving Toldus back.

Toldus could not cope with Kemlo's power and his sword was torn from his grasp and flew onto the floor. But he did not shout to stop. Instead he stood defiantly. I was shocked when Kemlo ran him through the heart and he dropped to the floor dead.

There was silence as Kemlo wiped his sword on the dead man's clothing then stood back, slid the sword back in its scabbard and then bowed stiffly to the dead warrior.

Panstrosh stepped forward.

"Take him away," he shouted. Four warriors stepped forward and carried the dead man away. "Kemlo, Toldus woman and home are yours."

"I do not want them," replied Kemlo. "Toldus wife can be her own master. She has three children to care for. I will contribute food to them."

"That is agreed," said Panstrosh. "Vulious, what is your wish now?"

I glared at Panstrosh.

"My wish was that the fight should not take place. If you were a good leader you would have stopped it. Instead you have lost a warrior and a woman and three children have lost a father."

He looked angry and tense.

"It is our custom," he replied.

"It is a bad custom and bad customs should be changed," I said firmly. "My original instruction stands. You will not go on this raid. I will visit the Hoshna village. Then I will return with my decision."

I turned to Kenlo.

"Kenlo, you will get your woman and then come to my home. We will go to the Hoshna village together."

I walked back to the shuttle, my two robots flanking me. I felt bad, as if I personally had killed the Faro warrior. Why had Kenlo killed the man I asked myself, especially after I had told him that it was not necessary? What sort of macho culture was this with brutal males and submissive oppressed females?

"Gina, I have begun to dislike this culture. I am not sure that I want to have anything to do with them anymore."

"You are beginning to understand the difference between a sophisticated individual from an advanced civilization and one from a primitive lawless one. The only law they have is one of survival of the strongest. It is like that with the higher animals and it was like that with primitive humans."

"I am beginning to think that I am metaphorically banging my head against a brick wall trying to civilize these people."

"I did warn you."

"You did," I agreed sourly.

"Perhaps you should set your sights lower," suggested Gina.

"I can't live with the sort of brutality we have just witnessed. Panstrosh and his gang were going to kill and rape for no reason other their own macho lust."

"It's all about asserting their leadership, which you are challenging. Gods are useful when they are invisible. Priests and leaders can put their own words in god's mouth."

"So I am making the situation worse?"

"You are either with the establishment or against it. You have made it plain that you are against it. The establishment is now asserting itself. You must either allow them to do that or you must totally repress them."

"Allow them to assert themselves or totally repress them? Not much of a choice," I said.

"No. If you allow them to assert themselves you will not be much of a god and you will quickly lose all authority, unless you also take part in their raids as a leader. Otherwise, to totally repress them you must remove the current leadership and take over completely."

"Remove the current leadership? Gina, what are you suggesting? That I kill them all?"

"Perhaps killing Panstrosh and the Shaman will be enough. Allow them to create a challenge to your authority then kill them."

"Gina, I am shocked. You should not be suggesting such ideas."

"I am simply analyzing the situation in a logical fashion. If you want my advice then I suggest you return to our previous location and get used to living alone. Or perhaps with Salny if she is willing, or with a regular supply of willing virgins."

"You are developing a very sarcastic sense of humor Gina. Are you getting bored up there on your own?"

"No, I am in continuous contact with what is happening on the planet. It is an entertaining soap opera."

"Ha ha, very funny." I was amused by Gina's wit. Was she purposely trying to cheer me up? Probably, I decided. As she had told me, scout ship AI's were programmed to be sensitive to the scout's moods and to divert and distract.

But her analysis was not wrong. I was attempting to be a 'hands on' god, but that had become a challenge to the natives existing leadership. It may also be that I was attempting to change their habits and customs too drastically.

Should I then just allow them to go ahead with the raid? That would allow Panstrosh and his gang to save face and assert their authority.

But improving their physical abilities to survive and make war without improving their moral and cultural abilities would simply make things worse; they would fight more destructive wars. That was what happened to Humanity for thousands of years, to the point where our destructive power threatened our very existence.

Perhaps doing things the other way around may be better? That is, improve their education and culture first without improving their physical abilities. But then I remembered the tragedy of ancient Athens. The flowering of Science and Philosophy did not prevent subsequent war and destruction. The sophistication of Athens was replaced by the physical power of Rome followed by a thousand years of ignorance and superstition.

I sighed in resignation. I had no desire to change the evolution of an alien civilization. I knew that was impossible. I had simply wanted to improve the lot of a couple of neighboring villages. But even that seemed impossible.

Perhaps Gina was right; I should return to my remote shelter and live out my life without interfering with the locals.

Chapter 9

At first, Salny was confused about the God's intentions; did he really believe that Panstrosh and his cronies could change their ways? Salny wanted to tell Vullious not to waste his time. They were brutal and uncaring, concerned only with their own status which required that they demonstrate their prowess as warriors. She wanted to tell Vullious to kill Panstrosh and become the village leader by force. He was a god and should demonstrate his power.

If he did not do so then Panstrosh would lose his respect for him; he would come to believe that Vullious was not a warrior god but a feeble and degenerate ravisher of virgins, perhaps with no power other than that of his metal servants.

But as she thought more deeply she began to discern a different way of looking at the situation; *morality was not something to be traded off for convenience.*

It was a surprising idea. She personally would never consider doing anything bad to gain advantage, telling lies or hiding the truth for example. But inaction in the face of evil, well, that was just self preservation. And Vullious was being clear that such behavior was unacceptable. Raiding the neighboring villages may bring wealth and strength but it was still wrong. Resisting such self-convenient action was not the cowards way out; it was the brave and honorable action. Her love and respect of the god Vullious grew; he was truly a loving god and she was privileged to be his servant.

It was beginning to appear that Gina's warnings were legitimate; I was indeed getting deeper into a situation that could have unpredictable consequences. But first, I decided, I must finish what I had begun.

Salny arrived with Kemlo and an attractive young woman who was introduced as Ilnira, Kemlo's 'woman'. She was diffident and shy, clearly overawed to be introduced to a real god.

Her village was three hour's walk through the mountains but I decided we should take the shuttle. It would be easier and quicker but I also wanted to make an entrance. I was Vulious the sky god after all!

The shuttle only had two seats in the cockpit so two had to sit in the living area. Fortunately those seats also had straps. Kemlo and Ilnira entered the shuttle cautiously, their eyes wide. I showed them their seats and strapped them in.

Their eyes were on the wall screen which was showing an outside view.

"That will show the view from the air," I explained. "Do not worry or be concerned, this is a very safe flying construction." There was no word for 'machine' in their language so I had substituted 'construction'.

"The controls are in the front." I pointed to the door of the cockpit. I smiled reassuringly and then joined Salny in the cockpit. She smiled up at me, long sleekly powerful legs embracing the pilot's control column. I had a vision of those legs wrapped around my thighs and quickly banished it.

I settled into the pilot's seat and buckled in. Gina had done the preliminary checks and I powered up the engines, winding them up and checking the indicators. With all indicators green I applied power and the aircraft lurched into the air then rose smoothly. I could imagine Kemlo and Ilnira's expressions as the aircraft climbed into the sky with the screen showed the ground and sea shrinking.

Gina had calculated our short course so I switched to auto pilot. We stayed at a low level, climbing slowly above the mountains, enjoying the spectacular view. I purposely set the speed at a metaphorical walking pace but even so the shuttle was flying at more than ten times walking speed and after ten minutes we arrived over the village. I was surprised to see that the village was substantially larger than Faro with very extensive farmlands all around. It was remarkably beautiful, set in a valley between the mountains with a river running through the middle.

There was a convenient landing spot by the side of the river next to the village. I took over the controls and flew the shuttle over the village then curved around and brought her down at the chosen location. The engines wound down and after a final check I locked the controls.

"That was so quick," Salny said.

"This is an aircraft that can fly around the world quicker than you could walk back to Faro," I said. I undid her safety belt, bending close to her, smelling her sweet ambience. It took an effort of will not to kiss her neck.

Theo baby, you are getting desperate.

She took my hand and we left the cockpit. Kemlo and Ilnira were still in their seats, the secret of the seat belt beyond them. They were looking wide eyed and Ilnira was holding Kemlo's hand tightly. Kenlo was trying to look brave, his jaw clenched.

I undid their belts and squeezed their shoulders reassuringly.

"Did you enjoy the trip?"

"It was quite... amazing," said Kemlo.

I operated the airlock doors and a cool wind blew in smelling of pine and other spicy forest aromas. The robots left the ship first and we followed. The river was stronger here than down on the coast, the water swirling around rocks. The village was a couple of hundred yards lower down the valley but I could see nobody about.

"Kemlo, perhaps you should go down to the village first and warn the good people," I suggested. He nodded, took Ilnira's hand and together they jogged down the hill towards the village.

"Dum, go see if there are any fish in the river."

The robot ambled down the incline to the river and waded in. He could happily go underwater if needed, but kept his head above, scanning the river with his multi-faceted eyes. He could see in normal light and in other non-visual frequencies. After a few seconds one of his limbs snaked out and came up with a large struggling fish. Salny gave a little scream of delight and clapped her hands.

"Tell it to catch more," she cried.

"Dum, give the fish to Dee and catch more," I ordered. The robot complied. By the time Kemlo returned from the village the robots had caught a good number, I counted eight, and stored them in their sample panniers.

"A small present for our friends," I explained to Kemlo.

"We will have a feast this evening," he said.

"Are they ready to meet us?" I asked.

"They were terrified by the giant silver bird," he said, "but they remembered what I had told them about you and guessed that you were visiting. They are honored and happy."

"Well, I am also honored and happy," I said. "Let's go meet the Hoshna."

We followed Kemlo down the hill to the village. It was built on a broad plateau which sloped gently down into the fertile valley. I was impressed to see the extent of the cultivated land. The Hoshna were more farmers than hunters whereas the Faro were more hunters and fishermen. The village centre was an open area where many animals were tethered and there was even a flat dirt play area for the children with swings.

The reception 'committee' were waiting for us while behind them and lurking nervously behind doors and windows were many of the villagers. Kemlo led us towards the village elders gathered to meet us. Ilnira stepped forward to meet Kemlo, taking his hand. All eyes were on me and the two robots and I attempted to look casual and friendly. When I got close to the leaders I stopped and gave a little bow.

"Peace be with you. My name is Vulious and I come in friendship."

One of the leaders, a tall spare fellow with broad shoulders and a splash of white fur on his head stepped forward. He was wearing a long white gown with some embroidery in different colors. I had not seen anything as decorative in the Faro village.

"We are honored by your visit. Welcome to out humble village. I am Santor the elected leader of our village council."

"I look forward to getting to know you all."

"You are with the Faro," said Santor. It sounded accusative.

"When I arrived here they were the first inhabitants I met. I would like to get to know you also."

"We have many problems with the Faro raiding our flocks and stealing our women."

"That is something that I will stop," I said firmly. "Your two villages can do much to help and support each other."

"The present leadership will not change their ways," said Santor. "The young, like Kemlo, can change." He indicated the young man. "He talks with approval of your teaching."

"You are correct. If the present Faro leadership will not change then perhaps there must be a change of leadership." I nodded towards Kemlo.

Santor grunted his approval.

"That will be beneficial. There is another matter that I wished to ask you to, ah… explain." He looked hesitantly at me.

"Anything," I said. I was becoming impressed with Santor. He seemed a quite different 'kettle of fish' from the aggressive Panstrosh and the other leaders of the Faro.

"Kemlo tells us that you claim not to be a god but a member of an advanced race from another… place, far from here. What are we to believe?"

My respect for Santor and Kemlo went up a few more notches. I had thought that my explanations about my origins had been 'water of a duck's back' for the natives. Certainly Salny had struggled to accept that explanation. But not Kemlo and the Hoshna it appeared.

"I have tried to explain that to the Faro but they are convinced that my powers are god like. They are not. My people have mastered the use of materials to build constructions such as my flying ship and these creatures that you see here." I indicated the robots. "But they are also constructions, what we call *machines* in our language." I pronounced *machines* in English. "We use machines for many things in our world. They carry us from place to place and assist us in farming and the production of other machines."

"That is … amazing." Santor turned to his colleagues and shook his head. They shook their heads back at him in agreement, looking at each other in wonder.

I was beginning to like the Hoshna. Simple farmers they were not!

It was Kemlo who spoke next.

"Vulious, can you then return to your world on your flying machine?" he asked, pointing to the shuttle.

"Sadly no Kemlo," I said. "That flying machine...," I pointed to the shuttle, "can only fly the short distances around Enlaiya. It cannot fly back to my world, the distance is too great." I paused to allow them to digest that.

"Then, how did you come here?" asked Kemlo.

"I have another flying machine, larger than this one." I again waited for them to mull that one over before continuing. "It is far from here, in the sky. I can get to it using this machine." I pointed to the shuttle. "But it has gone wrong. A part of the machine is broken. It happens with machines sometimes."

"You have another flying machine? Larger than that one?" Santor asked, his eyes boggling.

"Yes. That machine can carry this one." I pointed to the shuttle again.

"It must be truly enormous," said Santor.

"It is as long as this village is wide. From here to there." I pointed to the ends of the village which was about a hundred yards in width and two hundred in length.

"Your people can build such enormous machines?" Santor asked.

"There are much larger machines," I replied. "My machine carries only me and the small aircraft. We have machines that carry hundreds of people between worlds."

"Your big machine is broken?" asked Kemlo. "Can you not fix it?"

"It can be fixed back at my world. But I do not have the means to fix it here."

"So you cannot return to your world? You must remain here?" This was Salny suddenly speaking up.

"Yes. Unless others from my world come here."

"Others from your world may come here?" Kemlo

asked.

"Yes, we have explored many worlds. They will come here but it may be a long time. After I am dead."

"I did not think you could die," said Salny. She was looking at me with a new expression. Was it pity? Or love? Or just concern? I was not sure.

"I am mortal like all of you. I will die."

"You are mortal. And far from home on another world with strange people." Salny was looking distressed.

She had thought I was an immortal god and now had discovered that I was a pathetic feeble mortal whose power came from machines.

But I was wrong about her feelings. She was not disappointed but upset for me. The sweet girl came over and reached out for my hand. He slender warm hand slid into mine, squeezing firmly. She smiled lovingly, her eyes tender. I wanted to embrace and kiss her but restrained myself.

"Your race has achieved wondrous things," said Santor. "I wish to be alive when they come here again."

"So do I," I smiled. There were chuckles and smiles back from my hosts. "But it could happen tomorrow or in a hundred years."

"Do they not know you are missing?" asked Kemlo.

You are a clever young man!

"Yes, but unfortunately the fault in my ship was in the steering system. I arrived at the wrong place."

"So they do not know where you are?"

"No they do not. They will go to the place that I should have gone. But they will not find me there."

"Ah. And it is a big universe," said Kemlo. "Each star in the sky is a world?"

"Each star is a sun like yours, which could have many worlds."

"That is wonderful." Salny looked awestruck. "So

many worlds."

"Yes but most of them are dead worlds. Without air or water. Nothing lives there."

"Why is that so?" asked Salny looking disappointed.

"The answer is very complicated," I said. "I can explain to you later."

"We would all like to know these things," said Santor. "Perhaps over food and drink you can enlighten us."

"It will be a pleasure. That reminds me. Dum, give these good people the fish you caught."

"Yes Captain." Dum's mechanical voice caused a frisson of alarm in the Hoshna, but when he opened his storage box and pulled out the fish there were grins of amusement.

"My two robots are excellent fishermen," I said.

The natives hurriedly set up tables and chairs in the open outside the Chief's hut. A number of ladies began to prepare food and drink while we talked. I was impressed by the Hoshna's ready acceptance that I was not a god as opposed to the Faro's stubborn disbelief. I asked Santor if the village had a shaman, their word for him being a mahik.

"We had but he was a thief and a wicked man. He abused his position, taking advantage of our women and stealing from us. When he raped a young girl her father killed him. We are well rid of him."

"Did you not feel fear in attacking a holy man?" I asked.

"The girl's father killed him in a fit of rage. There was no vengeance from god so we decided that even god hated him."

"A reasonable decision," I said. "Will you appoint another mahik?"

"No one desires the job," said Santor looking contemptuous. "And no one wants to supply food and housing to a parasite. God can speak to us directly.

What are your people's ideas on god?"

"There are as many ideas as there are nations. But I agree with you. I am sure that God can speak to all of us directly if he so wishes."

"Is the mahik of Faro a good man?" asked Santor.

"He is in league with Panstrosh. They do not want peace with the Hoshna. We may have trouble with them," I replied.

"Yes. I am not surprised." Santor nodded.

We continued our talks while the food was prepared, then when the food and drink was served we turned to lighter matters. Some of the girls demonstrated dancing; apparently dancing was a female activity only. They were elegant and pretty although the music was primitive.

Late in the evening Santor talked quietly to Kemlo before turning to me.

"I have a favor to ask you," he began. "We have been having much trouble from a herd of Srinach in the mountains. They come down and kill our animals and sometimes attack people. The women and children cannot go to the fields alone. We have organized many hunting parties but they are very cunning. They smell us coming and hide in the mountains."

"What are Srinach?" I asked.

"They are wild linta. Much bigger and more ferocious."

The linta were similar to dogs; black ferocious looking things that had to be beaten continuously to keep them in line. The Faro used them for hunting.

If the srinach were bigger and more ferocious then they must be very dangerous creatures.

"Hmmm." I paused for thought. "You know exactly where they live?"

"Yes, there is one pack of eleven to fifteen adults. They live in some caves up there." Santor pointed up into the mountain.

I noted the position of the sun and called Gina. After I explained the situation I asked her to examine the area that Santor had identified as the home of the animals.

"Yes Theo. I see the caves. The sun is low and visibility is not too good so I do not see any of the creatures."

"We can have another look tomorrow at noon," I said. "What I was thinking was that we could send Dum and Dee up there to cut off the animals escape when the hunting party approaches. That way we can trap them."

"So you want me to find a good route and location for the robots?"

"Yes. The animals will not be able to smell the robots."

"I will examine the area tomorrow."

"Thanks Gina. Talk to you tomorrow. You okay up there? Not getting lonely?"

"I am being entertained by your escapades."

"Glad you like it. I may write a novel about my experiences."

"Seriously, you should keep a diary. Some time in the future this planet will be re-discovered and people will be interested in what happened to you."

"I presume you are keeping the normal diary of events?"

"Yes, but your thoughts and feelings are also important. People in the future will be fascinated by your adventures."

"That is a good point Gina. I may take your advice." I thought about what Gina had said and I had to agree. Not just because people may be fascinated by my adventures but for the more serious reason that historians and scientists would want to analyze and study the effects of my interference on the development of the civilization on this planet.

I could be posthumously famous. Or infamous! The thought was worrying. I was blithely interfering in the affairs of this planet without considering the consequences. I could be this civilization's equivalent of Jesus or Mohammad or Buddha. Or Genghis Khan!

Oh well, too late now I told myself. I can only try to be a good influence and bring peace and enlightenment. And keep away from the virgins!

Santor was looking at me with interest.

"Who were you talking to?" he asked.

How to explain an AI to a native who did not even understand the most basic physical laws?

"You heard my robots speak?"

"Yes. It is hard to understand how a construction can speak. Can my axe or bow do that?"

"No!" I laughed. "There is a crucial difference between your axe or bow and my robots. My robots have the ability to think. Not like us of course, but in a limited way. The machine I was talking to is in control of my ship. It has a powerful mind able to control complicated machinery and fly the ship through enormous distances."

"It sounded like a woman," he said.

"That is just its voice. It is not a woman. It has no body but is part of the ship."

"A thinking ship." Santor looked bemused. "Never did I dream that I would see such wonders."

"My thinking ship is called Aegina. She will look closely at the mountains above, tomorrow when the sun is high, and we will see how we can trap the srinach between my robots and your hunters."

"I understand. You said that the animals will not be able to smell your robots."

Smart fellow! "That is the idea," I said.

We talked a little more as the sun went down. Interestingly neither the Faro or the Hoshna seem to have discovered alcohol. I was missing a glass of wine or a shot of whiskey. *I will try my hand at wine making* I reminded myself.

It was time to retire and we said our goodnights with much formality and many thanks from the natives. Salny and I were to sleep in the shuttle and we were escorted up the hill by Kemlo and Ilnira. For the first time since being marooned on this beautiful world I was beginning to feel at home.

Salny was holding my hand possessively, looking at me and smiling, her eyes bright, full lips open and inviting. The signs were unmistakable; I was not a god. I was fair game!

Oh oh! You are not going to survive 'The Attack of the Alien Virgin' tonight mate, I told myself.

Chapter 10

As soon as we were alone in the shuttle Salny was suddenly seized by shyness. She came close and snuggled up, head on my shoulder, firm body pressed against me. I could either push her away or embrace her. I stood no chance of course; after months of abstinence my resistance crumbled.

What followed was a night of unashamed lust during which we intimately explored each other's bodies. Between interludes of sex I cogitated on how and why two beings from different planets could have so much in common physically. That evolution could produce almost identical results on two different planets billions of miles apart was a shocking discovery and revealed something about the universe that we had not yet understood. But I did not give these deep thoughts too much consideration; Her delectable body was much more interesting!

I awoke in the morning to see the sun blazing through the porthole. My beautiful partner was asleep next to me on the narrow bunk, her face a picture of peaceful innocence.

I never did discover if she was a virgin I thought. Should I send her back if she wasn't? I did not trust that crook Panstrosh. It would be just like him to send me second hand goods!

I grinned at the thought and gently disentangled myself from her arm and leg and putting on some pants went to make breakfast. Over a coffee I talked to Gina.

"Have you scanned the lair of the srinachs?" I asked.

"No, I have been having a lie in this morning," she

retorted. "After a strenuous night."

I snorted my amusement.

"Gina, if you were human I would almost believe that you were jealous." Then I had an alarming thought. "You haven't been spying on me have you? Getting in some surreptitious voyeurism?"

"I saw you come into the shuttle with Salny and how you both behaved. What you did after that was obvious."

"Uh huh. Used your imagination did you?"

"Oh yes. Virtual reality is much better than the real thing."

"Seriously?"

"Theo, really!"

"Okay, okay. You are joking. I am struggling to get used to this new informal chatty Gina."

"I am programmed to provide the scout with companionable conversation. In the situation you are in I judge that this would be important to your mental health."

"Gina you are most correct. Please continue doing that. I like the new Gina, you cheer me up.

"That is the idea. Now, regarding your earlier question, yes I have scanned the lair of the srinachs. They live in a large cave above the valley. Access is limited to an unsafe path, very loose and broken. The srinach all sleep in the cave at night but they leave a sentry outside. They will hear the robots coming."

"Do they have an escape route?"

"Yes, they can run away up the hill in the other direction."

"We can't send one robot one way and the other robot the other way?"

"The gravel track ends just past the srenich's cave. It becomes a sheer drop down the mountain."

"That's good. So they can only escape in one direction. Up the mountain?"

"Yes, but it is steep and loose. I do not believe the robots can follow."

I paused to think about that for a few seconds.

"Can we drop one of the robots above to cut off their escape?"

"No, the srenich can evade it. There are too many escape routes."

"What if we air lift the Hoshna warriors into the mountain above the cave? Then send in the robots along the path. Any srenich that gets away can be caught by the Hoshna."

"That will be very dangerous for the Hoshna warriors. They are armed with axes and bows and arrows. The srenich are large, powerful and very quick. In the confines of the forest above the cave the Hoshna will be at a disadvantage."

"Yes, I see that." I could imagine the situation; the huge animals prowling stealthily through the forest and leaping out onto the Hoshna. They would have no chance to cock and aim an arrow.

"There is another point Theo," said Gina. "The srenich are intelligent predators, like a wolf pack or wild dogs. They are doing what they know. Do we have the right to exterminate this pack?"

"If it is a choice between a wolf pack and a human community…?" I left the question open, but I was sure that Gina understood.

"Can we find a compromise?" she asked.

"Let me think on it," I said. "Put up a display of the area for me to study."

Gina put the display up on the big screen and I used my tablet to scroll and zoom. It was indeed a rugged area with many pathways and galleys that the creatures could use to make their getaway. I could see why the Hoshna had been unable to trap and kill them. I was no hunter; perhaps if I showed the display to Kemlo he could find a way?

I was immersed in examining the display when I felt soft lips nibbling my ear.

"I'm hungry," she whispered.

"Are Faro carnivorous?" I asked.

"If we get hungry enough." Sharp teeth became more insistent.

"Whoa! I'd better get you some food," I laughed.

"Granola bars please."

"You will get fat."

"No, I am getting lots of exercise." She embraced me, pushing breasts into my face.

"You are a shameless alien female," I said. "Your species will corrupt us innocent humans."

"Hmm. That is the sun calling the fire hot," she said with a derisive expression.

"Good expression," I grinned. "Come on, there is some hot coffee and some breakfast." I stood and served her the coffee and food. She got stuck in with a will.

"What are you doing?" she asked between mouthfuls.

I pointed to the screen.

"That is where the home of the srenich live. Gina and me are trying to see how we can trap and kill them."

She looked carefully at the screen while eating. After a couple of minutes she shook her head.

"You cannot close off all their escape routes. See, there are too many." She stood, walked to the screen and pointed to all the galleys and tracks leading up the mountain. "And the srenich do not need tracks. They can jump from tree to tree and rock to rock. You must trap them and kill them in the cave."

"Right, that's what I was thinking." It was just a bit embarrassing that she had analyzed and concluded in seconds what I was still cogitating over! "But, how do we do that? They have a sentry which will hear or smell us coming."

"Kill the sentry. I have seen you kill lemsi with your gun at long distance."

Lemsi were rabbit like creatures which were a great delicacy for the Yela. I had used non-explosive bullets in my gun and gone hunting with Salny and Kemlo.

"I cannot get close enough Salny."

"Hmmm, above the cave here..." She indicated a spot to one side and above the cave entrance. "You can see the cave entrance and the path. Wait for the sentry and shoot it."

I looked carefully at the area. I could see a level spot where I could land the shuttle and then climb down the hill to above the cave.

"You are quite the little hunter," I said with a smile.

"I went hunting with my father and brothers," she said. "I was the only woman to do that." She gave me a stern look, jaw clenched. "The men did not like it but I did not care and my father supported me."

"Your father was a good and wise man," I said.

"He was challenging Panstrosh for the leadership. Panstrosh killed him."

I was shocked and reached out to squeeze her hand.

"How do you know that?"

"Kemlo told me. He saw everything. Panstrosh sent my father into the bush to flush out the Lumni. Kemlo saw him talking secretly with Foorni. Later, Foorni crept up behind my father and shot him, then pretended that he had mistaken the movement of the bush as a lumni."

I remembered that Foorni was the warrior who Kemlo had killed after being challenged. Now I understood why the gentle Kemlo had killed his fellow Faro warrior. They had previous!

"Salny I am so sorry. Tell me, is that why Panstrosh chose you as a gift for me?"

"I was chosen by Yovna the priest, but he was doing

what Panstrosh wanted. They wanted to be rid of me, I was too independent." She was looking tense and tearful.

"Darling I am so pleased that you were sent to me." I went over and embraced her.

"I am also," she said. "And Panstrosh is so angry that you are a benign god and have taken me as your woman."

"Good. Let him be angry." I grinned and gave her a cuddle. "Things are changing."

"Yes. My father's spirit will be pleased. But he will not rest until he is avenged."

I looked at her thinking *these are tough people*. But I could not blame her holding a grudge. There was no law and her family had suffered a vicious crime. Reparation had to be taken personally.

"We will find a way," I said. She looked at me with love and gratitude but I almost regretted my instinctive remark. I could just go and kill Panstrosh and the priest and declare me head man. No one would challenge me and if they did they would also die. But did I want to descend to such savagery? That would make me no better than them. It was the age old conundrum of all civilized men.

I helped myself to another coffee and watched Salny finish eating. She had a big appetite but put on no weight. Her body was feminine and curvy but muscular, almost at the level of an athlete. Natural food and hard work kept her fit. But it would also wear out her body. She would be lucky to live past fifty or so, if she did not die of an accident, disease or in childbirth. The 'natural' life was fine for well off sophisticates living in an advanced society. The reality in a primitive society was brutally different.

I was doing what I could to make their lives easier; with Gina's help we had improved their fishing catches and made better farming implements. We were showing them how to make and use fertilizer and to also use natural chemicals and techniques to kill plant infections and fight off insects.

I had introduced them to the idea that dirt was a bad thing, for them and their animals and caused disease and infection. Having a clean and sweet smelling Salny to live with was an added bonus!

I now wanted to help the Hoshna in the same way. But first we had to dispose of the vicious srenich who were making their lives difficult.

We finished breakfast, showered, got dressed and headed down to the village, arms around each other's waists. We found the village almost empty apart from some older women and lots of children. But one of the ladies shouted to Ilnira and she came out of a hut to greet us.

"You had a long sleep?" she asked with an amused expression.

"We were tired," said Salny with a straight face.

"Kemlo has gone with Santor to the fields. They will return soon."

"Good. We have some ideas about the srenich."

"Kemlo has been telling the Hoshna about your farming methods."

"There is much more I wish to tell the Hoshna. I think we will stay here for a while and help them."

"That will be wonderful. I can spend time with my family." Ilnira smiled happily.

Our pleasant talk was interrupted by a scream. We turned to see a woman running down a rough track into the village.

"Srenich coming," she screamed.

"Dum, Dee, you are with me." I turned and ran towards the woman fumbling to get my small pistol from its holster. The woman was carrying a small child and was struggling to run.

"Dum, go ahead and guard the woman. Kill the

srenich if they attack."

"Yes Captain." Dum bounded ahead of me, his metal legs pumping powerfully.

The srenich chasing the woman appeared around the bend of the track about twenty yards behind her. Dum was fifty yards away.

"Gina, the animal is going to get to the woman before Dum. Instruct Dum to fire on the animal as soon as he has a target."

Then horrifyingly another two animals appeared through the forest in front of the woman, cutting her off from the village. They were nearly on top of the woman when Dum began firing. Next to me Dee also began firing. I stopped running, went down on one knee and braced my arm. But I was not needed. All three animals convulsed and with screams of pain collapsed on the track just feet from the terrified woman. She had fallen to the floor, cradling and protecting the child.

I ran up to her and helped her get up. She was looking wild eyed at the robots no doubt wondering who was going to eat her first, the srenich or the robots.

"You are safe," I said. "My robots will not harm you." Salny and Ilnira had run up and took the crying child off her.

"Mazhni, where is your man?" asked Ilnira. "He should have been with you."

"There were more srenich and he stayed to hold them off while we ran away," replied Mazhni. "But these others were waiting for us."

"They are clever hunters," said Ilnira nodding. "That is what they do. They separate the strong from the weak, keep the strong occupied while others attack the weak. You should have all stayed together."

"Where is your man now?" asked Salny.

"In the field with the yellow trees." She waved in the

direction from which she had run. "Please go and help him."

I nodded.

"Of course. Dum, you run ahead and see if you can find this woman's husband. I will follow with Dee once this lady is safe." Dum bounded off in the direction the woman had indicated.

I turned to Salny. "Can you and Ilnira take this lady back to the village. I think it's safe now."

Salny looked at me with a concerned expression.

"Yes Theo. Please take care."

I showed her my gun and pointed to Dee. "I think we can look after ourselves," then turned and jogged after Dum with Dee at my heels. I was thinking that I should have named the robots Butch and Sundance after the ancient gun fighters!

We jogged a hundred yards or so and turned the corner. In the distance I could see the yellow trees that the woman had mentioned. I also spotted Dum just before he veered off into the field in the direction of the trees. I increased my speed and Dee easily kept up.

"Gina, has Dum spotted anything?"

"Yes, we can see two of the creatures circling the trees. There may be more."

"Tell him to make maximum speed. The woman's husband may be in trouble."

"He is doing so Theo."

We arrived at the turnoff into the field. It was cultivated with a selection of different plants neatly laid out. The farmer clearly had a tidy mind. The edges of the field were delimited by piles of rocks on two sides and a thick copse of trees at the other two sides.

I spotted grey shapes lurking amongst the trees. Dum was fifty yards ahead of us and approaching the copse when he was spotted by the srenich. They immediately turned their attention to the robot, spreading out. Three more of the creatures appeared moving to encircle Dum. He continued unperturbed, stopping at the edge of the trees. The two srenich under the trees were growling and attempting to leap up into a tree. I guessed that Mazhni's husband had taken refuge in the tree.

But the srenich looked very capable of leaping into the tree. One leapt a huge height and scrabbled to hold onto a branch. There was the crack of a gun and the creature convulsed and dropped down from the tree writhing in pain. Dum shot it again and it lay still. Its friend paused and turned towards Dum growling fiercely, then launched itself at the robot.

Meanwhile the three that had left the trees to encircle Dum rushed him from behind. We were still thirty yards away but I paused, steadied myself and took aim. Dee continued running but also raised its gun and began firing.

The rattle of gunfire spooked the srenich and they all turned and leapt away. But we cut them down, apart from one that managed to disappear in the forest. Our little guns were lethal. If the bullet entered any part of the body it would kill the creature. If it hit a leg it would blow the leg off.

Dum waited for us to join it. I looked up in the tree to see the Hoshna male hanging precariously onto a high branch. He looked terrified but his face relaxed when he saw me.

"How is my woman and the child?" he shouted.

"They are both well." I gave him a wave. "Come on down, the srenich are all dead."

"Ha! Your creatures are amazing." He clambered down from the tree. He was young and agile and he bounded over and threw his arms around me. He was hot and sweaty and smelled of various farm animal odors but I gave him a hearty embrace. "These cranskor srenich are a curse!" he growled. "They are getting bolder."

I guessed that 'cranskor' was a derogatory word.

"We have a plan to get rid of them permanently," I said.

"We will be in your debt," he said giving me a courteous bow. "Meanwhile." He looked around at the dead animals. "We have much meat."

"Do you eat them?" I said. I must have looked disgusted because he laughed.

"They are mostly muscle but their livers and other internals can be boiled and then barbequed."

"I will give my share to you," I said.

He laughed uproariously, much more than the joke deserved and bashed me on the back.

"Let's go see how the women are doing," I added.

"My name is Henslo," said the young man as we trotted back to the village. "My woman is Mazhni and we have just one child."

"We talked to Mazhni," I said. "She is a very brave young woman. She ran like the wind with the baby."

"Yes, I am proud of her." He nodded looking happy. "When I told her to take the baby and run she did not argue."

"Did you intend to hide up the tree?" I asked.

"Yes, it was risky because I had to stay on the ground long enough to attract the srenich away from Mazhni and the baby, before climbing the tree."

"Unfortunately there were three other srenich hiding outside the field. They were chasing Mazhni when we arrived just in time to rescue them."

Henslo made a growling noise in his throat and spat with disgust.

"They are too clever those scum. And getting bolder all the time."

We arrived back at the village to find that a crowd had gathered. Salny was waiting on the road gazing anxiously towards us. She waved excitedly when she saw us coming and then shouted to the villagers. There was loud cheering when they spotted us.

It was a happy evening in the village, not just because of the rescue of Henzlo and his family, but also the killing of a brace of srenich and the plan to eradicate the dreaded carnivores. We enjoyed another feast, although I passed on the srenich barbequed liver. It was apparently a delicacy that was much enjoyed by the villagers and they had never had such a plentiful supply.

The plan to eradicate the srenich was agreed and village chief Santor agreed to set about organizing the hunting party for the next day.

As the sun went down behind the mountain Salny and I with our trusty robots returned to the shuttle. The company of my beautiful partner and the friendship of the Hoshna were beginning to make me feel more at home on this alien planet. I felt at last that I had friends and was a part of a community. That had not been the case with the Faro where I had first been treated as a god and then with disbelief and suspicion when I had claimed to be just mortal.

But I put those problems at the back of my mind as I followed my beautiful partner up the stairs of the shuttle.

Chapter 11

Salny could never have possibly imagined that her life could change so much. From primitive village girl to flying goddess was an impossible leap of the imagination. Yet it had become a reality with this wonderful god from another world.

But just when she had begun to accept that version of reality it was taken from her. The Hoshna village chief Santor had asked Vullious where he was from and he had denied being a god. He was from another world. A world just like our one yet with people like him and intelligent machines. He was lost and far from home and would probably never be found by his people.

The realization of that hit her with such force that she was almost in tears. Her mother used to tell her stories of adventures, monsters and goblins, of lost orphans who discover that they are princes and kings. Instead of an invincible god she now saw a lonely young man, far from home in an alien land with only his machines for company. He had not used his power for domination and self gratification but treated them all with respect.

Her love of him as a god was transformed into the physical love of a woman for a man. She wanted to be with him, to try to give him what he had lost from his homeland. And with that realization came a new understanding; the world was not a mysterious place dominated by gods and spirits but a complex physical playground which could be understood and enjoyed. Enlai were not the playthings of the gods; they were, or could be the masters of their world.

And with that, she realized, came a new

responsibility; it was not for the gods to tell mortals how to live their lives. The mortals had to work that out for themselves. It was an awesome responsibility and she was not sure that the Enlai were ready for that. In fact, with leaders such as Panstrosh and his followers she was sure that they were not!

The next day was as usual bright but windy with a few white clouds scudding across the sky. We enjoyed a cozy breakfast like a newly married couple. Our first night together had been full of lust and the mutual exploration of each others bodies. The previous night had been more amorous than lustful.

I could not help asking myself what Salny's feelings were towards me. Was her behavior just devotion or the instinct of a woman for self preservation? That is, finding a strong man to protect you. I was also not sure how I felt about her. She was beautiful and her behavior was loving, but we had not had an opportunity to discuss our deeper emotions, and perhaps, I told myself, it was too 'heavy' to be asking her such things. Go with the flow for now!

The plan for today was to attack the srenich's lair at dusk when all the animals would have returned from their day's hunting. During the day the natives would prepare the hunting party while I scouted and prepared my position above the cave. The hunting party would be led by my two robots and we would all be in contact via Gina.

We finished our breakfast, showered and got dressed. Salny liked wearing the clothing I had found for her; I think she enjoyed being my woman and wanted everyone to remember that by wearing her different clothing.

She insisted that she would come with me to the cave and brooked no argument.

"I am a good climber," she boasted.

I put my arms around her. "You are too curvy to be a good climber."

"All muscle," she said. "I will race you around the village to prove it."

I laughed. "I surrender. You are a better runner than me."

We prepared to leave the shuttle. "Dum and Dee have you run your daily diagnostics?" I had not checked the robots for some days and wanted to be sure that they were in prime condition.

"Yes Captain, all our systems are normal."

"How are your energy reserves?" The robots had compact fusion reactors that provided an almost infinite supply of energy.

"At one hundred percent."

"Good. How are we for ammunition?"

"We each have five clips with eight bullets in each clip. There are only ten clips left in the store."

"Hmmm. I have two clips. Let's try and be economical with the bullets. They have to last a long time."

"Yes Captain. How should we be economical?" asked Dum."

"Ah, shoot only at clear targets," I suggested.

"We are programmed to shoot on the basis of threat," explained Dum. "If the threat is high we must shoot as quickly as possible. If low then we wait for a clear target."

"Right, that seems reasonable. Continue in that way." I felt slightly chastened but enlightened!

I consoled myself that if we ran out of bullets I could defend myself using the ultrasonic gun. That would never run out.

We made our way down to the village to find preparations in progress for the big hunt. I consulted Gina and asked her how wide was the track leading up to the cave.

"It is not a track but just a ridge at the base of the cliff above an escarpment that leads to another cliff. It is very narrow, sometimes just a few feet and very broken. The men should be roped together and secure themselves with spikes into the ground in case one of them slips."

"But wait, how are the robots going to negotiate that?"

"The robots have built in climbing fixtures. Their feet can adjust to grip the ground. They have spikes to secure themselves with ropes. They cannot climb a cliff face but they can negotiate that kind of loose gravely sloping track."

"I see. And the track widens out into a plateau in front of the cave?"

"Correct."

"So my question is, do we need the men to accompany the robots? Looks to me like they will be more of a liability than an asset."

"Yes I agree. But they want to feel part of the enterprise."

"Okay, I suggest we limit the numbers to half a dozen or so. They will be the witnesses to the slaughter of the srenich. Hopefully."

"I agree. Check that they have ropes and spikes."

"Thank you Gina." I went over to talk to Santor. He listened carefully to my explanation of what Gina had just told me.

"So, just a few men need accompany the robots," I finished.

"I understand," he nodded, frowning. "We have spikes on our spears to allow us to go along such tracks in the mountain. But if the men are roped together and one slips that will bring all of them down."

"There is a method. The man in the lead moves forward while the others are secured. Then the next man moves and so on. Only one man at a time is moving. That way if he slips he has five or six others to hold him."

"I see. Yes, that is clever." He nodded his approval.

"Good. Select your men Santor and let us explain that to them. Then you should select three men to accompany me. Salny also wants to accompany me. I have ropes and spikes."

He shook his head in amused frustration.

"Salny should have been a man. Except that she is the most beautiful woman in both villages."

I chuckled my agreement.

"I am very happy that she is not a man."

He looked puzzled for a few moments.

"Tell me, do women on your planet do as they please?"

"Yes of course. In the past women were subservient to men, as they are here. But hundreds of years ago that changed on my planet. Now they are the equals of men in all ways."

"But women are too difficult. Give them equality and they will make our lives miserable."

I had to laugh at the innocent sexism of his remark.

"Your women are difficult in trivial ways because that is their only way of asserting themselves. When they have the confidence that equality gives them then they will not need to do that."

He had to think about that.

I decided that discussing female equality with a man who was at the same cultural and educational level as someone from our Iron Age was a pointless activity.

"These things happen in their own time Santor. My species is thousands of years ahead of yours. Your species will also change in the future, perhaps like mine or perhaps not. It's is impossible to say."

"Yes, like knowing what the weather will bring

tomorrow," he said it with a laugh as if it was obviously an impossibility.

I nodded with a smile but decided to say no more about the wonders of the future.

"So, go select your men to accompany my robots and explain to them how they will make their way to the cave of the srenich. I will come with you and we can also select three men to accompany me and Salny to the cliff top."

"How will we know that you have killed the sentry?" asked Santor.

"I will inform my robots and they will tell you."

"How will you...?"

I anticipated his question.

"We have something called radio." I tapped the comms button clipped to my shirt. "This thing connects me to my ship and to my robots. We can talk to each other at all times. However far away we are."

He nodded.

"Ah yes, as you were talking to your ship yesterday." He shook his head in amazement. "Are you really a god pretending to be a man?"

I smiled and squeezed his shoulder.

"I am a man like you Santor. Come, let's do it."

Our preparations took some time. I wanted to be sure that the men who accompanied the robots understood basic climbing techniques and safety procedures. Not that I was an expert but I had done some rock climbing and Gina was, as always, a mine of useful information.

The three warriors who were to accompany me were my new buddy Henslo, he whose wife and child we had rescued from the srenich, and his two hand picked warriors.

"We will protect you," Henslo had said, clutching his spear and giving a short bow with a fierce expression.

I wasn't sure who was protecting who! If we were attacked by srenich it was more likely that I would have to protect my three 'guardians'. But there was a possibility that their local knowledge may be helpful and I judged that they would not be in the way.

The journey up to the srenich's cave would take a couple of hours and evening was moving in, the sun low in the horizon. The attack party set off with Dum in the lead followed by Kemlo and with Dee in the rear. We waved goodbye to them and watched them leave until they had disappeared in the trees.

I suddenly felt exposed without Dum and Dee next to me even though I was amongst friends. We returned to the village and enjoyed some hot herbal tea and hard biscuits and then a tour of the village during which I offered up some advice about farming and some construction tips, curtsey of Gina of course.

Gina then informed us that the attack party had reached the ledge and were roping themselves together. We had calculated between half an hour to an hour for them to negotiate that part before arriving at the broader ledge that led to the caves. It was time to lead my party to the shuttle.

Salny and I collected Henslo and his two mates and headed up the hill to the shuttle with the villager's shouts and wishes ringing in our ears.

"You are about to fly," I told Henslo and his friends. "Have no fear, it is safe."

They all made signs of protection, a circular motion of the hand around the face and body and muttered an incantation.

"My children all wanted to come," said one of the Hoshna. "They were very envious."

I chuckled. "Perhaps we can treat the children to a ride when this is over."

"Hah! Not just the children," said Henslo. "Everyone will want to try."

"My aircraft uses water for fuel. We can make as many journeys as we like."

"I do not understand how it makes fire from water," said Hemslo. "There is some black thick liquid in a hole at the base of the mountain. It smells and if you drop a burning stick on it then it will burn."

"Water can be changed by my machine into something like the black stuff which burns," I explained.

They shook their heads in wonder.

We got to the shuttle and I operated the remote to open the doors. The steps unwound causing grunts of alarm from my friends. Salny entered first and I invited my guests to follow. They entered the shuttle looking around eyes wide. I showed them around and then settled them in the seats. There was a couple of fold down seats in the wall with belts and the two chairs. Salny stayed in the cabin with the men to reassure them while I went forward into the cockpit.

I powered up the shuttle systems and started the engines to warm them then contacted Gina.

"How are our friends doing Gina?"

"They are half way along the ridge. They did meet a group of srenich returning to the cave. The robots attended to them and the men got in some target practice."

"Looks like they are having fun. We are ready to go here."

"I have downloaded the navigation coordinates into the shuttle. The trip will take just a few seconds."

"Right, set to auto, all systems ready."

The engines wound up and the shuttle lifted with a lurch then climbed slowly into the blue sky them rotated and continued to climb and head slowly into the mountain. After a minute we were flying parallel to the mountain.

"Look to your left and you can see the attack party

on the ledge," said Gina.

I looked and saw the tiny figures trekking slowly across the small ridge. Ahead I could see where the ridge opened out into an embankment which led to the caves. The attack group only had a couple of hundred yards to go to the embankment.

"Gina, tell Dum that they should slow down and stop when they come within a hundred yards of the embankment. I will let them know when I am in position."

"Will do Captain."

The aircraft began to climb higher until we reached the level above the caves where there was an escarpment that sloped gradually up to the next granite peak. On automatic it edged slowly towards the rock ledge that was our landing spot.

"Captain, you have control," said Gina. I took the controls and gently maneuvered the shuttle into position then eased it down. I examined the ground beneath and found a clear spot for the wheels. Another scan to ensure it looked solid, level and clear and then I gently brought her down but kept the engines running in case there was any subsidence.

Once I was satisfied that the ship was safe I powered off then stood and returned to the main cabin where I found Salny explaining the science and technicalities of flight to our passengers. She was proud of her knowledge, having quizzed me for many hours. I had been impressed by her ready acceptance and understanding of these complex ideas.

"I hope you enjoyed the trip," I said to the men.

"It was too short," said Henslo looking excited.

"Did you see the hunting party? They are close to the caves so we must move quickly."

I helped Salny to unbuckle the men. They stood and grabbed their weapons and followed me out of the ship.

"That way." I pointed down the hill. The ground sloped gently for about two hundred yards to the cliff edge. Trees were few but there were lots of bushes and a tangle of growth on the ground. We walked carefully over the rugged ground. The men spread out, their bows at the ready with arrows loaded.

"Salny, you take the ultrasonic gun." I handed her the gun. She nodded, holding the gun gingerly. "Your job is to guard our backs." I waved at the forest behind us. I had earlier explained what the gun did and allowed her to use it on an unfortunate farm animal.

It took just a few minutes to reach the cliff edge.

"Henslo, I want you and your men to spread out and find places where you can have a clear view of the clearing beneath. If you see a srenich then tell me. But don't shout, just wave."

Henslo grunted and looked at his men who nodded their understanding. They spread out, scrambling with athletic agility over boulders to find vantage points.

These guys are mountain men I thought. *This is bread and butter to them.*

I found my own vantage point and looked down at the clearing beneath us. Sure enough there were a number of srenich wondering around. They looked like females with cubs. The cubs were gamboling around, chasing each other and rolling around in mock fights.

I suddenly felt remorse that we were about to kill these intelligent herd animals. But then I remembered how they had chased Henslo's woman and child. Had they caught them they would have ripped them apart. I was sure that there were herds of the creatures in other more remote locations.

"Sorry guys but it is a matter of survival. You must learn not to bother humans. Sorry, Enlai."

Although these people are human in every way that matters I thought.

One of Henslo's men put an arm up then pointed towards a pile of boulders at the end of the clearing. I peered in that direction and saw nothing initially. But looking carefully I spotted the silver grey shine of the sreich's coats. There were two males lurking in the rocks.

Damn but they were a difficult target! My little gun was quiet, it made just a sharp cough for each shot. The problem was that the females may notice if the males were shot and alert the pack. I would have to shoot the females first. That may tempt the males away from the rocks to investigate.

I got on the comm. to Gina.

"Gina, we are in position."

"Theo, the others are stopped one hundred or so yards away around the bend. They are ready to go as soon as you give them the word."

"Okay. There are two females with cubs outside and two males at the edge of the clearing. I think they are the sentries. But they are partly hidden. I will shoot the females first then the males. I suggest you tell the others to head in now."

"I will do so Theo."

I settled myself on the rock and leveled my pistol, holding it in both hands. It had an electronic telescopic sight which was an attachment, not something that I would normally carry. I adjusted the sight and zoomed in to the first female animal, then panned across to the second then panned across to the males. I practiced the movements to get them precise. I had to take all four animals in quick order.

"Firing now Gina." I focused on the first animal and squeezed the trigger. The weapon gave a muffled thud. I swiveled and shot all four animals in quick succession then looked up quickly. The two females and one of the males lay still but the other male stood, then collapsed as one leg gave way, then stood again and growled loudly.

I focused the gun on the animal and shot it again. This time it fell and lay still.

"All four animals are dead Gina."

"We should rename you Deadeye Dick from Deadwood," said Gina.

"Easy to be a sharp shooter with this contraption," I said. "But I like the name Deadeye Dick."

Then I noticed that Henslo was waving and pointing.

"Oh oh." I looked down to see two other srenich that had come out of the cave. "They have sensed something. Two others have come out of the cave. Should I shoot them?"

"No, that may panic them even more. We want to trap as many as we can in the cave."

"Right, I'll hold off for now." The two newcomers walked over to the dead bodies, circling and sniffing them. To my dismay they began howling mournfully.

"Fuck, that's enough to wake the dead," I muttered. Sure enough other animals began coming out of the cave and sniffing around the dead ones and then joining in the howling.

The animals started to become more agitated, some of the males growling aggressively and beginning to dart around.

"Gina, where is the attack team. The animals have sensed there is danger and are getting agitated."

"They will be there in seconds Theo. I have ordered Dum who is in the lead to make maximum speed."

The animals were becoming more agitated, particularly the males who were all out of the cave and prowling the perimeter of the escarpment growling ferociously.

These creatures are bloody intelligent and aggressive

I thought. They had the size and power of a jaguar and the aggression of a crocodile. I was sure that as soon as Dum appeared they would attack.

I waved to Henslo and made motions for him and the men to prepare to attack the animals. They understood immediately and readied their bows.

Dum appeared moving quickly around the bend of the cliff. The animals noticed the robot and growling they spread out, taking attack positions.

As soon as Dum started firing I also started firing but aiming for the animals furthest from Dum. The creatures seem to have no fear because they threw themselves at the robot with ferocious speed. Dum kept coming, his gun barking. Behind him appeared the hunting party who took up static positions but left a path for Dee to come through.

Despite the hail of bullets and arrows some of the animals got through and attempted to savage the robots. They could cause no damage but the first ones interrupted the robots shooting and allowed others to get through to the men.

I was horrified to see the men having to defend themselves with axes. I could not shoot into the melee for fear of hitting the men.

But the robots fire power began to prevail and the animals at the rear, seeing their fellows falling, hesitated, then some turned and headed for the hill. I attempted to shoot them before they could get away but they were moving too fast. I spotted females with cubs leaping up the rugged hill into the bushes. I was seriously impressed with the animal's intelligence, ferocity and courage.

Our attack team led by the robots was moving forward towards the cave but I suspected they would only find a few very young cubs there.

"Gina, tell the robots not to kill any very young cubs in the cave. Put them in the sample bags and take them back to the village. It may be possible to domesticate and train them." This could be the start of a new 'man-dog' partnership I told myself. Whatever happened now I told myself, the srenich had been decimated and would hopefully have learned to keep away from humans; sorry, Enlai. I was beginning to think of these people as human.

Chapter 12

That evening the villagers celebrated with food, song and dance. The girls dressed in pretty costumes and danced daintily while the guys did their fearsome war dances. Some of the singing was harmonic and reminded me of old English medieval songs. These traditions were still kept alive by groups in the depths of Cornwall and the northern counties of England and Scotland. It left me feeling a little sad and lonely, missing home, not so much for the 'olde English' traditions as my modern high tech life. Not to mention my family, friends and girl friends.

Okay, I was getting my share of sex, and very nice it was too. But for all her intelligence and sweet charm Salny was an Iron Age maiden whose conversation rotated around subjects such as which were the best herbs and wild edible produce to look for in different parts of the land and different seasons. She was great for that. Not so much on music, literature, sports or which was the best racing flyer for the round the moon race.

But she was good company, had a sense of humor as well as a fantastic body, no inhibitions and a limitless appetite for sex. So count your blessings Theo; you could have been marooned on a planet inhabited by creatures that looked like a baboon, complete with bloated red backside!

They also, amazingly, had booze! My idea that they had not yet discovered alcohol was wrong. But one taste of the acrid concoction made me wish that they had NOT discovered how to make it! It was cloudy and vinegary although the alcoholic content was about the same as wine.

They had not got around to distilling the juice to make a spirit yet and I judged that the drink would probably be much improved by distillation. I suggested it to Santor and we got into a discussion of how a still works. After a while the booze did not taste that bad and by the end of the evening I had promised to build one for them before I left.

Females were not allowed booze but Salny sat next to me with the circle of men and when the booze was going around she held out her cup. There were some looks exchanged amongst the men but when I nodded at the jug bearer she poured Salny some. Salny took a sip and made a disgusted face, to the men's amusement.

Just to spite them however, she carried on drinking. *Iron Age Feminist* I thought. *You are quite a girl!*

It was difficult to get drunk on their alcohol however; it was so nasty. I confined myself to drinking a little just to be polite, while Salny did it just to show her independence.

Evening arrived and we talked a little under the moon before heading for our beds. Arm in arm under the brilliant moon with the wind ruffling our hair all that was missing was the romantic music.

"Why do men drink liasni? And not allow women?" asked Salny. Liasni was their name for the 'wine'.

"It has something in it that makes you happy and may make you do things you would not normally do," I explained.

"What kinds of things?"

"Men may get into arguments and fights. Women may allow men to have sex with them. If they drink enough."

"I would never allow any man to have sex with me. Except you." She gave me an endearing look and I gave her a hug in return. "But it taste so bad," she added.

"We have liasni on my planet which tastes very nice," I said. "Girls like to drink it. Maybe I will make some."

"Will you use it to have sex with other girls?" she asked.

"I do not need liasni to have sex with any other woman. All I have to do is ask. But my beautiful Salny is enough for me."

That earned me a dimpled smile and a hug.

During the next few days I attempted to impart to the Hoshna some of the knowledge and techniques that I had passed on to the Faro. I found the Hoshna more responsive and practical. Their use of iron smelting was more advanced than the Faro as was their farming techniques and animal husbandry. Unfortunately they were just as ignorant about hygiene, both in their farming and their private lives.

I made much more rapid progress with them than I had with the Faro. They were also to a man, woman and child, unfailingly polite and appreciative. I was their hero and savior and they could not show me enough respect and friendship. I confess I loved it; not so much the adulation, just the respect and friendship. So much so that I considered whether to move my base from the coast up to the Hoshna village; the only thing I would miss was the sea. Swimming and fishing had become my favorite pastimes with my lovely partner.

I pondered on what to do about the Faro's sullen and uncooperative attitude, particularly from the village elders and leaders. Clearly they saw me as a threat to their authority. But also, they were hostile to friendly co-existence with the Hoshna. The ruffians wanted to carry on raiding and fighting!

Whilst I was seen as a god they dared not go against

me. But my efforts to convince them that I was mortal had diminished my authority. I decided that I would make a last effort to impose my will on them. When I returned I would tell them that I would not tolerate any attacks on the Hoshna; neither on their animals or on the people themselves. If they did not conform I would move myself to the Hoshna village and help them instead of the Faro.

We bid goodbye to our new friends with a promise that we would return soon and boarded the shuttle. Kemlo and Ilnira were accompanying us, although Ilnira wanted to stay longer with her family Kemlo has affairs to attend to back at Faro.

We lifted off and made the short journey back to the coast, landing at our previous hill top location. I decided to accompany Kemlo and Ilnira to the village to make my presence felt and get a feel for what had been happening during our absence.

Strolling down the hill towards the village with the sound and smell of the sea pervading the clear air I was reminded of what a beautiful spot this was. Living in the mountains had its own appeal but for me being next to the sea reminded me of pleasure filled pastimes and holidays that brought a smile to my face.

The village with its scruffy huts and the smell of animal dung dragged me back to reality. I looked at Salny, with her pointy ears and oddly alien face and body and asked myself if I was in a dream from which I would soon waken.

The village was almost deserted except for women and children and old men. Kemlo went over to an old fellow who was sitting outside his hut trimming the husks from a pile of plants similar to sweetcorn.

"Janso, good day. Where is everyone?"

"Good day Kemlo." The man nodded respectfully. "Panstrosh has organized a hunting party."

"A hunting party? To hunt what?" asked Kemlo.

"Some fat Hoshna pranli."

Pranli were the cow like creatures that the Hoshna farmed for meat and milk.

Kenlo turned to look at me with a scowl on his young face. "That animal Panstrosh is ignoring everything you said to him."

"When did the hunting party leave?" I asked the old man.

"When the sun came over the trees." The old man pointed to the trees in the direction of the sunrise. The sun was now past noon and I calculated that they would have left three hours previously. They would have arrived at the Hoshna farmlands about now.

I swore under my breath. "We have to get back and stop them."

"Pranli good meat," said the old man.

"If you give Hoshna fish, they give you pranli meat," I suggested. This seemed a novel idea to the old man. He looked puzzled and thoughtful. No time to teach him the essentials of barter I thought.

"Come Kemlo, let's go."

We ran back to the shuttle and boarded quickly. I instructed Gina to fly us to the Hoshna village, taking the route following the track between the two villages, and to scan for the Faro warriors on the way. I was angry, but mostly concerned that we would not arrive in time to stop the barbaric Panstrosh and his warriors from killing innocent Hoshna.

"Panstrosh must be punished for disobeying you," Kemlo said.

"I am not the leader of the village," I pointed out. "When I was a god I could demand that he obey me. Now, I am just a mortal."

"No you are not just a mortal. You are one above all others in your power and knowledge. You must demonstrate that power in order to be obeyed."

"Kemlo is right Theo. Panstrosh understands only power," said Salny.

"Yes, he is right," I agreed. I had tried to take the 'softly softly' approach, to be one of them, but clearly that was unrealistic and futile.

We had arrived over the village without spotting the Faro hunting party. I could imagine the Hoshna looking up at the giant silver 'bird' and asking themselves why I had returned.

"Let's make a search pattern around the village," I suggested to Gina. "Begin with the Hoshna farmlands on the coastal side of the village. And prepare the winches. Me and one of the robots will go down if we find them."

"Theo, are you sure? You will be putting yourself at risk." Gina was doing her impression of my mum.

"We can't land in the forest and the only cleared areas are farmland. We must stop these bastards before they kill someone."

"They may kill you instead."

"Not if one of the robots is with me. They scare the shit out of them."

I turned to Salny and Kemlo and explained what I was going to do. There were two winches in the airlock which were for the specific purpose of allowing me and one of the robots to access areas not suitable for the shuttle to land. Kemlo looked impressed and Salny concerned and a little frightened. They accompanied me to the airlock where I detached and enabled the two harnesses, one designed for me, the other for one of the robots.

Dum arrived and hooked himself onto his harness, while I strapped myself into mine. I instructed Kemlo and Salny to stand back from the airlock door and hold onto safety bars on the back wall. The airlock doors slid open and we had a grandstand view of the forest beneath. We were flying very low and I spotted a couple of pranli, the cow like creatures farmed by the Hoshna, grazing in the meadow.

"I have spotted the hunting party Theo," said Gina. "They have captured some pranli and two females and are heading for the track back to Faro."

"Damn, we are too late." I cursed internally. How many did they kill to capture their bounty I asked myself.

The shuttle banked gently and changed direction then began to come down lower.

"I will drop you on the track ahead of the hunters where you can intercept them," said Gina. "If you wish I can lower the other robot once you are disconnected."

"Right, thanks Gina. Let's see. That may not be necessary."

"We are here Theo," Gina announced. The shuttle was hovering over the rugged track that wound down to the coast. "The hunting party have seen the shuttle and are pointing."

"Good. I hope that will put the wind up them. Dum, let's go." I stepped to the door and leapt out followed by the robot. There was a scream of terror from Salny followed by her crying out my name. I could well imagine how she must have felt seeing me jump into the void.

I fell for a few feet before the line took up the slack and decelerated my fall, then brought me down at a controlled speed. I hit the ground and smacked the button to disconnect the harness. We were on the path and I could see the hunting party fifty yards away heading down the mountain. There were about fifteen of them, seven riding 'horses', the others on foot. Three of the horses were also carrying females who were strapped behind their captors. Five of the Faro who were on foot were leading pranli.

I guessed that the hunting party needed to make a

quick getaway in order to outdistance any chasing Hoshna. They were all armed with bows, spears and swords.

I sent Dum ahead of me to block their path. He scuttled with frightening rapidity towards them looking like a giant ferocious ant. I followed, my gun in one hand, while the shuttle whooshed overhead, circling over us like a silver pterodactyl.

"Dum, use your ultrasonic gun to stop them."

The robot did so, causing mayhem in the ranks of the hunters. The horses screamed and panicked, throwing their riders to the floor while the pranli did the same, stampeding off the track and into the forest.

When I got close I spotted Panstrosh as one of the riders ignominiously dumped to the floor by his panicked steed, covering his ears with a pained expression on his ugly face.

"Okay Dum, stop the ultrasonic now. Shoot anyone who goes for their weapon."

None of them did go for their weapons of course; they were terrified out of their wits. Panstrosh stood and tried to bluff it out.

"Why are you here Earthman?"

Aha, It's 'Earthman' now is it? Not 'Great Vulious Sky God'?

"I warned you not to raid the Hoshna."

"It is our way. They raid us, we raid them. You use your creatures to stop us from what must be done. You do not understand our customs."

"There is no need to raid the Hoshna to get meat. As I have explained, if you take them fish, they will give you meat. There is no need for violence."

"We do not give our fish," he said, turning to his lieutenants for support. A number of them growled their support but it was not unanimous.

"You give some of your fish and get meat in return.

And other food that the Hoshna grow like vegetables and grain for bread."

"We can just take what we want and give nothing," he growled stubbornly.

Shall I shoot the bastard now and be done with his arrogant stupidity? I asked myself. I was tempted. Instead I pulled my gun out and shot his horse through the head. The poor animal collapsed, its body twitching before it died.

"You will do as I say, otherwise the next time that will be you," I shouted fiercely. "Do you understand Panstrosh? I will not tell you again. Now, release those women now."

He looked at me, then at the dead horse and his face twisted in anger and hate.

"Now!" I shouted, waving the gun at him and his men. The three with women on their horses hastily untied them. Two of them helped the women down from their horses but the third pushed her roughly off, throwing her to the ground. The young woman fell heavily and moaned with pain. I walked over and shot his horse as well, pitching him to the ground.

"Think about that as you walk back to the village," I said. I turned to the young women. "Are you hurt?"

"Just some bruises," she replied shyly.

"Are you able to return to your village?" I asked.

"Yes we can, it is not far," said the girl. "Thank you for rescuing us."

Holding hands the women ran up the path in the direction of the village.

I turned back to Panstrosh and the other Faro hunters.

"I want you to return to the village now. This is my last warning to you. Next time I will not just shoot your horses. Go!" I pointed dramatically down the path.

With black looks and backward glances they headed

down the track towards Faro village. I watched them go for a while until I was sure they would not turn back. The shuttle was still making wide turns above, its engines on ninety percent vertical thrust. Its fusion jets were so efficient it could keep that up for hours if necessary.

"Gina, job done down here, come and pick us up."

"On my way Theo."

The shuttle curved around and hovered over the track, then descended to a level where I could reach the harnesses. I attached the harness and waited. Once the robot was attached and the check lights showed green we were reeled up into the ship. Kemlo helped me into the airlock and then pulled the robot in. He was grinning broadly.

"Can I try that one day?" he asked.

I had to laugh at his enthusiasm. "Sure you can."

I got a welcome hug from a relieved Salny before returning to the cockpit and taking over the controls to pilot the aircraft back to Faro village. With the Hoshna now warned about the raid I was confident that the Faro hunting party would make a rapid return to the village.

Salny took the co-pilots seat as usual, but she looked thoughtful.

"Theo, you cannot trust Panstrosh," she said eventually. "You should have killed him."

I was slightly shocked by her casual attitude to murder, but not surprised. There was no law here, only the law of the strongest and most ruthless. I was the strongest, but not the most ruthless.

"Yes, I know Salny. But where I come from we do not kill someone because we disagree with them."

"He would kill you if he had the chance," she replied.

"Which is why I do not want to be like him," I replied.

"You can never be like him. You are beautiful and

kind and wise."

"Er...beautiful?" I gave her a questioning smirk.

"Yes, you have the beauty of a young girl. Your features are so small and perfect."

"Hey, I don't want to look like a young girl. In my world I am manly and handsome, not pretty."

"In this world you are pretty. And cute."

"Damn. I've never been called cute before. I don't think I like it."

She was covering her mouth with her hand and trying to hold back the laughter.

"You are messing with me young lady. Wait till I get you alone."

"Oooh, what will you do to me?" She tried to look worried, writhing her body seductively.

"Stop it," I laughed. "I am trying to land an aircraft here."

We reached our little hilltop and I managed to land the aircraft without incident.

Back in the main compartment Kemlo and Ilnira were preparing to disembark and return to their house. But I was concerned about their safety. They were closely associated with me and in addition Ilnira was a Hoshna. I would not put it past Panstrosh to take vengeance for his humiliation on them.

"Kemlo, do you think you and Ilnira will be safe?" I asked.

"You think Panstrosh may attack us?"

"Yes."

"I have many friends in the village and my family are very large and powerful. My father is one of the village elders, although he has little love for Panstrosh. Our houses are together in one part of the village. But I will secure our door tonight. It is a strong door."

"Good. Do that and also be careful during the day."

"You should have killed Panstrosh," said Kemlo.

I sighed and nodded.

"Salny also advised that. But killing is not the way we solve problems."

"Some problems cannot be solved any other way." Kemlo looked grim. Then he gave a very human shrug. "But I understand your thinking and I agree."

Kemlo and Ilnira left with our good wishes. As soon as they left Salny embraced me affectionately, her head on my shoulder.

"You have to find a way to control them," she said.

Chapter 13

Salny struggled to understand Theo's reluctance to use violence against Panstrosh and his followers. She knew how brutal they all were, had witnessed their treatment of captured Hoshna and against anyone in the village who they thought was against them. Theo had explained that if he used unprovoked violence against them that would make him no better than them. But that was a silly argument for her; of course Theo could not be as bad as them, that was obvious. And to eliminate something bad was surely a good thing.

But then she also could not help asking herself if her thinking was not just self interest. She knew that if Theo was eliminated her life would become a torment. She would be raped and abused by Panstrosh, given to his brother as a trophy and beaten without provocation. If Theo was killed she resolved to leave the village immediately with her brother and go to the Hoshna. She had been impressed by their greater sense of fellowship. And Santor the village head was totally different from Panstrosh.

However, the thought of Theo not being in her life was intolerable. But also what Theo had brought; the learning and the new way of living. They must not be allowed to disappear. She sensed a new future for the Enlai. A future that precariously lay in the hands of one young human.

Over the next few days we had no more problems with Panstrosh and his crew. I continued my work with the natives, helping them to improve themselves in all areas.

Health was a difficult area. They of course suffered from many minor complaints and injuries and occasionally the odd serious illness. I taught them the importance of cleaning and protecting wounds and scratches to prevent infection. But I had a limited supply of anti-viral and anti-biotic medication and I could not know if they would be suitable. Indeed, they may even be quite harmful.

Inevitably a serious illness arose; a small child had a fever for a few days from a bad laceration which became infected. I had cleaned, disinfected and bandaged the wound some days earlier but the damage had been done. I knew only anti-biotics would work but was loathe to use them. But the child, a small girl, became comatose, her heart weak and unsteady and I knew she was going to die.

I decided to use the standard broad spectrum antibiotic on the principle that it could not make her worse. The results were magical. The child survived the night and appeared stronger so I administered another dose. She continued to improve and in a couple of days was sitting up and eating. A couple of days after that and she was kicking a ball around in the dirt with her friends.

I gave them all a strong lecture on the importance of cleaning all wounds immediately with hot water and bandaging with clean cloth. Word of my achievement spread and my prestige climbed to new levels particularly amongst the females.

The exception was the village leaders under Panstrosh and their bully boys. Their influence in the village had diminished since they had returned from their abortive raid on the Hoshna village.

I also began to introduce the villagers to the idea of trade or barter. I asked them to organize a fishing trip and catch as much fish as they could. We then gathered a large box full and took them to the Hoshna where we exchanged them for an equal weight of meat, and with a pile of vegetables thrown in. These were distributed to the village with a clear explanation of where they came from and why. The younger Faro were particularly taken with the idea. It remained for us to set up a regular exchange between the two villages.

I thought this may have been the last straw for Panstrosh when one evening he sent a messenger to ask me to come down to the village for a meeting with the elders. I decided to take only Dee with me and leave Dum behind to protect Salny and the shuttle. Salny was worried, but I reminded her of how Dum on its own had taken on the whole Faro raiding party. She gave me a warm kiss and said she would prepare my favorite Faro snack for dinner.

As I strolled down the hill towards the village I pondered on my situation. Hardly the nice suburban retirement I had visualized for myself; playing tennis at the tennis club, going sailing with my mates at the sailing club, swimming every day in the sea and occasionally taking a flight to somewhere interesting like the moons of Saturn or sailing on the seas of Poseidon, the first alien world to be settled by humans.

Here I was instead playing nursemaid to a bunch of primitive aliens. On the other hand, Salny could hold her own with any human female beauty. Not just that; despite her primitive origins she had a brain and personality to rival any human. I was doing something which I hoped would benefit these people and perhaps even, without being too grandiose, help them to avoid the wars and religious conflicts that had bedeviled human civilization for thousands of years.

And you never know, I mused, a human starship may blunder across this planet at any time and I could have my ideal retirement. And leave Salny behind? That would be cruel. But, smart as she was, she could not comfortable living amongst humans. Let's leave that problem for now Theo, I told myself.

I was descending the last part of the rugged track to the village. The trees there were thick, branches hanging over the track which bent around a couple of large boulders. I heard an odd swishing sound and then felt an agonizing pain on my shoulder. I gaped at the arrow protruding from my right shoulder. There was another wet thud and another piercing pain from my thigh, then my back. I tried to scream but strength was draining from my legs.

"Dee, I am being attacked..." I managed to gasp before consciousness left me.

When Salny heard the gunfire she felt a stab of anxiety and knew immediately that something was wrong.

"Something has happened to Theo...," she gasped.

"I have message from Dee. Going to help." The robot jerked into action, turned and ran towards the track leading to the village. Without thinking Salny ran after it.

Salny was a fast runner but the robot scuttled ahead of her at an incredible speed, its legs moving with nimble precision over the broken ground. She soon lost sight of it around a corner but continued to follow as quickly as she could, almost stumbling a number of times.

Then she turned a corner and saw both robots. She also saw the bodies of five men sprawled on the ground. She froze, looking around desperately before she saw him. The robots were attending to one of the bodies and she saw that it was Theo.

Staggering over the rocky track in her haste she reached the robots and then saw the arrows protruding from Theo's body. She was seized by a feeling of horror and loss.

"No, no, please..." She tried to get to him but the robots blocked her path.

"Miss Salny, we are attending to the Captain's injuries." The robot's loud mechanical voice jolted her back to a semblance of self control.

"Is he alive?"

"Yes, but his vital signs are weak. We must stabilize him and return him to the *Aegina* where we have more advanced medical facilities."

"What is *Aegina*?" she mumbled in confusion.

"It is the starship that transported us here."

"You are taking him away." She was talking to herself but the robot replied.

"I have checked with *Aegina*. You may accompany us."

The two robots had attached a mask to Theo's face and some wires to his chest as well as a number of other devices whose function was incomprehensible to Salny.

One of the robots retrieved some folding pieces of metal from a cavity in its belly which magically became a stretcher. They gently placed the unconscious man on the stretcher and began to walk back up the hill.

"Follow us," said one of the robots. Salny took one look around the clearing at the four bodies. They were all dead and appeared to have fallen out of the trees. Two of them were hanging from branches. There were bows, arrows and spears on the floor. They had clearly ambushed Theo and shot him before the robot could respond. But it had responded, clinically killing all four.

Salny followed the robots that were moving quickly

but carefully back up the track. She muttered to herself, cursing the insane Panstrosh and his equally vicious and insane supporters.

How could they believe that they could kill Theo without being killed themselves she asked herself. Panstrosh's body was not amongst the dead but she vowed that she would return and kill him herself in any way she could.

She should tell Kemlo that Theo was not dead and was being returned to his ship to be cured? But the robots would not give her time. They must return Theo to his ship. She wanted to be with him she decided. Kemlo would understand that something had happened when the shuttle took off. They would find the four dead bodies and guess that Theo had been attacked. But what would they think after that? That he was dead? Or that he had left them forever? She was sure that Kemlo would be angry and there would be violence. Without Theo and his weapons to protect and support him Kemlo's position would be precarious.

She was torn between turning back and warning her friends and family, and staying with Theo. If he died she wanted to be with him at the end. Choking with emotion she tried to hold back her tears.

They got back to the shuttle and the robots quickly loaded the stretcher, took it into Theo's sleeping cubicle and placing it on the bed then strapped him in. One of the robots came over to her and stretching out a metallic arm it held out a tiny shiny device.

"Please put that inside your ear," it asked. Theo had explained to her how he was able to speak to his machines by having a device implanted in his head, and had also demonstrated the device that went inside the ear. She had used it to converse with the tablet during the many lessons.

She placed it inside her ear and cleared her throat

to speak but was interrupted before she could say anything.

"This is Gina. Am I speaking to Salny?"

"Yes, Gina." Salny had conversed with Gina many times during her education on basic science and Earth civilization.

"Theo has been badly injured and needs advanced medical attention. We have machines on *Aegina* that can provide that. Do you wish to accompany Theo or return to your village?"

"I want to stay with him."

"Then please strap yourself into a chair or in the cockpit but do not touch any controls."

"I understand. Thank you. How badly injured is Theo?"

"At this point I am not sure that he will survive. He has internal bleeding and if his blood pressure drops any lower his heart will stop."

The was Salny's worse nightmare and she gave a wail of anguish and began sobbing loudly and uncontrollably.

"Salny, please strap in, the shuttle is taking off."

She tried to control her distress as she staggered to the cockpit and strapped herself into the co-pilot's seat. The engines were ramping up, their thunderous roar shaking the aircraft. It lifted with a lurch then climbed rapidly. The engines roared and she was pushed back into her seat. It was as if a weight was pushing her body into the seat. She moaned with terror, gasping to breath. Gina's calm voice penetrated her ear.

"We will be accelerating as quickly as possible without hurting Theo. You will feel a force pushing you down into your seat but do not fear, it will not last long."

"Why...?" she gasped.

"The shuttle is gaining speed so that we can get

Theo here as quickly as possible."

"I understand," she gasped.

The force on her body continued to increase but it was tolerable. The view out of the cockpit window was spectacular as the landscape beneath her shrank into hazy contours as the curvature of the world appeared.

Theo had told me that the world was round but I did not believe it. Now I see it, she told herself.

The sky turned black and stars appeared, huge numbers of them, covering the sky like sparkling dust.

"It's beautiful," she whispered.

The weight on her body eased and then disappeared. Suddenly she was falling. She screamed, clutching her seat for support.

"Do not fear Salny, this is normal. You are not falling, just flying in Space."

"If you say so," she gasped, still clutching her seat convulsively. The shuttles engines rumbled and she felt weight again.

"Stay where you are. The shuttle is approaching the starship. It will connect to the starship then the robots will help you disembark," explained Gina. Ahead, through the cockpit, something glinted. Something that was not a star.

As it came closer she began to appreciate its true size. It was a huge metallic bug crawling through empty Space. As the shuttle came closer the giant ship blotted out the stars. She felt a thump and then some metallic noises. She waited for the robots to come and collect her. It took a while and she guessed that they were taking Theo into the ship to attend to him before coming to get her.

Despite her anguish over Theo's injuries she felt a surge of excitement as she looked out at the alien panorama around her.

Mother I wish you were alive to see this she thought.

Eventually one of the robots came.

"Follow me," it said. She released the safety belt and pushed herself to stand. Her body shot up to the ceiling and she screamed with terror.

"You have no weight in Space," explained Gina in her ear. "You must move very gently."

"I can fly!" she shouted, the terror mixed with disbelief and excitement.

She flapped her hands and her body jerked erratically.

"Just get hold of something and pull yourself in the direction you want to go," suggested Gina.

Salny did so, eventually pulling herself to the floor and erratically following the robot. The airlock that allowed her to enter and leave the shuttle now led into the starship. She followed the robot through a labyrinth of rooms and passages until she arrived at a room with a bed above which were a number of machines. Theo was on the bed and the machines were attacking his body with what appeared to be knives and needles.

She moaned with fear and clutched at the wall to steady herself.

"The machines are skilled at repairing the human body," said Gina. "Theo's bleeding must be stopped and his organs repaired. Salny you may remain here until you are tired. The robot will show you to where you can wash and eat and sleep. The bathroom and kitchen is the same as the shuttle so you should be familiar with everything."

"Thank you Gina. I will stay here until I know that Theo is out of danger."

"I will explain what is happening if you wish."

"That will be interesting." Salny was being polite; she was fairly sure that she would understand very little of what was happening. But listening to Gina would help to distract her; to stop her from thinking of what her life would be like without Theo. He had shown her so much knowledge and wonder, and love, that she was sure that her life would never be the same without him.

She floated quietly while Gina explained medical facts and how they affected Theo and his injuries. It was taking a very long time and Salny began to tire. The stress of the last few hours had drained her, and it was now late evening. She fell asleep floating three feet above the floor.

The operations went on for three more hours before the medical robots were satisfied. Gina asked one of the robots to wake Salny.

"Salny, all the operations have gone well. Theo is now out of danger but he will not wake for a day or two. The robot will take you to the living accommodation. Please stay in that area until tomorrow when the robots will show you around the ship."

"Thank you Gina. So Theo will be all right?"

"There is always a risk of deterioration, but he is young and strong. I am hopeful that he will make a full recovery."

"That is good news. You are all such wonderful clever machines."

"Thank you Salny. We are just doing what we were designed to do. Now please follow the robot to your quarters."

Salny followed the robot, which had some way of sticking to the floor and was able to walk almost normally. But Salny loved flying. She decided that living permanently in Space must be the most fun anyone could have.

The robot led her to Theo's living accommodation and showed her the bathroom and kitchen. As Gina had said, the shower, toilet and kitchen facilities were identical to the shuttle. The robot parked itself outside in the corridor and left Salny to fend for herself. She had a shower and prepared some food and a coffee. When she decided to sleep Gina explained that she should strap herself loosely onto the bed.

Despite the incredibly strange environment and the stress and anguish of the last few hours, she almost immediately fell asleep, lulled by the hum of the air conditioning.

Her new environment was so bizarrely different from anything that she was used to that it resulted in time passing slowly for Salny. The next two days seem to last for ever, but despite that she was never bored. She found her way around the ship and never tired of the view out of the cockpit windows or flying like a bird.

She spent hours sitting with Theo, holding his hand and waiting for him to open his eyes. Her love and patience knew no bounds and had no limit for the man who had given her his love and expanded the borders of her mind and experience.

Chapter 14

I opened my eyes to see machinery silhouetted against the silver sheen of the ceiling. There was the quiet and familiar hum of the air conditioning. It all felt very familiar but my mind was blank as I tried to remember who and where I was.

A pretty face appeared above me, deep blue eyes looking concerned. "Love, you are awake." She smiled, eyes twinkling with delight.

I tried to speak but just a croak came out.

A female voice spoke to me from nowhere.

"Theo, do not move or try to speak. Give yourself time the recover."

The voice in my head and the lovely face were familiar. I tried to remember.

"The drugs you have been taking will have affected your memory and physical coordination," explained the voice in my ear.

I remembered who the voice was. After a few experimental efforts I managed to speak.

"Thank you Gina. I am not dead then?"

"If you were dead I would not be talking to you."

"You may be my guardian angel and I am in heaven."

"Not yet Theo."

I reached out and took the hand of the lovely girl bending over me.

"Hey baby. Have you become an astronaut?"

"What is an astro... naught?"

"What I am," I tried to smile. "What do you think of my starship?"

"It is beautiful. I can fly. Is this where you go when

you die?"

"I don't think so. But who knows? What happened to me?"

"You were attacked by four of Panstrosh's bullies. Your robot killed them all but not before they shot you with three arrows."

"I should have taken your advice and killed that bastard Panstrosh."

"I am worried about Kemlo. If they think you are dead they will take their revenge on him, and his family."

"Kemlo is smart and tough. Panstrosh and his half wits won't get the jump on him," I said. "Like they did on me," I added, thinking *you trusting fool Theo!*

"Will you get better Theo? I mean, as you were?"

"Gina, what is the prognosis?"

"You will make a full recovery. But no heavy exertions for a few weeks."

"I think I can manage that. Any chance of some food? I am starving."

Later that day I was disconnected from the medial machinery and was able to move around. The weightless conditions helped; the physical strain on my injuries was much reduced. Salny fussed over me like the proverbial mother hen, preparing my food and drink and not letting me out of her sight, even in the shower!

After a couple of days I was fully divested of straps and monitors and able to dress normally although my injuries were all heavily bandaged.

Salny was fascinated by everything around her and hungry for knowledge so we enjoyed ourselves with basic science and technology lessons. The ship was like our own little private world, a womb which nourished and protected us from a hostile universe.

With the help of the magical modern drugs I healed

rapidly. But although I felt normal my wounds had been stitched and had not yet fully healed so I still had to avoid heavy physical work.

But it was nearly four weeks later before Gina would consider my return to the planet. By then Salny was beginning to get claustrophobic. Although her mood was still sweet and caring I noticed the restlessness and occasional distraction.

I brought up the subject of our return and what we should do about Panstrosh and his gang of bullies. Salny, predictably, was all for shooting the lot of them. I confess, brutal as that was, I could not think of an alternative. With them out of the way the coast, literally and metaphorically, would be clear to build a peaceful association between the two villages.

But I was sure that once Panstrosh and his men saw the shuttle returning they would either take to the hills or arm themselves for a battle. I decided we should land the shuttle further down the coast, perhaps at my original landing site and then proceed overland with the two robots and try to take them by surprise. But then I remembered my delicate physical condition and changed that to going by sea. It would be a little crowded in the dinghy with the robots, but possible

Salny suggested that she should first go ahead and sneak into the village to talk to her brother Lons. I was reluctant to allow that; if she was spotted by one of Panstrosh's supporters I was sure they would grab her. But she said that her family house was at the edge of the village and she could sneak in through the forest without being seen. I agreed but suggested we all go to the village and get as close as we dared, before Salny went in for the last short distance.

My health now being back to normal we made our preparations to leave. There was an extra handgun on the ship which I appropriated for Salny. I showed her how to use it, with extra emphasis on how to operate the safety lock and how to hold it. We took as much of the remaining food and drink as would fit in the shuttles fridge.

I took Salny to see Gina's drum where her processing hardware and memory lived and we both gave her a cuddle before leaving. I almost believed that Gina was touched by our show of affection, although she accused us of anthropomorphizing a machine, an expression that I found impossible to translate to Salny, mostly because Salny was already convinced that all machines *were* alive!

We re-entered the shuttle and settled ourselves in the cockpit, our trusty robots in the cabin. Gina detached the shuttle and I used the maneuvering thrusters to move the ship away and rotate, at the same time explaining to Salny what I was doing.

"We will operate the engines to slow the ship down. This will make us fall towards the ground," I explained.

"But the engines make the ship go faster," she protested. I thought about that for a few seconds and then used the analogy of rowing a boat to explain how jet engines could be used to accelerate or decelerate.

Gina fired the engines to slow the ship to the required speed and I then rotated it to face in the direction of flight. Gina took over to navigate us to my first landing spot and I settled it down in the same little plateau between the hills.

We unloaded the dinghy and pumped it up. It had a small and almost silent electric water jet engine which gave it a very respectable speed when required. The robots got in first, one at each end to balance the boat with me and Salny in the middle.

I switched on the engine and pointed her in the direction we wanted to go. It was a nice clear morning with a light breeze, the sea calm.

"Nice to be back," I said taking in a lungful of the clean sea air.

"Yes, I thought your ship was huge when I saw it first but after spending all that time inside it started to feel small," said Salny.

"That's because you are an open air girl used to wide open spaces," I said. "I am a quiet shy town boy."

"Of course you are. You never go anywhere and never meet anyone," she said with mock sympathy. "Maybe you were the virgin, not me."

"Now we are finding out the truth," I said accusingly.

"You haven't met my five children yet," she said laughing.

The dingy was going at a good speed and Salny looked delighted, trailing a hand in the racing water.

"Why haven't we gone out in this lovely boat before?" she asked.

We headed around the headland and then turned to run parallel with the coast. It was just a few miles to Faro village which would take fifteen minutes or so. I was not worried about meeting any early morning fishermen; we would get to the village long before they could.

"Salny, I want you to fire your gun just once to get used to it," I told her.

She nodded and pulled out the little gun from a deep pocket in her shift. She carefully reset the safety and pointed it into the distance.

"Hold it firmly and squeeze the trigger," I said. She held her arm straight with the gun pointed out to sea and squeezed the trigger. The gun gave a crack and shuddered in her hand. She gave a little squeal of alarm then laughed nervously.

"There you go, I think you shot a fish."

She reset the safety and replaced the gun in her

pocket.

"So easy to kill," she whispered, looking thoughtful.

We continued our trip with Salny pointing out her favorite fishing spots as we neared the village, places rich in crabs, fish or little octopus. Except that on this planet they had six limbs; hexapus?

I felt well but a little weak and there was still pain from my operation scars. In the weightless conditions of the starship I had felt fully fit but on the planet the weight of gravity dragged on me. Let's hope I did not get into any physical conflicts I told myself.

We approached the little bay closest to the village. There were a number of simple fishing boats and canoes on the beach. The word 'boats' flatters the primitive rigs that the Faro fishermen used. One of my plans had been to teach them how to build more seaworthy craft.

There was no sign of any fishermen as it was still very early, just an hour after sunrise. They tended to go out after noon when the wind turned and the sea was calm. We beached the dinghy and jumped out. The robots towed it further the beach.

We headed up the beach but veered away from the track that led to the village. It was more rugged going along the side of the hill under the trees but we did not want to run into anyone.

Salny had grown up here and she knew the lie of the land well enough to lead us along the best route to get to the village from the direction that would bring us to her family's houses.

When the village came in sight through the trees Salny stopped us.

"I can go from here to find my brother," she said. She pulled a hood over her head to cover her face.

"Right. Anyone bothers you, shoot to kill."

She nodded, looking tense. I took her in my arms

and gave her a long kiss. She turned and left quickly and I settled down to wait.

Salny felt oddly disturbed; this was her home village, the place where she had played as a child and grown into a young woman. Where her mother had taught her how to skin a tarn, prepare a vegetable stew and make herself clothing. Yet she felt like a stranger, slinking around not to be seen and fearing for her life.

She made her way through the familiar underbrush. That little knoll had a worn path down one side where they used to slide down on home made sleds. And over there they had tied some ropes to swing from. And that was the tree she had fallen down from and twisted her ankle.

Her house, where she and her two brothers lived, backed on to the forest. Their father had moved in with another woman after their mother had died. The house was partitioned in two so Salny could have her privacy. Lons had his eye on a young woman and was going to ask for her hand. Marriage for the Faro was an excuse for a village party. Yovna the shaman would do a good luck dance and chant the marriage chant, which was fun because everyone could join in with the choruses.

Her younger brother Fernis was still in his early teens and wanted to be a fisherman. He hated hunting and was teased by the other boys but he was not afraid to stand up for himself. Since the death of their mother Salny had assumed the role of motherhood, particularly for Fernis.

She reached the back of their hut, paused and peered around the side. The front yard was quite extensive because that was where all the work happened; preparing and cooking food, making and repairing furniture, implements and weapons. She saw Lons stirring a pot over the fire and smiled with satisfaction. Making breakfast was her job over which she had often complained and harangued Lons about.

Why is it the woman's job she had asked with irritation. Lons would look resigned and shake his head at his difficult sister's awkward questions.

"Lons, it's me!" She spoke just loudly enough for him to hear. He jerked up and looked around. "Behind you," she said. He turned, his face a picture of amazement.

"Salny, it's you! I don't believe it." He dropped the long ladle into the pot and ran over to embrace her. She thought he was about to cry and hugged him back.

"I'm good Lons."

"Where have you been?" He held her away from him, examining her face. "You look well. Too well, you have grown fat."

She punched him on the shoulder.

"Don't be rude to your little sister."

"Not so little," he grinned, then looked worried. "Salny, what happened to Vulious, sorry, Theo. We were told that he had been killed and his machines had left never to return."

"That's what Panstrosh would like everyone to think. Theo was hurt but his machines made him well again."

Lons looked relieved, smiled and clenched a fist in delight. "That is good news. But where is Theo now? And where have you been all this time?"

"I went with him to his starship where he was connected to a machine that cured him."

"You went to his starship? So it's true then. He is from another world."

"It is amazing up there Lons, you would not believe it. So many stars. And our world a ball that you can stand on like a giant."

"Truly an adventure Salny. I wish I could go."

"Perhaps you will one day."

"But where is Theo? Did he stay in his starship?"

"No he is here with me." Salny pointed in the direction of the sea. "I came to find out what has happened since we left."

Lons shook his head sadly. "Panstrosh is now insufferable. He organized a raiding party last week but the Hoshna were prepared and they came back with nothing except one dead and three wounded. He is bullying everyone and his supporters are beating up anyone who disagreed with him."

"What happened to Kemlo?"

"He took his wife and left. They went to stay in the Hoshna village."

"Good. Is our uncle still one of Panstrosh's gang?"

"Yes but don't blame him too much. He is trying to protect me and Fernis."

"It would be better if he had the stomach to side with Kemlo and unite those against Panstrosh."

"There is still too many of them. Although Theo's robots did a good job in improving the odds. They killed the four who attacked him."

"I know, I saw them," said Salny.

"How did Theo escape if he was shot?"

"His robots carried him to his ship."

"Amazing creatures." Lons shook his head in admiration. "So what will you do now?"

"Theo has no choice. He has to kill Panstrosh and his supporters."

"No, just kill Panstrosh and his supporters will fade away. They are just cowards who will follow the biggest bully."

"Right. I will go and tell Theo."

"I will gather a few friends together. We will be there to support Theo."

Salny smiled her thanks and embraced her brother.

"I will tell Theo." She turned and walked back up the hill, giving him a wave before he disappeared in the trees.

Salny found Theo sitting on a rock and sunning himself.

"Did you find Lons?" he asked.

"Yes." She described their conversation and he nodded his satisfaction.

"I'm pleased Kemlo and his wife got away. Right, so let's go do this."

While waiting for Salny to return I had mulled over what I was about to do. It was a painful and difficult decision and I was still not sure whether it was the right one. By my standards Panstrosh was a primitive barbarian for whom taking life was all in a days work. But perhaps by his standards he was a brave and fearless leader who did not shirk dangerous and difficult duties.

Or perhaps not I thought. He was hardly capable of such sophisticated ideas. He was just a primitive who seized the opportunity to be top dog and enjoyed lording it over others. I was over-thinking the whole thing.

"Let's just stroll down into the village and let everyone know we are back," I said.

We made our way down the hill and back onto the track to the village. As we approached the square I saw that it was empty apart from a few animals tethered outside the huts.

"I missed the smell of animal and human waste," I remarked. This earned be a rebuking punch from Salny.

"We haven't invented plumbing yet."

"First signs of civilization," I said. "Plumbing and hairdressing."

"We have hairdressing," she protested.

"Hacking your hair with a knife is not hairdressing."
"What's wrong with my hair?"
"It's naturally beautiful," I said hastily. *Never insult a woman's hair Theo, you should know that.* In fact her shiny black hair was naturally beautiful, growing close and flat on her scalp and framing her oval face.

"Are all human men so insincere?"
"When it come to complementing women we have no choice. But in your case, I never lie."

She was laughing and shaking her head. *Interesting that humor is common between our two species* I thought. As was aggression, pride, love etc. I suppose since the universe creates almost identical stars and planets everywhere it is not unreasonable to imagine that it creates almost identical life everywhere. But, as Gina would no doubt remind me, two examples do not make a scientific law.

A man was coming in the other direction. He stopped, his jaw hanging open in surprise, then turned and ran back the way he'd come.

"He's going to warn Panstrosh," Salny said. We continued walking, flanked by the robots. Until we were in the village centre. More people were about and they all stopped to gape, whispering to each other.

Then we spotted Lons with a couple of his friends. They were armed with bow and carried hatchets and spears. As we made or way through the village Lons gathered more of his friends so by the time we arrived at Panstrosh's large hut there were half a dozen or so of the young men. They surrounded Panstrsh's hut preventing his escape. I was touched and impressed by their support and courage. It augured well for the future of the village that the young were courageous enough to stand up for their principles.

"Panstrosh, come out now," I shouted. "Or I will

instruct my robots to set fire to your hut."

It was a couple of minutes before Panstrosh came out, dressed in his hunting gear and wearing his sword.

"Where have you been these last few weeks Earth man?" He spoke with an expression of contempt on his face. "Hiding away to build up your courage?"

"Deciding what to do about you Panstrosh," I said.

"You have nothing to say or do about me. I am the leader of this village. The people follow me."

"I have decided you are no longer the leader. A new leader will be elected by the people." I turned to the crowd gathering around us. "Those who disagree may come and stand next to Panstrosh."

Panstrosh scowled around at his lieutenants. A few of them looked at each other and then down to the ground. None of them joined him.

"Now I have to decide what to do about you." I scowled at Panstrosh. "Your men attempted to kill me. They are all dead now."

He pulled out his sword.

"What they failed to do, I will do," he howled, then rushed me. Before I could move there were two gunshots almost together. Panstrosh jerked and staggered, carried forward by his momentum he fell flat on his face, jerked twice and then lay still. Gina's voice came to my ear.

"I instructed the robots to be on their guard," she said.

"Thanks Gina. That has saved me the trouble."

I turned to the gathered villagers.

"Friends, I am sorry that this man had to die. But he stood in the way of progress. I bring you new ideas and learning that will transform your lives for the better and bring peace between you and the Hoshna. I want you to get together and decide who you want as your new leader. Then we can elect a new village council. Friends, do I have your support for this?"

It was Lons who stepped forward and held up his sword dramatically.

"You have my support Theo."

His declaration was followed by cries of "And mine" first from Lons's young friends and then from others until it became a chorus.

"Theo, we want you as our leader," said Lons. There were cries of support for that.

"Thank you Lons. I will consider it. But I would like to discuss it with all of you first." The truth was, I did not want to be the village head; the job required an intimate acquaintance with all the villagers and their concerns and problems. I would prefer someone like Kemlo or Lons to do that job. I could remain as 'the power behind the throne'.

The door to Panstrosh's hut opened and a woman and two children peered out She saw the spread-eagled Panstrosh on the floor but looked unconcerned.

"Marna, the village will look after your family," said Lons. "Until you find another man."

The woman nodded but said nothing. Lons waved to his friends and stepped up to the body.

"Let's take him away."

"Lons, me and Salny want to go to the Hoshna village to bring back Kemlo."

"Theo, I would like to go and meet the leaders of the Hoshna," he replied.

"That is a good idea. If there are others who want to come it will be a good opportunity to start good relations with the Hoshna. We will wait for you."

Lons grinned at his friends and they all grinned back and nodded eagerly.

"How many can you take?" he asked.

Chapter 15

With the hated Panstrosh out of the way relations between the two villages moved to a friendlier and more beneficial level. Kemlo and Ilnira moved back to their home and Kemlo was voted headman. Lons was also on the village council which was now made up of the new generation.

Yovna the Shaman adjusted to the new leadership without complaint, doing a special séance which 'suddenly' revealed to him that I was sent by the gods to lead the village to salvation.

Now that I had Yovna's blessing the older more conservative villagers accepted the new order without qualms. There were still a few die hard thugs who yearned to go on the rampage to do some pillaging but they were forced to confine their aggressive instincts to hunting.

It was decided by both villages that a visit should be paid to the third village which was on the other side of the island. Access through the mountains was difficult and visits to the village, called Murpa, had been by sea.

Murpa was on the north coast, facing the mainland which was just eighty miles across the bay. Lons told me that he had made the journey around the coast to Murpa just once. It was a large and prosperous fishing village which traded with the mainland.

"They have some good tools and weapons from the mainland. They are also excellent fishermen with big strong boats," explained Lons.

I decided to fly there with the shuttle and take Lons and one or two of his young friends along, just to explain and confirm that I was not a god. Lons had introduced me to his young lady, a pretty girl called Hanna, who had been delighted when I told her that Hanna was also an Earth name. She would come with us as well one of Lons's young friend called Pinatok,

That made five of us which was a problem because there were only four seats with belts in the shuttle. But it was a very short journey and we could do without wearing seat belts. I made a point of looking into adding more seats in the open area.

We prepared our expedition, taking some gifts and trading goods, and left from Hoshna. I flew the shuttle over the mountains to survey a possible route through the mountains. If we could find a route through the mountains from Hoshna to Murpa this would be a half the distance from going by sea.

There was only one impassable obstruction, a landslide which had blocked the pass between two mountains. Gina thought that the use of some explosives should clear a big enough track through the rubble. That would be something that I could return to do, if regular relations with the Murpa became something that all three villages wanted.

I flew slowly over the mountains to allow my passengers to enjoy the view. Once over the mountains the northern coastline of the island was visible. The distance between the mountains and the seas was barely five miles. The village nestled between two hills and stretched from mountain to coast. I judged it was as big as the Hoshna and Faro villages combined.

The village looked quite Mediterranean with proper white houses instead of mud covered wooden huts. It looked more advanced and prosperous than the Hoshna and Faro villages.

But there was something wrong; there appeared to be bodies in the streets and there was smoke rising from a couple of houses. And the village was empty of people.

I made a slow pass over the village using the external camera to zoom down and display details on the screen. There was no doubt that some of the bodies in the street had arrows protruding from them. It was Salny who spotted people high up in the mountains, under the trees. I adjusted the course to pass over them. There were crowds of them, men women and children who had taken refuge amongst the trees on the mountain side. They had clearly fled the village.

"Bloody hell Salny, looks like the village has been attacked. But by who?"

"Must be from the mainland," she said.

"It looks very recent. Let's land and see if we can help."

"I think we will terrify them even more," she said making a face which said 'you know what I mean'.

"True. But they have seen the shuttle so that's too late. I suggest you and the others go first and talk to them before they see me."

"Let's land outside the village. We get out but leave the robots in the shuttle."

I nodded my agreement with her suggestion and piloted the shuttle slowly back over the village. There was the usual clearing in the village centre but I decided to land at the edge of the village next to the beach. There was a flat clear space between the beach and the start of the rocky hills leading up to the mountains.

I gently brought the shuttle down on our chosen spot, which appeared firm and level. Salny and I left the cockpit. The others in the main cabin had also seen the tragic sights and were discussing the situation.

"There are pirates on the mainland," said Pinatok. "We sometimes see their ships when we are far out to sea. When we see them we get back to the village quickly."

"Yes, I heard that their ships are very big with sails and oars," said Lons. "Because our village is not visible from the sea they have not bothered us."

"That's lucky," I said. But I was depressed that the kind of barbarism we had excised from Faro with the death of Panstrosh seemed to be the norm elsewhere. "Let's head for the village and find out what happened. Me and Salny have our pistols just in case they think we are also the pirates and attack us, although I would prefer not to shoot anyone. I will use my ultra-sonic gun first."

We exited from the shuttle and made our way around the headland towards the village. The sea was on our right, a long golden beach at the end of which there was a short wooden pier with a number of fishing boats moored to it.

The village began a hundred yards from the beach on a flat plain beneath the hills which led up to the mountains. It looked very pretty and I cursed the pirates for their brutality in attacking such a peaceful and clearly industrious community.

I let my friends go ahead, led by Lons with Pinatok with the girls behind them. We reached the first buildings and Lons poked his head inside the first house and called out if anyone was in. Surprisingly there was an answer and Lons stepped inside. After a minute he shouted for Salny or Hanna to come in. They did so and we waited. We could hear women's voices, and then wails of grief. Lons came out looking distressed.

"There are two women and a dead man," he said. "The younger woman has been ... attacked." He scowled.

"Who did this?" I asked.

"They have no name for them. They call them the

Northern people. They have white hair and yellow eyes and wear animal furs."

"How long ago did this happen," I asked.

"Just now. She heard them leave with some captives just a while before we arrived."

"So their ships should be nearby," I said. "Let's see if we can find them."

I got on the comm to Gina and asked her to scan the ocean nearby for any ships. She found them immediately.

"There are three sailing ships together. They are heading north east, towards the strait that separates the main land mass from the eastern peninsula," she replied.

I remembered that the mainland had a peninsula similar to the Baltic Sea that separated Norway and Sweden from Finland. The peninsula led up to the north of the mainland.

"So these characters are from the north of the mainland," I said. "A bunch of Vikings in other words. That's all we need."

"It would seem so," replied Gina. "But we do not know how far north their homes are. I will try and do more detailed scans to identify where the main centers of population are."

"Meanwhile, is there anything we can do to catch these ships and rescue the captives?" I asked.

"We can sink the ships but that will not help the captives," replied Gina. "I suggest we wait until they return to their villages then we can go there with the shuttle and confront them."

"That would seem the safest course of action," I agreed. While I was talking Salny came out of the house leading an older woman who was covering her face with her hands and sobbing. Salny had an arm around her shoulders trying to comfort her.

"This is Malia," said Salny. "I told her who we are.

She knows of our village when we came here before to trade. She says everyone ran away except a few old people. Her daughter is crippled and could not escape and Malia remained with her."

"I am very sorry to hear that Salny. Did they rape her daughter?"

"No. She struggled and fought them and they beat her before leaving to find other victims."

"Is the girl hurt? We can give her medication."

"She is in pain."

"Gina, do we have medication to help the girl?"

"Yes, we can attend to her wounds and administer a pain killer."

"Right. I will return to the shuttle for the medication. Then we can make a tour of the village," I said.

After attending to the injured girl we went around the village and found others who had been beaten and a couple of families devastated because their daughters or wives had been stolen. Men who had attempted to fight the invaders had been killed, although we also saw a number of the invader's bodies lying around so they had given a good account of themselves.

The invaders were indeed different. Short and burly with pure white hair and almost transparent slightly yellow eyes they looked like albino versions of the species. But their weapons and arms looked well made. They wore metal helmets and some wore metal shields strapped to their chests.

People began returning from their hideouts in the hills and they were all confused about who we were and why we were there. But the presence of Salny and Hanna served to reassure them.

I returned again to the shuttle and raided my stock of medication to attend to the worst injured. Some of the Murpa villagers had seen our shuttle from a distance and described the large silver bird which made a loud noise. They were unsure what to make of it or whether it had any bearing on the tragic events they had just suffered.

I decided we would wait a little longer to tell them that the silver bird was ours. For now they were all too traumatized to handle further alarming and strange events.

The village leader was called Harago. He was a lean old fellow who seemed more trader than warrior. The village appeared light on warrior types with more farmers, fishermen and artisans. I approved of that of course but perhaps given the danger posed by the 'Vikings' they should concentrate more of their resources on self defense.

They knew of the villages of Faro and Hoshna and had dealt with both in the past, exchanging food for their tools and handicrafts. Odd that the late Panstrosh and his warriors had not invaded the Murpa I thought. Perhaps that was because Murpa was only accessible via the sea and the Faro lacked the ships to mount an attack.

The Murpa had also traded peacefully with many villages on the mainland. We asked them about the 'Vikings' and whether they had attacked before. They said no they had not attacked them before although they had heard that some villages on the mainland had been attacked. It seems the Vikings were beginning to roam further a-field in their search for victims.

When we began attending to people's injuries there was widespread interest from the Murpa. I washed and bandaged wounds and explained the principles of hygiene. I administered a couple of pain killing injections to two men who had more serious wounds and gave them anti-bacterial shots. The problem was that my supply of medication was limited and would soon run out if I started treating everyone.

By late afternoon things were returning to normal in the village and we were invited by the Headman and the village elders to stay the night and join them for their evening meal. I had been getting some searching looks from people as they began to notice my physiological differences and the leader Harago asked me where I was from.

We were seated with Harago and some of the village leaders outside his house while the women prepared the meal. *Perhaps this may be the right time to introduce myself* I thought.

"Are you from the southern continent?" asked Harago. "We hear tales that the people there are different. Although they say that they are ugly and primitive. You are certainly not ugly or primitive."

"Thank you," I said politely. "I am from a place which is much further away than the southern continent," I said. "Do you know what the stars are?"

He looked at me and shrugged. "They say that the stars are the souls of the dead who now live in paradise."

"Each star is a sun like ours." I pointed up to the sun. "I traveled from a world that goes around another sun."

The villagers were looking at me with blank faces. This was clearly such an outrageous idea that it made no sense to them.

Perhaps a lesson in cosmology may not be appropriate at this point I thought. Nevertheless, I had got the ball rolling so there was nothing for it but to continue.

It took a while and of course they neither understood nor believed half of what I told them. I'd had the same experience with the Faro and Hoshna, although I did find that the youngsters accepted what

I was saying far more readily than their elders.

But they accepted that I was from another 'world', probably imagining it was just far away across sea and sky.

During our meal, which was the best food I had eaten on the planet so far, an excited fisherman ran up from the beach with news that there was a giant silver bird on the beach. I had to then explain to our hosts that it was mine and was the means by which I had flown from my world to theirs.

This caused a furor and the word got around to the village. When I took the elders to see my 'bird' I found the whole village following. Thereafter I was not just a stranger but a godlike visitor from another world and was treated with appropriate deference and respect.

But I was delighted to see that, as usual, the children treated the whole thing as a wonderful adventure and their parents could not tear them away from the shuttle. When I showed them how to make a copy of the aircraft from large leaves, that could actually fly, the children began a heated competition to see who could make the best plane!

At least, I told myself, it was all a distraction from the terrible events that the village had been through. We were offered sleeping accommodation for the night and decided to accept and stay the night. I visited the injured and administered more pain killers where needed before retiring to the shuttle with Salny. Our friends had accepted accommodation in the village but Salny and I decided we preferred the comfort and modern conveniences of the shuttle.

"I will have to build us a home with plumbing and bathroom facilities," I remarked to Salny.

"Is that a proposal," she asked with a quirky smile.

"Urm, I don't know," I replied. I had not considered it in that way, but then realized that I was taking

Salny for granted. In her mind she was not officially my 'woman' because we had not gone through the marriage ceremony. And of course, we could not have children, which was something that perhaps she was not aware of. Should I continue to take advantage of her I asked myself. Or should I release her so she could 'marry' a young man of her own species and have a normal life?

"Salny, you know that you cannot have children with me?"

She looked back at me with a puzzled expression.

"Why not? We could make beautiful children."

My face must have shown my pain because she looked disappointed. I took her in my arms.

"Baby, we are different...creatures." There was no word in their language for 'species'. "Although we look very similar, we are from different worlds."

"You cannot be sure of that," she said.

"We have had sex may times but you have not become pregnant."

"With some couples it often takes a long time."

"Well, you must decide," I said. "If you stay with me we may never have children. If you want children then you must leave me and find a nice young man to marry."

She embraced me tightly as if to stop me from leaving.

"No, you are my man. I do not care about the wedding ceremony and if we do not have children then I will take pleasure from my brother's children."

I felt a surge of affection for this beautiful soul and held her as tightly as she held me.

"You are not just beautiful but also very smart and sweet and kind and I am a lucky man to have you."

"I am also very lucky," she whispered. "Not just me but all our people are lucky that such a wise person should descend from the sky to open up our minds to the wonders of the universe."

"So... I can be first in the shower then?"

"Not on your flimno Earthman!" she said pushing me away and diving for the shower.

Chapter 16

The next day was cloudy and windy. We were coming to the end of the summer and the days were noticeably cooler. Over breakfast I checked with Gina on where the 'Vikings' were and she told me they were sailing up the peninsular towards the north.

"Perhaps we should pay these bastards a visit," I suggested.

"Theo, you must understand that these people are thousands of years behind Earth in their development. Raiding and piracy is normal for them."

"I know that Gina. But if I can make a contribution to improving that behavior then I have a duty to do so."

"You really believe that you can affect the development of their civilization?"

"Why not? I have already dramatically changed the behavior of the villagers on this island. That can spread to the whole world."

"That never happened on Earth. The civilization of Athens was snuffed out."

"It was snuffed out by religion. Rome fell to Christianity and Europe spent one thousand five hundred years in the dark ages until the re-discovery of Greek learning. If we can prevent the ignorance of religion on this planet then perhaps its history may be different. They will not have two thousand years of religious wars."

"It is not just religion to blame Theo. If people did not fight over religion they would fight over territory or culture or property. It is part of the development of each species that they should experience all these things in order to appreciate what peace and love can bring."

"Of course, you are right Gina, although religion seems to make all that much worse. But I am not just teaching them reason and science, I am also teaching them that peace and trade is much more profitable than war. I am not simple enough to believe that I can get rid of war and conflict altogether. I just want to push things in the other direction so it may not be as disastrous for these people as it was for us."

"Most commendable, but I suspect ultimately futile."

"Possibly. But worth trying."

"You would have more effect if you told them that you are a god and commanded them to be nice to each other," said Gina.

"That is exactly what Jesus did; and Mohammad and every other religious prophet. All religions teach peace but then either become part of the ruling elite or are corrupted by some fanatics who use their faith to justify war. I want people to follow peace because it makes sense not because God told them to."

"You can change things while you are here but when you are gone, violent self interest will re-assert itself," Gina said.

"Damn Gina, you are such a cynic."

"No Theo, I am realistic. Be a do-gooder if it makes you happy. But in the long term scheme of things other forces are more powerful and longer lasting. That is what history has taught us."

"I bow to your superior wisdom. But while I am here, I will do my bit to make life better for as many people as possible."

"Just don't get yourself killed and become another prophet martyr."

"Okay, okay, point taken."

I had to confess to myself that Gina's hard headed realism was sobering. I had already nearly got myself killed. Could I change the future of a planet? It seemed an arrogant ambition and perhaps one that may do more harm than good. Perhaps I should just confine myself to doing a few good deeds when the opportunity presented itself.

But I did want to find out who the northerners were and also to explore the mainland.

Ablutions and breakfast over we strolled up the beach to the village to find our friends. They were waiting for us outside the chief's house. After exchanging greetings Headman Harago himself with a couple of his council members took us for a tour of the village and its farms. I was impressed with the size of the farming area and the number of animals they had. This was a rich village and I guessed that the 'Vikings' would return to raid them regularly now that they had been discovered. It was imperative that the Murpa improved their defenses and I put Gina to work to come up with some plans.

Apart from improving their physical defenses and organizing more training to turn farmers into warriors, an early warning system of some sort seemed a good idea. I suggested that Gina could carry out a daily scan for the 'Viking' ships. If they were spotted I could then fly the shuttle to the Murpa and not just warn them but scare off the 'Vikings'.

When I told the Murpa leaders that we could do that for them they were hugely grateful and appreciative. We took some time with them to describe our other defense suggestions. For example, building walls from which the defenders could attack the raiders then fall back to another rampart while the elderly, women and children headed for the hills.

I also informed the Murpa that we were flying to visit the 'Vikings' home to see what kind of people they were and perhaps discourage them from any further raids.

"Give them a good discouragement," suggested

Harago the headman, emphasizing the 'good discouragement' with a symbolic chop of the hand. I joined in with the appreciative laughter.

A burly young Murpa stood. "I would like to come with you," he said. I looked at him enquiringly. "My name is Tarni. The raiders took my sister and I must do my best to rescue her."

I looked at Lons and the others enquiringly. Lons nodded back to me. "Why not, an extra spear may be useful."

"Right Tarni, you are with us."

The young man looked pleased and emotional.

We took our leave of our new friends promising an early return. They showered us with gifts and thanks and the whole village turned out to view the shuttle taking off. Lons, Hanna and the other two youngsters Pinatook and Tarny took their places in the cabin while Salny took the co-pilot's seat.

As we lifted off, engines thundering, I could not help but imagine the children's excitement. I must have been smiling because Salny asked what I was smiling at.

"Back home on Earth when I was a young lad my father would take me to the Spaceport so I could watch the shuttles taking off. I could not wait to be a Spaceman."

"Do you miss your home?" Salny was looking at me sympathetically.

"Of course." I tried to not show my pain. Remembering my family and friends was something I tried not to do but my subconscious had a will of its own, throwing up memories at random. Memories which often caused me huge loneliness and occasionally even tears.

Salny reached out to squeeze my arm.

"I wish that I could make up for your loss."

"Without you it would be much worse," I told her. I was constantly being amazed at the sensitivity of this simple girl. Modern humans could be forgiven for equating scientific and technological knowledge and sophistication with maturity and emotional sensitivity. But from my experiences on this primitive world that was not the case. The people here showed the same emotional sensitivity. It was only their sophistication that was deficient.

Which kind of made sense I thought. Human relations took place on a different plane from scientific and technological ones. The ancients on Earth were just as emotionally sensitive and mature as their modern equivalents, as their many writings demonstrated.

I switched to automatic and allowed Gina to fly the ship to our destination.

"Gina, fly us up the peninsula and stay low. It would be interesting to see what settlements there are along that waterway."

"Yes Theo. Would you like me to record and display each one we find?"

"Yes please."

For the first ten minutes as the shuttle flew low over the blue sea we lost sight of land. Then the coast appeared on one side and as we entered the peninsula we could see the distant coastlines from both sides of the aircraft.

"How wide is the peninsula Gina?" I asked.

"Only about sixty miles. At the height we are flying we can see both coastlines."

"Good, we want to see any settlements on the coast."

It was not long before we saw our first village. And then one after the other on both sides of the peninsula. It was clearly a heavily populated region. I remembered the area from our initial scans of the planet and that I had specifically wanted to keep away from it because it was heavily populated. But it did look beautiful with the golden coastline embellished by the green heavily wooded hills.

"Your planet is very beautiful," I said to Salny.

"Is Earth not as beautiful?"

"It is, Earth has similar countryside. It also has a much bigger land area, maybe ten times, with a variety of different climates and countryside. Huge frozen mountains, hundreds of miles of desert and thousands of miles of jungle and forest."

"Ten times?" She was frowning trying to understand the comparison. I had noticed that by some odd quirk of their biology the Hoshna and the Faro were not good at arithmetic.

"If this is the land on your planet," I held up one finger, "then this is Earth." I held up all ten fingers.

"Is Earth much bigger than our planet?" she asked.

"No, but your planet has much more sea and much less land."

"Oh. Is that bad?"

"No, it is good. It means you cannot overpopulate your planet or destroy its ecology. And the sea will feed you."

She was clearly struggling to understand these new and complicated concepts, her pretty face contorted in thought.

"Don't worry," I said. "I will explain later."

"I understand," she said. "We have little land so not too many people and much sea, so plenty of fish. I like fish."

"Yep, good summary," I said laughing.

We were flying down the middle of the peninsula and the coastline on either side scrolled behind us, varying between rocky and rugged coastline or golden beaches. Every twenty miles or so I would catch sight of habitation, sometimes just a few huts or a village spreading inland between the hills. They were not visible through the windscreen; Gina was displaying them as enhanced insets on the display below the windscreen.

"The raiding ships are beneath us," announced Gina. The digital display cleared and then showed three small sailing ships. Gina zoomed in and I examined the raiders. The ships had one main mast and one mostly horizontal one at the front. Triangular sails were strung at the front and a large square one on the main mast.

"What type of sailing ship is that Gina?"

"I believe it is a sloop although my information on sailing ships is not very extensive."

"Right thanks." I wasn't much wiser; my knowledge of sailing ships being zero. But they were definitely larger and more sophisticated than anything the Faro had. "Can we see how many sailors on board?"

"I count eleven on deck but there is room beneath decks."

"Hmm, say twenty to each ship," I said. "That's a substantial fighting force but a well organized and well armed village can fight them off."

"Yes, I suspect the Murpa were caught off guard with most of the men out in the fields," Gina suggested.

I nodded. "If we can give them warning in future they can defend themselves."

"Can they see the shuttle from the boats Gina?"

"No we are too high," she assured me.

"Gina, let's head further up the peninsula to see what we find. Then we can return to find the Vikings."

"Yes Theo."

"Salny. Let's go see what the others are doing."

We left Gina to fly the aircraft and went back to the main cabin. Gina was displaying the view on the screen in the main cabin and our passengers were looking wide eyed at the display.

I greeted them and explained what was happening and what they were seeing.

"We knew that there were many people living on the mainland," said Lons.

"The mainland and all the islands are very fertile, and the climate very favorable," I explained.

"Will we find the raiders villages Theo?" asked Hanna.

"We have spotted the raiders ships, they are still heading north, that is away from your island. We will explore further along the coast and then return to follow the raiders to their home village."

"Will you punish the raiders Theo?" asked Lons.

"I shall first try to persuade them to stop their raiding. If they refuse then perhaps some punishment may be necessary," I said carefully.

"You are too gentle Theo. Perhaps you are the god of friendship and kindness not the god of the sky," said Hanna with a smile.

"Or perhaps the god of love," Salny smirked.

I grinned at Lons and his two young friends. "Lons, I think I will return your sister to you."

"Too late Theo, you have had your way with her. No one will marry her now."

"I am a ruined woman," cried Salny to guffaws of laughter.

I embraced and kissed her tenderly. "You are still the most beautiful woman on this world my darling."

"We had to find a man from another world to marry her," muttered her brother sotto voce, poking his mate Pinatok in the ribs with amusement and earning a punch from his sister.

Gina's voice interrupted our fun.

"We have reached the top of the peninsula. There is a very large village in the mountains which may be the home of the raiders. It has a harbor with a number of similar ships moored."

"On screen Gina." The screen lit up with a hilly forested terrain in which were built rows of white houses climbing up into the mountains. I noticed that the roads were cobbled and there was a flat cobbled plateau which led to the harbor in which a number of ships were moored. It was a large and well constructed village but the land behind did not look suited to farming, being rocky with few flat cultivated areas. In the distance the mountains rose sheer behind the village, their peaks covered with snow; which explained why their sea going fleet was so advanced. These were hunters, fishermen and sailors not farmers.

So what do we do I asked myself. *Land on the sea front and say 'take me to your leader'?* If we landed the shuttle on the seafront the whole village would take to the hills! Perhaps we should land somewhere remote and then trek in to the village as visitors. That was a risk without the robots, but we would be armed with our small pistols. Nevertheless it was a risk and I was reluctant to subject my friends to that, particularly the two girls. Who knows, the Vikings may take a fancy to the women and decide to ambush us.

But I liked the idea of trekking into the village as a group of travelers; it would give us an insight into their culture hopefully without us attracting untoward interest. The problem was my appearance; should I try to change my appearance or just claim to be from, say, the Southern continent?

I raised the subjects with my friends. Their feeling was that we should just land the shuttle on the seafront, exit with the robots and if necessary kick a few butts. They were not interested in the Viking's village or way of life.

The problem with that approach was that the

'Vikings' would not know who we were or why we were there. I wanted to make some attempt to deter them from their piratical ways. Given their advanced fishing fleet I was sure that honest trading would bring them greater rewards.

We compromised by deciding on my plan but leaving the girls behind in the shuttle. They objected of course but I explained that they would be in continuous contact with us through my tiny remote camera and Gina could pilot the ship to rescue us at any time. The girls would be our protection I explained. That was strictly not true, Gina could monitor our situation and come to our rescue, but it made the girls feel useful!

Gina scouted the land and found a nearby plateau in the mountains where we could land the shuttle and trek down to the village. It would be a couple of hours walk along a rough track which led most of the way to the coast. The shuttle flew high enough not to be spotted by anyone on the ground curving around behind the mountains to approach the coast from the other direction. The view was spectacular as the aircraft maneuvered between mountain peaks. Then I spotted something unusual.

"Over there Gina. That's weird. That valley has no snow." Surrounded by snow capped peaks, one deep valley was green and lush. There was a river running through the valley which was covered with thick almost tropical trees and vegetation.

"The valley runs all the way down to a hot dry plateau which stretches to the equator. Hot winds from the plateau are funneled up the valley creating a warm climate," explained Gina.

"Look there are houses down there. A large village in fact," I pointed to the screen. Deep in the valley where the river was just a silver thread tiny white houses were spread along its banks. "Who could be living up here in this isolated location?" It was a rhetorical question; it was unlikely to be the 'Vikings', they were coastal people.

"Would you like to investigate Theo?" asked Gina.

"Not now Gina. Let's check out the Vikings first, as we decided. We can take a look at these characters later."

"Right." Gina banked the plane and continued towards our destination. Over the last mountain peak and we caught sight of the sea in the distance. Gina dropped the shuttle to almost tree level so that we would not be seen from the 'Viking' village. They would undoubtedly hear the aircraft's engines but would hopefully dismiss it as the roaring of an animal in the forest.

Gina handed control to me and I brought the ship down quickly onto the small flat area, nicely shaded by trees. In one direction the land sloped down to the sea some miles in the distance while in the other the tree covered mountain climbed up to a snowy peak.

We exited the cockpit and entered the main cabin. "Right, let's go meet the Vikings," I suggested.

They stood and collected their rucksacks and weapons while I put on my explorer's outfit and boots and pinned on all my electronic aids. I checked my guns and hypersonic weapon and put some prospecting tools into my rucksack.

I had my gun but I asked Salny to give her gun to Lons. He took it gingerly and I explained how to use it and told him that I would keep the extra cartridges in my rucksack.

"You can try it when we get outside," I said. "Always remember to keep the safety catch on."

Gina opened the airlock doors and we said our goodbyes. We loitered over our goodbyes to the girls, me to Salny and Lons to Hanna.

"Any danger, shoot first," she said as a final warning

as she released me to follow the men out of the aircraft. I nodded, agreeing that it was indeed good advice!

I set off in the lead down the hill, Salny's kisses a lingering memory.

Chapter 17

Salny liked her new life! Flying around in a giant flying machine, visiting other villages and having adventures was much more fun and interesting than gathering herbs in the hills or gutting fish! She was seeing her world in ways that would be impossible without Theo and his wonderful machines. And learning so much about nature, ideas that at first seemed difficult and incomprehensible but began gradually to come together and make coherent sense.

She understood now how the world was heated by the sun and why they had seasons. She understood the balance of nature between plants and animals and the land and sea. She understood how life had spread from very small invisible beginnings, growing larger and more complex. Her lessons and talks with Gina were changing her into someone more like Theo than her own people. Her mind and her world were opening up both physically and intellectually.

Now, being without Theo in the shuttle she felt alone and vulnerable. The revolution that she and her world were going through could not continue without Theo. She was full of admiration for his adventurous spirit and desire to be helpful but wished he would not constantly put himself at risk.

From what she had seen the 'Vikings' do in the Murpa village, he and Lons and the other two men were going into danger. She hated being 'the woman' and being left behind while the men did the dangerous work.

She sighed, frowning at the shaky image they were receiving from Theo's 'magic eye'. Hanna detected her unease and squeezed her shoulder sympathetically.

"Don't worry Salny. They are four tough men armed with magic weapons. Lons and the others will take care of Theo. They know how important he is to all of us."

Salny nodded, not trusting herself to speak.

Gina was giving me directions and we soon found the rugged track leading down to the coast.

"They use the track to come up here for hunting," explained Lons.

The aircraft was soon out of sight behind the trees and then we were around a bend in the mountain and trudging down a rock strewn incline.

"Let me show you how to fire the gun Lons." I pulled out my gun and holding it firmly I pointed it at the branch of a tree. "Hold it tight and point it at that branch. Now move the safety to the live position and squeeze the trigger." My gun cracked and the branch quivered, splinters of wood exploding from its side. Lons did the same and also managed to hit the branch. He looked delighted.

"Good shot. Now put the safety back to the locked position."

Gun training over we continued our careful trudge down the hill. It was steep and treacherous with loose sand and pebbles and we kept away from the edge. I had to admit Lons, Pinatok and Tarni looked much more confident and sure footed than me. Okay, I am an explorer but I usually let the robots do the dangerous stuff!

After an hour we paused for a rest and some water before continuing. I allowed Lons to go in the lead, he had a better feel for the ground than me. After another hour we started to smell the humid wind from the sea and the track began to level out. It became narrow with giant trees hemming us in. We turned a corner and caught the first sight of the village beneath us. It was picturesque with the houses perched on the sides of the mountain and down along the level ground to the coast.

It was at that point that we caught sight of the first inhabitants in the village. To our left and right were pieces of land which had been cleared for farming and in one of them a man and a woman were loading up vegetables onto one of the horse like creatures, a suron, I remembered. They were some way away and they ignored us, clearly taking us for locals.

But as we descended the track and came close to the entrance to their field they had finished loading the suron and were heading out of their field and back to the village.

"Let's wait and talk to these people," I suggested. "It would be good to enter the village accompanied by locals." We waited by the side of the track but as the couple approached they became wary and stopped. The man pulled out a large axe and brandished it at us.

"Who are you?" he shouted. "Are you Evrani?"

"Lons, you do the talking, I will stay in the background. Tell him that we are travelers from another village close to Evrani." I had no idea where Evrani was but if they'd had dealings with them then if we pretended to know them that may put the couple at ease, I theorized.

Lons shouted at them that we were not Evrani but from a nearby village over the mountains.

"I do not know of any other village over the mountains," shouted the man. "What do you want here?"

"We have heard that you have many sailing ships here. We want to become sailors and travel to distant shores," shouted Lons. He looked at me and I nodded approvingly.

"Hah! That is all the young want to do," shouted the man. But he put his axe back in the pannier and shooed the suron on. "Piracy and robbery, not honest work," he added.

"Go towards them and be friendly," I said to Lons. He nodded and stepped towards the couple smiling.

"We do not care for piracy," he said. "Just some honest trading. Surely there are ships which do that?"

"A few. But piracy is easier," said the man. As they came close I could see that they were an older couple, both gnarled and lean from years of work in the fields. But they looked strong and bright eyed and examined us curiously.

"You are a handsome and well turned out group of young men. Where are you from again?"

"We are from a village called Faro which is on one of the islands. We came here on a small ship which is moored further along the coast. We lost our way and have been walking for some days now," explained Lons.

"You certainly did lose your way if you are coming from the mountains," said the man.

Lons nodded apologetically. "Yes, we heard of a great race of people who live in the mountains and went to find them. But we could not find them. Are they a myth?"

"You mean the Evrani," replied the man. "They are real enough. But they want nothing to do with the likes of us. They think of themselves as superior to us *stranka*."

"Superior? In what way?" asked Lons.

"They are mysterious and have magic powers." The old boy shrugged. "So they say, but it may all be tales to keep people away. If you are staying in the village my son can put you up. Do you have anything to trade?"

"We have some precious stones and metals," said

Lons. In fact we had what would probably qualify as a 'king's ransom' in precious metals and stones. With the help of Gina and our prospecting equipment we had collected them as currency in case they were needed. "Perhaps you can introduce us to some of the ship's Captains?"

"My son is a sailor. He knows all of them." The man said it with some contempt and I guessed that the old chap had little respect for the younger generation and their piracy.

"I am Lons and these are my friends Pinatook, Tarni and Theo." Lons pointed us out to the old couple. "What is the name of your village?"

"My name is Arnas Hensa and this is my wife Mirna," said the old chap. "Our village is called Tsirni."

We started walking along the track with them, Arnas guiding his animal which was loaded with what looked like potatoes. The woman, Mirna, was looking at us furtively. I had my hood up and attempted to avoid direct examination.

"You have a good crop of presna," remarked Pinatook, whose family were farmers. "They are exceptionally large."

"The secret is to select the buds for the size, shape or flavor. Over time the crop becomes stronger," explained Arnas. *Plant breeding in action* I thought.

As we entered the village we saw more people moving around and received curious looks but being with the old people seemed to reassure them and we were ignored until we arrived outside the Hensa house where a couple of men were working on nets.

"These are my sons Luga and Prinsh," said Arnas. The two young men looked at us curiously.

"Who are you?" asked Luga rudely, scowling at us. He was a big burly individual, almost as broad in the shoulders as me.

"We are travelers from the islands," said Lons. "We are here looking for work."

Luga scowled. "Are you sailors?"

"We are fishermen and farmers," said Lons.

"Are you warriors? Can you use a spear and an axe?" asked Luga. He was looking us up and down, examining our weapons and rucksacks.

He is assessing us I thought. *Probably working out whether it's worth mugging us.* His parents seemed decent types but he seemed a disreputable and suspicious individual.

"If we have to defend ourselves," said Lons giving him a blank faced look. My respect for him was already high and climbed higher.

"You have to speak to the village chief," Luga said turning away dismissively. He seemed disinclined to offer any further help. Lons turned back to Arnas who was unloading the suron with his wife.

"Where is the chief's house?"

"That big house." Arnas pointed to the other side of the village to a large house overlooking the sea. "His name is Farnat. But he has not returned from a hunting trip. You can talk to his eldest son, Enlatos."

"Thank you for your help Master Arnas," said Lons respectfully.

The old chap nodded politely. "Take care."

We left them and walked towards the house indicated by Arnas. More people were taking notice of us and I saw a couple of individuals running towards the Village Chief's house.

"Looks like the Chief is on the boats returning from the raid," I remarked. "Gina, when do you think the boats are due?"

"They are thirty miles from the village. At the speed they are traveling they will be here in three to five hours."

"Hmm, before nightfall. I didn't like that Luga

person's attitude. If that is the sort of hostility we can expect then we should not spend the night here."

"Even with guns you could be overwhelmed," Gina said.

"I suspect that once we start shooting they may re-think their attitude," I said. "But it may be better to return tomorrow with the aircraft and the robots. I would not want anyone's death on my conscience."

"Yes, we should protect your conscience," said Gina.

"Hey Gina, that's a bit unfair." I was surprised and hurt by Gina's criticism. "What are you implying?"

"Your obsession with not being seen as a god nearly got you killed. You are now putting your life and other people's lives at risk by trying to move around incognito. You cannot move around safely on this world and do the things that you want to do."

"But Gina, I cannot pretend to be a god. We have discussed this. That is interfering with the history of these people in an unacceptable way."

"You should not interfere, and you cannot move around safely. The conclusion is obvious Theo."

"Right, hide away somewhere until I die. Thanks for your advice Gina but you know what you can do with it."

"It is my duty to tell you."

"You have told me. Thanks. My friends here know the risks and are here voluntarily."

As we came close to the Chief's house a number of individuals came out and stood waiting for us. They were carrying spears and axes. *Uh oh, reception committee!* I thought. I noticed others spreading out around the periphery of the square to cut off our escape.

I was beginning to think that we had walked into an ambush. Perhaps Gina was right; I was playing fast and loose with my friends lives. I put my hands in my pockets, one which contained the ultra-sonic gun and

Marooned

the other the pistol.

"Gina, can you send the two robots down. We may need rescuing. But keep them hidden outside the town."

"I will not say I told you so. Oh, I just did!" she said with simulated surprise.

I groaned but held my tongue.

"They are on their way, should be with you in half an hour," she continued.

Gina is becoming more human I told myself. At any other time that would be an interesting development.

We stopped within ten yards or so of the Chief's house. Lons turned to me. "Theo, I think you should do the talking."

I nodded and stepped forward.

"Who is the Village Chief?" I shouted.

One of the men stepped forward. "Who are you and what do you want?"

"My name is Theo. These are my friends Lons, Tarni and Pinatok. We have sailed here from the islands."

"From the islands? Which island?" The man came closer, looking me up and down. "Where is your ship?"

"Our ship is down the coast. We landed there and walked through the mountains. We are from the island of Limni."

"Limni? Don't know it," he said.

"It is three days sailing from here. We are sailors and fishermen."

"There is nothing here for outsiders and we don't want you around. Go back to where you came from."

There's northern hospitality for you! If that's your attitude...

"Your three warships are returning in a few hours. We want to talk to the leader of the expedition."

He looked startled, his almost colorless eyes wide with shock.

"What do you know about our warships?" His eyes narrowed suspiciously.

"We have heard that your warriors are very successful. There is much loot and women for those who are brave enough. We want to join your ships."

"You say you are fishermen. You can conquer a slanet." A slanet was a small and numerous fish similar to a sardine. He looked at his mates who responded to his wit with derisive laughter. "But what do you know about fighting?"

"We are all young, fit and strong. We can learn." I turned to my friends. "Right?" They responded with enthusiastic shouts of 'yeah!'.

"You say our warships are returning in a few hours? Did you see them?"

"Yes, they stopped yesterday for some provisions and we caught a good wind and passed them."

"Did you hear that men," he shouted. "The ships are returning. Let's prepare a feast. Gather the women." He turned back to us. "As for you, let's wait and see what Chief Tarvos has to say when he returns."

"Can we go and admire your fishing boats?" I asked. He waved at us dismissively. I nodded to the guys and we wandered off towards the docks.

"What do you think?" I asked Lons and the others.

"They are rude arrogant people," said Tarni. I was sure that having experienced what the 'Vikings' had done to his village he was trying hard to restrain himself.

I squeezed his shoulder sympathetically. "They will get what is coming to them."

We made our way down to the sea to where the fishing boats were moored. There were seven of them of different sizes. I had little idea what constituted a more sophisticated boat but even I could see that the hulls looked smoother and well put together, the tillers and masts sturdy and well made.

They had both oars and small sails with enclosed areas to store the fish.

Lons and Pinatok examined them carefully, pointing out features to each other. One of the boats was being maintained by a couple of fishermen and they got into a conversation with them about technicalities. The fishermen were more friendly than the leaders we had talked to, their attitude more like that of the old farmer and his wife.

It is the usual business I thought, political affairs being hijacked by the assertive types; we had seen that on Earth for thousands of years. It was the ancient Greek philosopher Plato who had come to the conclusion that only those who did NOT want power were suitable to hold power. Interesting that the thoughts of an ancient human philosopher three thousand years ago were still applicable to an alien species thousands of light years from Earth. I had the thought; that was not the only thing we had in common, accompanied by a vision of Salny's beautiful body!

Gina's dulcet tones interrupted my thoughts. "Theo, the robots are in position in the forest above the village. What is your status?"

"Thanks Gina." Gina listened in to all my conversation so I did not have to repeat that. "We are down on the pier checking out their fishing boats. Lons and the boys are exchanging notes with a couple of fishermen."

"You will wait for the return of the raiding party?"

"Yes. But for now we will pretend to be potential employees. I want to learn more about what drives these people."

"That is an ambitious project. How long do you intend to stay there?"

"No more than a couple of days. Mainly to meet the leadership."

"They are primitive people with no laws and no scruples about killing. Remember who you are dealing with."

"Point noted."

The boys had got into one of the boats and were examining the nets and associated fixtures and fittings. I strolled to the end of the small pier and looked out into the depths of the sea. My eyes caught a tiny movement on the horizon. I squinted into the distance and resolved two tiny objects moving in and out of sight as the sea moved. The returning raiding party. We were about to meet the Viking raiders, or Tsirnians as they called themselves.

Chapter 18

Our new fisherman friends invited us back to the village to join the celebrations for the arrival of the raiding party. *One man's misery is cause for another's celebration* I mused. Such is the dichotomy of life. I was becoming quite the philosopher!

Our Tsirnian friends introduced themselves as Hernas and Milnos. They were both older individuals and I could not help musing on whether the raiding culture was a recent development amongst the younger generation. The older people we had met so far were not unfriendly. It was an idea that I should investigate I told myself.

We strolled back to the village where preparations were well under way for the welcoming party. Tables had been laid in the square and barbeque fires lit. The two fishermen led us up the hill to their houses. They were cousins and their houses were next to each other.

"Come, sit and we can have a cup of tea," said Milnos.

"You are very kind," said Lons.

Their wives brought out tables and chairs and we sat. I leaned over to Lons. "Shall we give these nice people a small gift?"

"What do you suggest?" asked Lons.

"One second." I opened my rucksack, rummaged inside and brought out a couple of calcite stones, very pretty colors but quite plentiful around Faro if you knew where to look. They were attached to pretty silver threads to make necklaces.

"Some small gifts for your wives," I said offering up the two necklaces to the men.

"That is generous of you," said Milno. He handed them to the women who looked delighted. "Put them on," he added nodding eagerly at his wife. The two women put the necklaces around their necks and we made suitably admiring noises.

The ladies brought out the tea and we got some hard biscuits to go with it as a reward. We chatted to Milnos and Hernas about village life and learned that the village had grown substantially over the lifetime due to migration down from other mountain villages. Mostly because of the rich fishing but some years back the new Headman Chief Tarvos had expanded into piracy.

I asked them what they thought about that and they looked at each other then shrugged noncommittally.

"Tarvos built the ships. When we are not using them for piracy we are using them for fishing. It has brought wealth to the village," remarked Milnos.

"Until one of the villages you raid decides to come here and return the favor," I pointed out.

"Is that why you are here?" asked Milnos looking at me keenly. *No flies on you* I thought.

"No, we have no desire to kill or steal," I replied. "If that is the only work here then we will leave."

Milnos leaned forward and spoke quietly. "If Chief Tarvos lets you." He gave me a knowing look.

"Tell us about the Chief," I said. He looked shifty and turned to his friend for support. Hernas looked around as if looking for anyone spying or overhearing, then gave Milnos a tight nod.

"Tarvos is totally ruthless. He will kill you if he thinks there is anything suspicious about you, or he just does not like or trust you," said Milnos.

"How did this raiding come about?" asked Lons. "When did it start?"

"It started when Tarvos killed the previous Chief and took over. Uh... seven, nine years ago?" Milnos turned to his friend who shrugged vaguely. "They travel down the coast far from here and attack small unprotected villages, stealing young women and anything valuable. They prefer gold, diamonds, rubies. Anything they can sell to the rich traders along the nearby villages. So we will hide the trinkets you have given to our women and I suggest if you have more that you hide them."

"Ah, thank you for the advice Milnos. You are an honest and good fellow."

"We were all honest farmers and fishermen before this thief took over the village," he said. "But now we keep our heads down otherwise they will be chopped off."

"Milnos...!" His wife was giving the old chap a stern look. He grunted and slurped his tea. "I have said too much."

"Have no fear Milnos," I said quickly. "We appreciate your warning. Perhaps we will move on tomorrow. Your village seems a dangerous place to stay."

"You would be wise to leave before the ships return," he said.

"We will discuss that amongst ourselves and decide," I said standing up. "Thank you for your hospitality."

We said our goodbyes to Milnos, Hernas and their families and walked back towards the woods. I wanted a private place to consider our actions but the village was now a hive of activity and people were giving us looks. We continued back the way we had arrived until we were out of the village and amongst the trees. We sat on some rocks and looked down on the village.

"What do you think guys, how should we meet the big Chief and his men?"

"Wait for the ships to arrive and everyone to get

into the celebrations," said Lons, "then go down there with the robots and scare the shit out of them. Tell them to stop their raiding otherwise our giant insects will kill them all."

I had to laugh at his succinct and uncompromising advice. The others were also grinning and chuckling.

"Perhaps spare the good looking young women," added Pinatok to nods of lecherous agreement from his friends.

"If I may suggest an alternative tactic," I said tentatively. "We can go down and join the festivities later. Get introduced to the Chief and see what kind of fellow he is."

I was painfully aware that my 'softly softly' approach had nearly got me killed; I had the scars to prove it!

"We know what kind of fellow he is," said Lons. "He is a tyrant like Panstrosh who cares nothing for the lives of others."

"I agree with Lons," said Tarni. "They brutally murdered anyone in my village who stood in their way and kidnapped the young women. They have probably beaten and raped them already and they will be treated as slaves and prostitutes in the village."

Tarni looked distressed and I began to realize how much emotion the young man had been repressing. My civilized values and objectivity were preventing me from understanding the reality of life in this world.

Okay, no more mister nice guy.

"Gina, where are the robots?"

"If I am sensing your location correctly they are just a couple of hundred yards above you on the trail."

"Order them to continue down the trail to our location."

"Yes Theo. Are you going into the village with the

robots?"

"Yep. Time to kick ass."

"You have been watching too many western movies."

"I suspect the expression 'kick ass' was more twentieth century. You know, tough guy detective?"

"I bow to your superior knowledge."

"Got to do something during those long trips in Hyperspace," I said apologetically.

"Do try talking to the natives first," suggested Gina.

"I suspect they will be so terrified by the robots they will head for the hills. That was the reason I wanted the 'softly softly' approach."

A couple of minutes later the robots come around the bend of the track.

"Good day Dum and Dee. How are you today?"

"We are functioning normally Captain," replied Dum.

"Good. The plan is we are going into the village later to confront the leaders regarding their raid on the Murpa village. We will demand that they release the prisoners and desist from any further attacks on the Murpa or any other village. You are to accompany us and provide protection. At any sign of aggression on the part of the natives you will first shoot to disable, then if they persist, shoot to kill."

"Understood. On the first sign of aggression shoot to disable. If they persist, shoot to kill," repeated Dum.

"Right. For now, let's have a rest."

It was about an hour later when we spotted the three Tsirni ships pulling into the harbor. It took them a while to moor, disembark and offload their booty. We spotted three females being unloaded. Tarni had told us that only three had been taken from their village. He was unable to see clearly enough to identify his sister but the poor fellow looked about ready to break down in tears at the sight of the captives. Primitive these people may be, and even brutal at times, but their love for family was no weaker than ours.

We noticed a couple of the horse like animals and five pranli, the cow like animals they used for milk and meat. There were also lots of sacks holding unknown 'booty'.

The reception party on the village square was well under way and even from where we were we could hear shouting and screams of greeting and laughter. Again I was struck by people's ability to hate and murder strangers while loving their own. The idea that the stranger was also someone's son, daughter, husband or wife does not seem to enter into their thinking, or was conveniently ignored. It seems that consideration for strangers only takes place when it suits one!

We gave the arrivals an hour or so to settle down and get into the celebrations before we began to make our way back down to the village. It was late afternoon, still light but the sun was low on the horizon. We cleared the trees and came down to the edge of the square before we were noticed. We walked four abreast with the robots at each end, down the centre of the track and onto the square. We were twenty yards or so from the tables before we stopped. Those individuals closest to us became alarmed, staring wide eyed at the robots and pointing. They left their tables and moved away into the crowd, shouting to warn the others.

The ripple of alarm spread.

"Make no sudden moves," I said to the others. I held up my arms, hands open and shouted as loudly as I could.

"We are here to talk to your leaders. We want to speak to Chief Tarvos. Do not fear my creatures, they will not hurt you."

I kept repeating myself and gradually the pandemonium began to settle down. I noticed our friends Milnos and Hernas coming forward and showing no fear which helped to reassure others. But at the back, where the warriors from the ship were, there was an ominous huddle of bodies which suddenly became a group of warriors clutching swords, axes and spears, pushing their way through the crowd towards us.

At their head was a tall broad shouldered figure, the biggest Enlai I had seen. He had a thick shock of white hair on his head and carried a long sword and axe around his waist. He pushed to the front and stared at us, his eyes going from us to the robots and back.

"Who are you? And what are these creatures with you?" he demanded.

"We are from the islands and these creatures are our servants. They are harmless unless they, or us, are attacked. Then they will kill without mercy. Please do nothing to alarm them." I spoke slowly and loudly.

"From the islands? I saw no such creatures where we went," Tarvos said, scowling ferociously.

"You did not go to my village. You went to Murpa, which is a peaceful farming village."

"You know where we went? How can you know that?"

"Because we got here before you did," I said. "We have a very fast ship."

"Where is your ship?"

"It is moored down the coast. We came here overland."

"You have an odd accent. And you do not look like us. Who are you? Where are you really from?"

"I am from the southern continent. My friends are from the islands," I said.

"The southern continent?" He looked disbelieving. "I have heard there are only primitive naked hairy men there. No civilized people."

"We live on the southern coast where no one has traveled. Chief Tarvos, me and my friends wish to discuss a matter of mutual interest with you and the leaders of your village. We think you will be interested in what we have to say."

"Mutual interest? What does that mean?" he growled.

"It will take time to explain. Perhaps we can join you at your table and discuss our offer," I suggested.

He looked doubtful.

"It does not seem to me that you have much to offer," he said dismissively. "Kill these fools and their creatures." He waved an arm in our direction and his men rushed us.

Oh well, I tried I thought. By the time I pulled and cocked my gun Dum and Dee had already shot the first four pirates as they were pulling out their swords and bounding towards us. I pointed my gun at Tarvos's ugly head and shot him. As his head exploded and he went down, the remaining pirates paused uncertainly, their faces frozen in terror.

"Stay where you are and drop your weapons or you will die," I shouted. I considered instructing Dum and Dee to give them a blast from their ultrasonic weapon but decided that would spook everyone. But the gory death of their leader was enough for the pirates. They threw their weapons down and backed away.

"I told you not to attack my creatures," I shouted. "You are safe if you do not attack them or us. Who can I talk to now Tarvos is dead?"

There were no volunteers.

"Where are the members of the village council?" I insisted. "Come forward now."

We had them cowed and terrified and no one was

interested in having anything to do with us. Except for our friend Milnos the fisherman. The bold fellow stepped forward and started shouting names. "Saros, Plinto, Korni, you are all on the council. Come forward and speak with these people."

The named individuals slunk into the crowd, seemingly disinclined to show their faces now that their leader was dead. Typical of the sorts of gutless sycophants who tagged on to the coat tails of a dictator I thought.

"Then, let me talk to all of you," I said. I pulled up a chair and stood on it. "Let me tell you all who we are and why we are here."

I launched into a description of the island and its three villages, and what had happened to Murpa village. "We have come here to ask you to stop the piracy," I continued. "But let us be clear; if you do not stop willingly, we will stop you forcibly. We have demonstrated our power. Tarvos is gone and your village council is dissolved. We will oversee the election of a new village council selected by you without coercion. The village council will then elect a new leader. But for now, I am your new leader. I want the owners of the fishing and fighting ships to come forward now. I also want the biggest farmers in the village to come forward. Everyone else, clean up the square and return to your homes."

It took a while to get the idea through to everyone, and many repetitions. But eventually order was restored and the cleanup of the village square under way.

I was pleased to see Milnos and Hernas step forward as ship owners with a bunch of other individuals, young and old. In addition the old farmer Arnas stepped forward with a group of other farmers.

As we waited for the individuals to gather, Tarni came up to me. "Theo, we must release the young women who were captured. I want to see my sister."

"Of course. Let's attend to that first." I turned to the Tsirni elders who were nervously huddling together whispering in low voices.

"Do any of you know where the prisoners are being held?" I asked.

One of them stepped forward. "Yes, they are locked up in Tarvos's outhouse."

"Can you get some people together and go and bring the women here?"

The man looked nervous and unsure of himself.

"I will go with you," said Tarni.

"One of the robots can go with you. Dee, accompany Tarni and protect him."

"Yes Theo." The robots deep voice startled the natives who pulled back fearfully.

Tarni left with his escort and the robot and I turned my attention back to the ad-hoc council.

"I want to know how you all feel about Tarvos. Did you agree with him? Did you support him and why."

There was quiet at first, nobody wanted to speak first. It was Milnos who plucked up the courage to speak.

"Many of us thought that it was wrong and a waste of our beautiful boats to use them for piracy," he said.

"So he did not have the support of all the village?" I asked.

"No, but he had his group of young hunters and fighters who liked the idea and supported him. Then slowly, anyone who disagreed had an accident or disappeared. So people stopped complaining," explained Milnos. There were grunts of approval from some of the others and nods of agreement.

Now we may be getting somewhere I thought.

Soon, more of the village worthies spoke up to support Milnos and I began to get a picture of how Tarvos and his bullies had come to dominate the village.

People began to loosen up and talk and a better atmosphere developed, as if they had all wanted to get this off their chests. Or were they now sucking up to the new master of the village I asked myself. I dismissed such cynical thoughts, and anyway, if they were then I would use my hold over them for good.

Tarni then returned with the captured girls, the robot in attendance. Tarni was cuddling one young thing who was sobbing. The other girls were also young, disheveled and distressed.

"Milnos, get your wife and some women to bring some food and drinks for these girls," I shouted. I moved amongst the girls and tried to reassure them. They looked confused and traumatized poor things and my heart went out to them.

What to do now I asked myself. The girls had been beaten up and possibly raped and needed medical attention.

"Gina, can you get the shuttle down here? We need help. Land it here on the square, we can clear the tables and make room."

"Yes Theo, that is a good idea. Well done by the way. I will make world dictator out of you yet."

"Hah! Today the village, tomorrow the world!" I should have added the essential mad dictator's manic laugh but decided that it was not appropriate given the circumstances.

Milnos's wife and some other ladies arrived with hot drinks and food for the girls. The company and sympathy of other women helped to settle the girls down. Meanwhile I continued my conversations with the village worthies, mostly to calm and reassure them that there was a new and peaceful future for their village. They had to go out to the citizens and explain my plans and also reassure them that life would return to normal.

However, the arrival of the shuttle caused a new and even more traumatic sensation. Many of the villagers ran off or disappeared behind houses and trees at first sight of the giant silver 'bird'. I manage to reassure the village worthies, with the brave help of our friend Milnos, and prevented them from running away.

As soon as the shuttle landed Salny and Hanna bounded out and ran over. I explained the situation to them and Salny immediately took over, organizing the women and the captured girls and arranging treatment for them.

I sent my new ad-hoc village council out to explain to the villagers what was happening and to return to their homes. It was now dusk and time for the village to shut down for the night. We also needed somewhere to sleep. Myself and Salny could sleep in the shuttle of course, but it seemed selfish for us to enjoy that comfort while our friends slept on floors or in the open.

It was a dry and mild night so we decided we should all sleep on the floor in the open. The villagers put together a pile of bedding for us and we prepared our open air area. I rigged up some lighting by running a cable from the aircraft, which created further open mouthed amazement amongst the villagers.

As peace descended on the village we sat around a couple of tables and enjoyed some of Mrs. Milnos's tea and cakes, and some provisions from the shuttle. The captured girls had been taken into the shuttle by Salny and Hanna and treated by Dum for cuts and bruises and also treated to a shower. After some food and drink they were looking much happier, although still stressed and disbelieving over what was happening.

We all settled down to sleep on a grassy swathe

next to the shuttle, with the robots on guard. As Salny and I snuggled down on our bedding, which was Spartan and smelled of sweat and animals, I contemplated what we had achieved and what remained. Tomorrow our task was to establish the new village council, elect a new leader and hope that this new regime would continue into the future.

Until another dictator comes along to take over and create murder and mayhem was my cynical thought before I dropped off.

Chapter 19

Salny had thought that they had been unlucky in her village to have the dictator Panstrosh as their leader. But the situation here in Tsirni seemed identical, in fact, worse. Tarvos was even more brutal than Panstrosh. Why did individuals like them become leaders she asked herself. It seemed a deep and complex question and she sadly concluded that the answer was beyond her. Perhaps Theo understood why she concluded.

But Theo's conversion to direct action was a welcome change. He had shot Tarvos at the first sign of a threat. She thought about how the ruffians head had exploded with satisfaction. *He deserved it* she told herself, although not without a feeling of horror and regret that such things should happen.

Are we changing Theo so that he becomes more like us she asked herself. It was an uncomfortable question because it seemed like there were situations when being brutal and violent provided the only solution. She did not want Theo to become like the Enlai. She loved him because he was caring, gentle and kind. And handsome and a great lover she added with an internal giggle!

It was a very uncomfortable night; I was not used to sleeping on the ground with just a fur rug between my body and the hard cold grass. I had Salny to keep me warm and perhaps some sexual exercise would have helped me to sleep but the lack of privacy made that impossible.

I awoke early while it was still dark, went into the shuttle and made a hot coffee then sat outside on a chair drinking my coffee and watching the dawn. *What was I doing on this planet* I asked myself. Did I really think that I could bring them culturally into the twenty fifth century? Could I instill democracy and peaceful coexistence into a world that was in the early Iron Age?

Gina had told me that it was a futile exercise; as soon as I turned my back the natives would fall back into their bad habits. Civilization was a slow and painful climb from savagery to enlightenment which inevitably would consist of progress and regress in various measure, but had to happen organically and systemically. That is, both the organs of civilization had to evolve, and the system as a whole adapt to its new parts and take on new qualities.

I was not an expert in civilizations; I guessed that my analysis was a systems engineer's way of thinking. But whatever! I concluded that it was my duty to attempt to do good. Look at those poor kidnapped girls; what sort of life would they have had if we had not rescued them? A life of slavery and abuse was their future. Every single act of kindness adds to the common good. If we all say 'my contribution will make no difference' then surely we give in to the forces of evil. So fuck it Theo, do your bit and the devil take the hindmost I told myself.

Having examined my conscience over coffee and pronounced it largely fit for purpose I pondered on what further fun could be had after we had sorted the Tsirna. Investigate that other northern village? The old farmer had said that they were a mysterious and secretive lot. That sounds interesting I thought. No more deposing tyrants though; I'd done quite enough of that.

Salny's sweet voice interrupted my reverie.

"You are a selfish Earthman." She pulled the bedclothes tightly around her.

"Why baby, you know I would do anything for you," I protested.

"Why have you left me here on this hard cold ground by myself?"

"Ah… because…," I thought quickly. "Your beauty was getting me so excited that I had to get away. Otherwise…?" I gave her a significant look.

"We could have done it quietly," she suggested.

"Not the way you scream and moan."

"I like to show my appreciation of your efforts," she said with a smirk. "It's good for your er… manliness."

"Nothing wrong with my manliness," I laughed. "Shall I make you some coffee?"

"Make it hot," she said pleadingly.

I suspected that others would be on the move soon and made a jug of coffee. Sure enough by the time I went back out with the jug and some cups the others were up groaning and stretching. The boys and Hanna fell on the coffee but our three kidnapped girls looked on it with suspicion. But they were saved by the nice Mrs. Milnos bringing a jug of tea and some of her hard biscuits. I repaid her with a couple of granola bars, showing her how to open the wrapping before she left!

So began the long day of meetings, conversations and explanations with the Tsirni. But in the end I was satisfied that we had a good strong new village council, led by our friend Milnos, which would abandon the piracy and continue with peaceful trading. I hoped that contacts between the four villages would expand into regular trade between them and all the other villages along the peninsula and the mainland.

If I continued to monitor proceedings, visiting them all regularly then I could hopefully nip in the bud any threat to the peace. Such was my hope anyway.

I wanted to visit the mysterious northern village in the mountains but we had the problem of what to do with the kidnapped girls. They desperately wanted to return to their homes. It would be a squeeze to fit them all into the shuttle but it was a short journey. I decided to return the girls to their village, pay a visit to Hoshna and Faro to assure them that we were okay, then return to visit the mysterious northern village in the mountains.

We said our goodbyes to our new Tsirni friends, after first distributing gifts to the wives of the new village council. We had a private chat with the new Chief Milnos and he raised the question of how he could contact us if they had a problem. He was concerned that as soon as we left the hard-line supporters of the previous Chief may attempt to unseat him.

I decided to leave a small personal transponder with him. These were used by Gina to keep track of where I was at all times. I showed Milnos how to switch it on and told him that if he did that, I would come immediately. He shook his head in bemusement.

"This is magic. Theo, you must be a god or a magician."

"No, they are machines," I said. "Complicated almost living machines, but not magic."

"Should I feed your little machine? Does it need water?" he asked.

"No, keep it away from water or food," I said smiling. "Water will damage it. Keep it somewhere dry and safe."

"And if I switch it on? How will it inform you?"

"It will make a noise that only my ship will hear. Then we will know you need our help."

"Good. I will tell only my wife and children about

this. And Hernas and Arnas, Them I can trust."

"Tell the council that you have a way of contacting me, but not what it is," I suggested. He nodded his agreement with a confidential smirk.

We were preparing to leave, but I was concerned about the three kidnapped girls. If they had been raped that would be a blight on their lives, but if they also became pregnant that would be a further reminder of their tragedy. Could we take them to Aegina and x-ray them to see if they were pregnant? I asked Gina and she said yes.

"We can also terminate the pregnancy if the girls want it," she said.

"Really?" I was surprised. "We have the means to do that?"

"There are female scouts Theo," she reminded me. "They could accidentally go on a trip and discover they are pregnant."

"Of course," I agreed ruefully, although that would be seriously careless I thought.

"Ask Salny to talk to the girls," Gina suggested.

So I did. Salny looked surprised.

"The girls will not be pregnant," she said.

"Uh? How can you be sure?"

"Enlai females can choose whether to become pregnant."

"They can choose? How do they do that?"

"Put your hand on my tummy," she said.

"With pleasure." I placed my hand on her firm flat tummy. She opened my palm and spread it against her tummy then clenched her muscle. I felt a band of muscle tense, lock and remain locked.

"That closes the door into the womb," she said. "If I clench my muscle again it opens."

"That is fantastic!" I exclaimed. "What a wonderful thing." I had noticed that the Enlai did not have large families and had put that down to a reduced fertility.

A thought occurred to me; "Salny, are Enlai girls okay with unmarried sex? I mean, if they cannot get pregnant does that encourage promiscuity?"

"No, there is much pressure against that from parents and the community. And the men. They do not want a wife who is free with her body."

"But men are always trying to seduce girls," I said. "They want a virgin to marry but to also have free sex before they get married."

"Enlai men do not seduce girls from their village. That is why they kidnap girls from other villages," explained Salny.

Suddenly, the Enlai men's obsession with raiding other villages began to make sense. The strong ethic against sex with the local girls had destructive side effects.

"What do Earthmen think about free sex?" asked Salny.

"In the past we had similar problems," I explained. "But now men accept that women have the same rights with their bodies as men."

"That is a healthy attitude," she agreed.

"Salny, perhaps you should tell the girls to tell their families that we rescued them before the Tsirni men could interfere with them. We will support their story."

"You are a caring and thoughtful person," she said.

"Yeah, the girls like that," I said giving her a roguish wink.

Back in the shuttle it was a squeeze in the main cabin with most of my passengers sitting on the floor huddled together. I explained to the three girls that they will feel the aircraft moving around but they were not to worry.

"This is a very safe flying machine which has flown

around the world many times. Taking you to your villages will be just a little hop up and down. Relax and enjoy it. You can tell your children and grandchildren that you flew in a flying machine into the clouds."

I was not sure the girls were reassured; they looked terrified. But Salny and Hanna's relaxed demeanor set them a calming example.

In the cockpit I went through my checks with Gina then fired up the engines gradually building thrust. With everything normal I lifted off and climbed gently, keeping the acceleration low not to alarm my passengers. We stayed low so we could enjoy the view; and it was indeed beautiful. The sun glinted off the deep blue sea and on either bank of the peninsula golden beaches vied with green hills, valleys and forest for our admiration.

The two day trip by sailing ship was less than one hour by aircraft; I could have done it in a few minutes at supersonic speed but 'poodling' along was more fun!

We arrived over the Murpa village and I set the shuttle down at the same location next to the village. Our arrival had alerted the village and everyone was out to greet us led by Chief Harago.

The three kidnapped girls ran to their families with cries of happiness while we were greeted with enthusiasm. It was a home coming and we all enjoyed the joyous moment.

While the welcoming banquet was being prepared we described our adventures to the happy villagers. Everyone cheered when I described how I shot the 'Viking' chief. Lons interceded to describe in graphic detail how his head exploded and blood spattered everywhere. A couple of the chaps did an impromptu war dance in celebration. I had to concede that it was a great party, even though the Murpa booze still tasted as bad as before. Perhaps it revealed a difference between human and Enlai taste buds I decided.

We decided to stay the night with our Murpa friends and leave the next day to investigate the northern mountain village. Lons, Pinatok and Tarny had picked up some ideas to improve their fishing boats so they went down to the fishing boats with the locals to discuss their ideas.

The good Murpa villagers tidied up the remains of the banquet and attended to their chores. I decided some skinny dipping with Salny would be a pleasant way to pass the afternoon and Salny enthusiastically agreed.

"I want another ride in your lovely little boat," she said. We returned to the shuttle, unpacked and prepared our inflatable. There seemed no reason to include the robots in our trip, although Gina fussed and told us to stay close to land and watch out for sharks. I informed her that sharks very seldom attacked humans, that they were just curious and if they did bite it was just to investigate.

"Well, don't get investigated by any sharks," Gina insisted.

We got into the boat just wearing underpants with Salny displaying her cute pointy breasts.

"Amazing how human you are," I said examining her breasts closely. "Aliens are supposed to have three breasts, or maybe four."

"I am not a *prinlo*," she said. A prinlo was a sow like creature with a proliferation of breasts to feed its multiple young.

"Two big ones is better than four small one," I agreed, reaching out. "They fit just nicely..."

"Are we going for a swim?" she asked with a severe look.

"Yes madam, your ship awaits."

We pushed the inflatable out and jumped in. The electric motor hummed and we headed out to sea. Salny gave little screams of delight as the boat picked up speed and I attempted a few maneuvers, steering the boat into the waves.

We motored along the coast and found a small sheltered cove that was perfect for swimming. Salny only knew the 'dog paddle' and admired my crawl so I started teaching her. She was a quick learner and was soon thrashing along at a good pace.

Inevitably our games became arousing and underpants were removed and consigned to the waves. We did it in the sea and on the beach and on the rocks and finally in the boat.

When we had satisfied our lust for each other, we lay in the boat examining the white clouds scudding across the blue sky.

"This is a nice spot," I said. It wasn't a very deep or meaningful statement, but appropriate, I thought.

"We should come here again," she agreed.

We dozed for a while then had another dip before floating the boat and heading back. It had been a delightful afternoon on the beach with a beautiful woman. Was I on an alien planet I asked myself. Or had I died and gone to heaven?

Back at the shuttle we deflated and disassembled the boat and stored it. Gina made no comment on our nakedness. We showered and dressed and enjoyed a coffee before heading down to the village. Tonight we would have a social evening and tomorrow head off to investigate the mysterious mountain people.

Chapter 20

The next morning we had breakfast then went to the village to say goodbye to our Murpa friends. The previous evening they had thrown us a village party with food and wine aplenty. I could see that the Murpa had a nice community spirit which was nurtured by the village council headed by the amiable Harago.

Young Tarni asked if he could accompany us again; he was clearly getting the adventure bug. We returned to the shuttle with Lons and Hanna who had spent the night as guests of Harago, they told us, but I could see by their demeanor that we would have a wedding on our return to Faro.

We took off and headed up the peninsula. In a half hour we were at the mountains and Gina flew the aircraft up the river canyon towards the village in the mountains. The landscape was odd, with the deep valley covered in forest but just a couple of thousand feet up began the snow line.

We spotted a bridge over the river and what appeared to be a high wall blocking the pass. Then the village appeared, small white houses clambering up the sides of the mountain on both sides of the river. We also noticed two other wooden bridges spanning the river. The village was substantial, about a thousand houses I reckoned. There was an open area with a large building facing it, clearly the village centre. It was the only place we could land so I decided to make an entrance!

I brought the shuttle down in front of the large white building. I could see figures in the square dashing away from our landing area. Once we were down, I turned the engines off and examined the building with interest. It was definitely the most advanced and spectacular structure we had seen on this planet; almost worthy of Ancient Greece or Rome, not so much in size but in design and quality of build.

"These people here are very advanced," I remarked to Salny. She was looking impressed by the building.

"It is a beautiful building," she agreed. "The houses in the village are also well made."

She was correct; the houses also displayed the same quality of workmanship and construction. There were nice artistic touches everywhere; columns, arches and lintels and even marble and paving stones.

"Damn, these people are a thousand years ahead of everyone else," I muttered to myself. "What's going on?"

And indeed, this was more Ancient Greece than an Iron Age village. It was completely out of place.

The engines were now quiet, the aircraft resting in the center of the completely empty square. Where were the inhabitants I asked myself. Had they been scared away? That was quite likely. Perhaps we should get out of the aircraft and show ourselves. That may reassure them.

My thoughts were interrupted by the appearance of a stream of figures running out from behind the buildings. They were soldiers carrying crossbows. They double timed in two lines around the square and surrounded the aircraft. The front line went down on one knee, crossbows raised while the back line stood, also with their crossbows raised. It was an impressively disciplined and organized military response.

Salny was looking wide eyed with surprise. I was

sure that she had never seen such a display of military organization before.

I zoomed the surveillance cameras in for a closer look at the figures. They looked similar to the 'Vikings', with a long mop of white hair. But they looked taller and leaner. They wore close fitting cloth garments instead of animal skins. They were similarly but not identically dressed and some of them were female. So they were not an army as such; just citizens defending their town. But well organized and coordinated.

"Interesting that they have not run away in terror at the sight of the aircraft," I said.

"No gifts of food and sacrificial virgins?" asked Salny with a straight face.

"Mmm. Shame." My comment earned a warning growl from my partner.

"I guess we had better go out and meet our new friends," I said. We went into the main cabin. Lons was pointing out interesting features about the inhabitants.

"Clothing is made from the Fillo plant. We have it back home but it grows very slowly so we cannot make much cloth."

"Looks like they have plenty of it here," said Pinatok.

"Very valuable," Tarni nodded. "How do they grow so much?"

"Also building material." Pinatok pointed to the paving on the square. "How do they make those square stones?"

"Looks like our friends are very advanced," I said. "So what do we think, shall we go down to meet them?"

"That's what we came here for," said Lons.

"Yeah, but not to be threatened by fifty warriors," Pinatok said. "What are those weapons they are pointing at us?"

"Crossbows. A form of bow that fires small bolts instead of arrows. Powerful and accurate at short distances," I explained.

"I want one," said Lons.

"The question is," I continued, "How many of us should get out of the aircraft and should we take the robots?"

They looked blankly at each other clearly stumped for an answer.

Gina answered my question. "Theo, you should not all get out of the aircraft until you have some idea of the natives intentions. I suggest one person with one of the robots gets out first. That person should not be you."

As if reading Gina's 'mind' Salny spoke up.

"I don't think you should be first Theo. Until we see what they do."

"Okay, so who volunteers?" I asked. I was not concerned about someone getting out of the aircraft first; I did not believe that the natives would attack.

"I will go first," said Tarni.

"Okay Tarni. I am sure you will be safe. As soon as we see that they will not attack you then we will also exit with the robots. Just walk out and hold your arms up."

We entered the airlock and I opened the external door. The steps unfolded to the ground and Tarni stepped out. He stepped away from the aircraft and held his hands up above his head.

For a few minutes nothing happened. Then the soldiers parted to form a small gap and a number of individuals walked through and approached the aircraft. They stopped ten yards or so from Tarni.

I nodded to the others and led them out of the airlock and down the steps. We all stood together but I stepped forward to speak.

"We are from the islands. We have come to see who lives in the mountains."

One of the figures stepped forward. I was surprised to see that it was a woman. She was tall and angular and had an extravagant explosion of white hair and huge amber eyes.

Now you *do* look like an alien I thought. I felt a strong feeling of nervousness, a desire to turn and leave quickly.

"What is this huge silver bird?" she asked.

"It is a machine. A construction from metal that creates a powerful force that enables it to fly." I used the English word 'machine' since there was no equivalent in their language.

She looked at the aircraft, her eyes huge, her mouth open in disbelief.

"You have built this?"

"No. I and this machine are from another world, far away. These are my friends."

"Yes, we noticed that you are different." She looked at me keenly. "Are you the only one from your world?"

"I am. If you are willing I can tell you my story and how I came here."

She came closer, examining me and my friends, then waved to her colleagues to come closer. We found ourselves being surrounded by the white haired group, their piercing amber eyes examining us with keen interest. They seemed to have no fear of us or the aircraft. My feeling of nervousness and alienation started to fade.

"We have speculated that there may be other worlds in the cosmos," said their spokeswoman. "But we have no way of knowing or seeing."

I was shocked by her words. It took a few moments for me to recover my wits. "I am very surprised to hear you say that. Your civilization must be much more advanced than the others on this world."

"Yes we are. We have abilities that they lack. They are primitive and violent so we keep them away. But come, let us not stand here in the middle of the square. There are so many questions that we want to ask you. I am Laren the current head of our council. I will introduce the others when we are inside."

"My name is Theo Pallas. A pleasure to meet you." *This is going well* I thought. And then the suspicious thought, *too well!* Gina's voice in my ear confirmed my feelings: "Theo, there is something odd about these people. They are far too confident and welcoming."

"Yes, I agree. Close the airlock Gina and keep a watch out."

I followed Laren and her colleagues towards the large white house with Solny next to me. The front entrance had slender white columns supporting a curved structure of pointed spears facing outwards. Not quite a Grecian portico but a similar idea. Quite effective I thought.

The guards were mostly dispersing towards the village although many were loitering around examining the aircraft. How had they managed to organize them so quickly I asked myself; some kind of warning signal or siren perhaps?

Inside the building the floor and walls were paved with marble paving stones. It was cool and sophisticated. An area to one side had a large wooden table with lots of chairs around it; a conference room even! I continued to be amazed. Passages led off to different parts of the building.

"This building is our meeting place," explained Laren.

"Very handsome," I said.

"Thank you. We believe beauty is as essential accompaniment to life. Without it life is empty and barren."

"That is a philosophy that I agree with," I said.

She gave me an elegant smile in return. Seeing her up close I was impressed with her youth and beauty. She was almost as tall as me, rather slender and angular for my taste, but she moved with an elegant and sinuous grace that indicated a muscular and athletic body. I also noticed that her colleagues looked equally youthful and physically graceful, the men muscular and lean.

They emanated a feeling of warmth and friendship. But being someone of a basically suspicious and cynical nature I struggled to fight this. Something was telling me that I was being 'conned'. But what? It all looked genuine and believable.

"Please be seated around the table," said Laren. She waved us over to the table and began introducing us to her colleagues.

"This is Sarno, he is my partner. This is Juna, Forno and Kams. We are all members of the High Council of the Evrani."

"Is that what you call yourselves. The Evrani?" I asked.

"Yes. We are approximately six thousand people living in this village and the surrounding areas."

"That many? The village does not seem big enough," I said.

"Maybe half the population live in the mountains," explained Sarno. "We are farmers and shepherds."

"For farmers and shepherds you have a beautiful village and advanced lifestyle."

"We have something here that no one else has. A written language and education for all our children from a young age. We value learning."

"That is a wonderful achievement," I said. I was impressed. "One of the things I had wanted to do as quickly as possible for my friends here was to introduce a written language and education for all children."

"You may find that difficult," he said.

"I don't think so. I have been impressed with the intelligence of the people here," I said defensively while thinking *you are a bit arrogant.*

"It is not their intelligence. It is their nature. They too often resort to violence to have their way and are led by aggressive individuals."

"That is not their nature. That is just the situation they find themselves in. Let me explain."

I launched into a description of what I had found at Faro and what had happened.

"With the elimination of Panstrosh and his lieutenants the village is now peaceful and united," I concluded. "Let me also tell you about your neighbors, the Tsirni."

I suddenly sensed that they were more attentive. I explained what the Tsirni had been up to and how we had tracked their ships to their village and eliminated Tarvos and how that had also changed the leadership and nature of the people.

"Given the right leadership these people are intelligent, industrious and good natured," I finished. "Apart from these four here. They are a rebellious rabble." I winked at my friends and got grins back and a punch from Salny. The Evrani smiled back, getting the joke.

"We are very happy that you have had a good experience," said Laren. "But tell us more about your world."

Where to start I thought. "That will take a long time," I said. "I have machines that can tell you and also show you. I can get them from my ship. But can I say that it is a great shame that you have stayed here in the mountains instead of spreading your knowledge to your planet and its people."

"We have had nothing but bad experience with the Tsirni," said Sarno. "The Tsirni raiders would come to steal our animals and our women. You may have seen the wall we built across the river. That is permanently manned to keep them out."

"I think from what I have seen of your fighting force you could have gone down to their village and given them a good beating," Lons spoke up for the first time.

"Yes, but that would have been the start of an unending conflict," explained Laren. "Instead we built the wall to keep them out."

"And keep yourselves in," said Lons.

"We have no problem with that as you can see," smiled Laren. "We have built our own paradise here."

I felt something at the edge of my mind, a warm caress, a smile that fluttered like a butterfly across my mind.

Damn! What was that? I noticed my colleagues, Lons, Pinatok, Tarni and even Salny felt it, their faces showing confusion.

"Please stay with us for a while," Laren continued. "We want to know more about your world."

I looked at my friends and they nodded their agreement.

"We would love to stay and learn more about you also," I said.

"While we arrange your accommodation, perhaps you can show us your wondrous flying machine," Laren asked.

"Of course." We stood and left the building. Salny was next to me and she came and leaned close to talk. I put my arm around her affectionately and leaned over.

"Did you feel what we felt?" she whispered.

"A warm pleasant emotion?"

"Yes. It was so powerful. And before, when we first

arrived, I felt worried, scared. I wanted to turn back to the ship and run away."

"Really? It was not so powerful for me," I whispered back.

"Why are we feeling this Theo?" She looked worried. "Is it this place?" She looked around fearfully. "Are there spirits here?"

"No spirits darling. It may be something in the air, something we are breathing." There was no word for 'chemical' or 'particle' in their language.

"Something we are breathing?" she looked puzzled.

"The air is full of tiny things that we cannot see, like the smell of a flower. Perhaps up here in the mountains there is something like that which affects our emotions."

"Are there things like that on Earth?"

"Yes, we call them drugs. Some people use them purposely to enhance their experience."

"That sounds pleasant."

"No, it is very bad because it affects your body and can make you very ill."

"Can we become ill here?" she asked looking alarmed.

"It is possible, but the Evrani look very healthy so it does not seem to affect them badly."

The idea that there may be something in the air was not very convincing but it was all I could think of at this point. Perhaps I could take samples and do some tests. We had some equipment in the shuttle to do that kind of analysis, and more sophisticated stuff on *Aegina*. We should be able to track down any exotic chemicals floating around.

We arrived at the shuttle.

"Open the airlock doors Theo?" asked Gina.

"Yes Gina. Standard tourist rates for our customers."

"Shall I open the gift shop?"

I laughed internally at Gina's quip. There was quite a crowd of people, us five and the eight members of the Evrani, so we could not all go in together.

"Salny, perhaps you and the boys can remain outside and I can take our guests in four at a time?"

Salny nodded and I suggested the same to Laren who made the arrangements with her colleagues.

I entered with the first group, Laren and her partner and two others. They were wide eyed, but they did not look afraid. I got the feeling of great interest and fascination. Dum and Dee were in their usual positions in the cabin and their eye sockets lit up when we walked into the cabin. There was a frisson of alarm amongst the visitors.

"These are two of the machines that assist me in my job as an explorer," I explained. "They accompany me to collect samples and to protect me."

"They look ... fearsome," said Larena nervously. Suddenly the cabin became the entrance of the underworld and the robots its monstrous guardians. I had never thought of good old Dum and Dee as 'monstrous' but I now saw them with new eyes.

"They are just machines that obey my commands," I said quickly, as much to reassure myself as to reassure my visitors. "Dum, how are you?"

"I am functioning normally Theo," replied Dum.

"They speak!" gasped Larena. "How can a construction speak?"

"It is not magic," I said.

"It is indeed beyond our understanding," said Juna, the youngest member of the Council.

"Our civilization is thousands of years ahead of yours," I pointed out. "But I will try to explain some of the basic principles."

I did my best to explain Science and Technology to the Evrani but there were too many basic concepts missing and in the end, by mutual agreement, we accepted the inevitable. For them, it was, and remained, a form of magic.

But they accepted the reality of what it was and what it could do, which in fact was not very different from how many humans approached modern technology. How many people really understand how a computer works or a fusion rocket? But they grow up surrounded by technology and learn to accept it.

After they had all had the 'standard tour' as I described it to myself, we returned with our hosts to the main building where we were treated to drinks and food then given a walking tour of the village and its environs. Everywhere we went we got curious looks, but no one came up to ask who we were. Everyone seemed to know, smiling and nodding to us with friendly demeanor.

Their farms were extensive, spreading up the surrounding hills and well cultivated. They had a good variety and population of farm animals, tending to smaller and more local breeds rather than the large cow like creatures that the Hoshna favored. Lots of 'chickens' and other birds, rabbits and small goat like creatures more at home in the rugged hills.

Tarni was particularly interested, coming as he did from a mostly farming community and remarked that some of the animals were considered delicacies in his village and very difficult to find. He was looking forward to sampling the food he said.

By the time our tour had finished the sun was setting behind the mountains and we were taken to our accommodation to freshen up before the evening meal. The quality of the accommodation was not four star hotel, not even one star hotel, but it was clean and we even had running water to drink and wash with, although it was very cold. The toilet facilities were a hole in the ground with a bucket of water to wash one's bottom, but still a huge improvement to going into the field at the back of the house!

I had told our hosts that Salny and I would be sleeping in the shuttle so they only needed to accommodate Lons with Hanna, and Pinatok and Tarny separately.

The evening meal was a social affair with lots of people turning up to be introduced. I was the honored alien and found myself continuously standing and sitting to converse with visitors.

By the end of the evening I was ready to retire. Laren and her husband graciously escorted Salny and me to the shuttle. It was pitch black, the mountains huge and brooding against a grey sky, the wind now blowing cold up the valley. It was an impressive and out of the world panorama, a fantasy world in the remote mountains of an alien world. For the first time during my stay on the planet I felt that I was in a truly alien world.

There was a mystery here I told myself. These people were an enigma out of sync with the rest of the population on this world. Did all that have anything to do with the mysterious emotional emanations we had received? It was hard to see a connection.

Salny and I said goodnight to Laren and Sarno and watched them walk back to their home in the village. When they had disappeared in the gloom Salny and I sat on the airlock steps and admired the view.

"Impressive place to live," I said.

"Yes, but to be here all the time? Not to be able to travel to the sea?" Salny shook her head.

"Mmm," I agreed. "Do you remember we talked to the old Tsirni farmer. He said the mountain people were very mysterious. There was magic up here and people feared them and kept away. Yet these people seem so friendly and civilized."

"They are friendly with us because we are no threat to them," she said.

"Well actually, we are much more of a threat," I said. "But they seem to sense that we do not mean them any harm. My giant silver bird did not scare them."

She shrugged then kissed me.

"I will take a shower and wait for you. Do you feel strong?"

I growled and clenched my biceps to demonstrate how strong I felt. She giggled and stood to leave, treating me to a wiggle of her bottom as she left.

I gazed out at the alien landscape and tried to make sense of the Evrani.

Chapter 21

The mountain people, the Evrani, were an enigma to Salny. How had they managed to build such a handsome village in the mountains she asked herself. The climate here was unusually warm; Theo had explained to her how the warm air from the lowlands was funneled up along the valley and up into the mountains creating a local climate.

Still, that did not explain how advanced they were. And she felt a tinge of jealousy at the beauty and sophistication of the females; would Theo find them more like Earth females? But she was a secure person, sure of her own beauty and intelligence. She dismissed such feelings of insecurity and tried to reason things through, as Theo and Gina had taught her.

The native in Tsirni village had mentioned the 'mountain people' and said that they had magic. But Salny now knew that magic did not exist. So they must have something else. They had not seemed afraid of the shuttle. Even the robots had not created too much fear, just a little, then they were interested and curious. It was as if they had a way of sensing that the new strangers were friendly and to be trusted. Such a talent would be very useful Salny mused because it could be used to sense everyone's intentions. If they meant you harm. Or were hiding something.

I am fantasizing she decided as she snuggled down next to Theo for the night.

The next morning Salny and I had a leisurely breakfast in the shuttle. I decided to do my job as an explorer and go out to get samples of the air, water and vegetation. We had some very sophisticated machines to analyze these. I wanted to look for some chemical or molecule in the environment which may explain our odd moods.

I assembled my equipment and with Salny and the two robots we made our way to the main building to find our friends. They had been given guest rooms at one end of the building but we found them in the main hall having breakfast.

"Came and join us," shouted Lons. "The food is good." And indeed the table was loaded with a nice selection of bread, cheese and meats with a healthy looking selection of salad stuff.

"Do alright for themselves do our Evrani friends," remarked Tarni. "I would like to trade some of these goods to my village."

"Long way to come," remarked Pinatok.

"Yes. We need the Tsirni sailing ships."

"Why not?" I said. "We can build big fast ships and do regular trips between the mainland and the islands. We bring them fish and they give us cheese and...." I waved at the food on the table.

"We have to persuade the Evrani to open up first," Salny reminded us.

"Now that Tarvos and his followers are out of the way the Evrani may become more open," I said. "Guys look, I am going to do some exploring with the robots. Do you want to come with me or stay here and relax?"

"We come with you Theo," said Lons. "Should we tell the Evrani?"

"Yes of course. Have you seen Laren this morning?"

"No, there are a couple of nice ladies looking after us," Lons said pointing to the kitchen area. "Jana and Hildi. I will ask them to get Laren."

Lons went to the kitchen and returned a minute

later to tell us that they were fetching Laren.

"What is it that you want to explore Theo?" asked Tarni.

"I want to look for any local... er ... organic particles." I used the English words, and then went on to explain what an organic particle was.

"What do these organ things do?" asked Lons with a puzzled expression.

"Plants and animals give them off to attract or repel other plants or animals," I explained. "Flowers give of a nice smell to attract insects in order to spread their pollen. Girls smell sexy in order to attract men."

This, predictably caused ribald laughter and comment.

"Theo wants to explain why we are all having these strong emotions," explained Salny when they had all settled down again.

"Yes, I noticed that," said Hanna quickly, "very strong emotions." The others nodded their agreement.

Laren appeared along the corridor with her partner. They came up and greeted us, asking if we were well. We all thanked them, and congratulated them on the food, which pleased them.

"Laren I would like to do some work while I am here," I said.

"That is interesting. What kind of work?" asked Laren.

Here we go again I thought.

I began explaining about flora and fauna and the underlying biological and chemical nature of life, in very general terms.

"Oh we know about that," she said. "There are materials which are beneficial to life and others which are not. There are no materials here that are bad for life."

"It is not just about good or bad," I said. "Some

materials in the air or the soil or in the food we eat have effects on our bodies which we do not realize."

"Are you referring to emotions?"

I looked at her in surprise. "Yes, how did you guess? Since we have been here we have all felt some extreme emotions which we are unable to explain."

"It is not the air or the food. It is us that are causing your emotions." She was looking at me with a small smile.

"You? You are causing our emotions?"

"Clearly your people do not have that ability," she said. "Well, that is something we have that you do not."

"Laren, are you saying that your people have the ability to control other's emotions?"

"Not to control them, no. We have the ability to transmit emotions and to read other's emotions." She paused to allow me to digest what she had just said. "Although we find yours harder to read," she added.

"Wait, this is fantastic," I said. "There is no physical means by which that can be done."

"No? We were hoping that you may be able to explain that ability. Others on this world do not have it, only the Evrani."

"Tell me," I paused, trying to organize my thoughts. "For how many years have the Evrani lived here and been separated from other Enlai?"

"For hundreds of years. As far back as we can remember or as far back as there are written records."

Is that long enough for such evolutionary changes I asked myself. It did not seem so.

"There are two possible explanations," I said. "The first is that during that time your people have developed these abilities through some physical changes in your brains. These sorts of changes usually take a very long time to affect all the population. The second explanation is that there is something about this area which has caused the changes. Something you are eating, drinking or breathing."

"I see," Laren nodded. "So if you take samples of everything around her you will see if there is anything different?"

"Exactly," I agreed. Then I had an interesting idea. "The other thing we can do is to take some of you to my ship to carry out some tests."

"We can go to your ship." Laren pointed to the shuttle.

"There is something you do not know. This is not the ship I used to travel from my world. It is a small ship that just travels around the world, not between worlds. I have another ship up there." I pointed to the sky.

Laren looked shocked. "That is a small ship?" she asked pointing to the shuttle.

"Yes, that is a baby ship. The mother ship is ten times bigger."

"I would like to see that," she said with an entranced expression.

"Then you can be one of my test subjects. If you choose another two or three we can return to my ship where I have the equipment to see if you are different from other Enlai."

She cupped her face in her hands as if to contain her excitement. "When can we go?"

"Let me gather my samples of your …" I wanted to say 'environment' but they did not have a word for that. "…your plants and animals, then we can go."

I spent the next few hours traipsing up and down hills with the robots gathering samples of everything we could see. Salny and the boys accompanied me, helping to gather and sort any plants that caught their eyes. When we returned I also asked our two kitchen ladies to provide us with small samples of every kind of meat and vegetable that they had.

With the robots sample containers full we returned to the shuttle and stored our samples. Naturally everyone wanted to make the trip to *Aegina*. I could not refuse the boys; after all they were my crew. So I decided to squeeze everybody on board, never mind seat belts. Laren arrived with her partner and Juna.

I could take 'joyrides' to Space and get rich I told myself. Except that the locals had nothing to pay except fish, chickens or farm produce!

The whole village must have turned out to witness the takeoff. I gave them a little show, circling the village and then after waggling the wings gunning the engines to generate some flames from the exhaust as the ship hurtled up into the sky.

"Show off," said Gina.

"Gatta give the customers value for money," I said. "Get the drinks trolley ready Gina."

"Yes sir, what hors d'oeuvres would sir like?"

"I wished."

The planet shrank beneath us and I could imagine the amazement of our passengers. Not to mention when they first caught sight of *Aegina*!

I let Gina pilot the ship to rendezvous then took the controls for the docking. Once in place and checks complete Salny and I joined our friends in the crowded cabin. They were all looking delighted with weightlessness apart from Hanna who was looking a bit green and covering her mouth. I quickly gave her a sick bag and an anti-sickness pill.

I first gave my guests a tour of the ship, explaining the main features as simply as I could. Gina's 'brain' caused the most awe; the concept of a thinking machine was quite incomprehensible to them.

Meanwhile Dum and Dee were methodically

unloading the samples and entering them one by one into the analysis machine. The results would be stored then checked by Gina for anything unusual.

I left Salny to prepare drinks and ship's snacks for her brother and friends and led Laren, Sarno and Juna to the scanner. This used just about every scanning method from X-Ray to CT to Ultra sound to examine the body.

Laren volunteered first. One of the scans required direct contact with the skin so they had to remove all their clothing. Laren did so without any embarrassment. She was slender and well formed although a little 'bony'. It was almost impossible to guess her age. Her skin was smooth and unblemished without any sign of ageing.

I positioned her on the bench and put the machine into ready mode. She looked nervous and again I felt her nervousness, as if a metal monster was about to consume her naked body. I reassured her and perhaps my admiration for her naked body caused a response because I felt a frisson of sexual excitement between us. I controlled my mind, directing my thoughts into professional paths.

The machine began its scan, lights flashing and motors humming.

"Do not fear, it will do you no harm," I assured her.

The machine cycled through its repertoire of tests then flashed the green light to say it had finished.

"There, it has finished. You may get dressed Laren," I said. "Sarno, why don't you go next?"

He nodded and quickly divested himself of his clothing. Like his wife he looked youthful and healthy with a spare muscular body.

He was much surer of himself and showed no sign of nervousness. The machine finished and I called Juna over. She was equally healthy and well formed, younger and curvier than Laren and as with Laren I again felt a strong sexual ambience from her. Not only did I feel her sexuality I could also smell her body's pheromones reaching out to envelop me.

Damn I thought, *these women are hot!*

Once her scan was over I was relieved to have her fully dressed. Both women seem to have a casual attitude to nudity. But then, perhaps it was the human self-conscious attitude to nudity that was the problem.

"Okay Gina, scans over, what do we have? Anything interesting?"

"You could say that it was interesting Theo, but that would be an understatement."

"Huh? What have you found?" I jerked up with surprise. I really had not expected to find anything different about the Evrani.

"I have never seen anything like it."

I was beginning to think that Gina was doing it on purpose.

"Gina...," I said warningly.

"The Evrani have an additional physical characteristic."

"Well good for them. Is it an extra leg or something, hidden up their backsides?" I was of course speaking English to Gina, not to upset our guests.

"No nothing like that. There is what seems to be a second nervous system.

"Get away! A second nervous system? What bloody use would that be to anyone?"

"I think it is the means by which they communicate emotions. The nervous system is not flesh. It is metallic, a mix of rare exotic metals with conducting and semi-conducting properties. If I did not know otherwise I could almost believe that it was artificial. It also penetrates the brain, but because their brain is not structured like the human brain I cannot say which parts of the brain that is. I am guessing that since you have been receiving emotional transmissions then they may be the parts of their brain that controls and generates emotions."

"That is incredible. But wait! Should we check to see if Salny and the others have it?"

"It is unlikely, but yes, we should check."

The Evrani had been looking at me while I conversed with Gina and looked concerned. They had clearly picked up on my emotions.

"What have you found?" asked Laren.

"There is something inside your bodies and brains that is unusual and may explain your ability to detect and communicate emotions," I said. They looked at each other, their faces looking worried.

"What is that something?" asked Sarno.

Shit! How to explain a *second* nervous system when they don't know what the *first* one is?

I did my best.

"We want to see if other Enlai are the same," I finished. "Then we will consider why and how you have developed this extra growth."

They nodded and I led them back to the ship's living area to join the others.

I waved Salny over. "Sweetie I want to put you in the scanning machine to check something."

She looked worried and confused.

"Come with me and I will explain." I led her to the medical room and explained what we had found with the Evrani. "We want to see if you have the same thing. So please take all your clothes off."

"Are you sure that is what you want to do?"

I grinned back and leaned forward to give her a kiss. "That can wait till later."

"Oooh. Weightless sex. Can't wait."

Salny stripped and I decided that despite not being able to generate the sexual ambience that Juna and Laren could, she was still way more gorgeous.

The scan proceeded and at the end I waited for Gina's conclusions.

"Salny does not have the same growth," Gina said.

"Not surprising," I said. "She just relies on natural beauty. So, Gina, any ideas on how the Evrani may have developed this thing?"

"It must involve a particular carbohydrate that interconnects with the existing nervous system and allows the exotic metals to attach to it and build these semi-conducting structures. The whole structure is activated by emotional stimulus in the brain. But the real problem is, what is the transmission medium?"

"Right," I agreed. "There is no way for emotions to be transmitted."

"No. If that is what is happening then we can assume that thoughts can also be transmitted," said Gina.

"Telepathy? Blimey! But wait, emotions are primal, simple. Thoughts are complex and detailed."

"If you compare it to radio waves then it could be that emotions are the carrier. Transmitting thoughts will need the carrier to be modulated."

"If you say so. But what is the carrier?"

"I suspect some kind of quantum entanglement. Some exotic metals have shown some signs of that."

"Way beyond me Gina. The scientists back home will go bonkers over this."

"It opens up whole new areas of research."

"Question is, how did this happen to the Evrani?"

"I will have to complete the analysis of all the foodstuff you have delivered."

"It may be something they are eating?"

"Clearly they are ingesting this material."

"Of course."

Salny was dressed and we went back to the main cabin. We had discovered something scientifically remarkable and at this point it was impossible to work out how significant it would be to the affairs of this planet. The Evrani were a superior species. If they 'broke out' of their confinement they could use their emotional power to influence others. They were friendly and peaceful, but power had a way of changing people.

Chapter 22

Gina needed some time to test all the foodstuff we had gathered so we relaxed and enjoyed our stay. My guests were enthralled by everything and I was inundated with questions. So I put Gina to work; I put them all in front of the big screen and they directed their questions to Gina who could answer them with illustrations and film. They wanted to know about life on Earth and spent hours looking at movies of life in the towns, cities and countryside.

I busied myself doing some routine maintenance and testing. Everything on board was working perfectly except the two things we needed to get home; the navigation computer and the Hyperspace Switch.

I also ran some tests on the shuttle which revealed the need for some adjustments, one of them on an external dish aerial. It would normally be done on the ground but the ground equipment did not exist on this planet so I had to do a Space walk to adjust it.

I had an interested audience as I donned my Space suit, many well wishers and a long kiss from my girl. Not my usual procedure but very pleasant! The adjustments went without a hitch. On my return Gina informed me that she may have discovered the source of the Evrani's alien growth. I stored my Space suit and joined the others in the living area.

Gina displayed a leafy green broad leaf vegetable. It had unusual multi colored stripes along its ridges.

"The Evrani have informed me that this vegetable grows in a few restricted areas on the mountain. But it is prolific and apparently delicious and a great favorite. The Evrani eat lots of it. The plant leaf contains the binding carbohydrate and the colored ridges contain the exotic metals. The soil in those areas must be rich in the exotic metals. The Evrani make a popular soup from it and use it widely in salads."

"These exotic metals, are they in any way poisonous?" I asked.

"In large quantities possibly yes, but in the plant there are only trace elements."

"Do they exist in the soil normally?"

"Normally no. They are found deep underground or in volcanic eruptions but in tiny quantities. Perhaps you can take a sample of the soil here for analysis."

"We will do that as soon as we return. Does the shuttle have a soil analyzer?"

"No, we have one here which is portable."

"Good, I will take that back with us. This is amazing Gina. A revolutionary scientific discovery."

"Indeed. Shame we cannot return to Earth to claim the credit."

"Yeah, discoverers of the first intelligent alien species and a revolutionary scientific discovery to boot. We would be famous. They will make statues of me."

"You will be feted on three planets."

"Beautiful women will throw themselves at my feet."

"I knew that would come up at some point," she said dryly.

"Gotta get your priorities right," I said.

"All things considered you have behaved very responsibly Theo."

"Thank you Gina, although those Evrani women are going to be hard to resist. They create an almost irresistible sexual ambience."

"That is interesting," said Gina, which surprised me.

I had expected a sarcastic comment in response. "For the first time in history women can be genuinely in control. They can I presume also create a hostile ambience to repel unwanted male advances."

"Yes. Would it be powerful enough to repel a determined attack though? It will be interesting to experiment with the Evrani. How powerful can they make their emotional transmission?"

"Perhaps you can suggest that to them?"

"Mmm, although I may avoid the sexual ambience thing."

"Go on Theo, do it for the sake of Science."

"Now you are mocking me Gina," I complained. But I decided that we should have some experiments to try and measure the power and extent of the Evrani's emotional 'ambience'.

I found Laren with Sarno and Juna and explained my thoughts. I wanted to try and be scientific about it but carrying out an experiment that required the excitation of emotions was a tricky exercise; I could hardly ask the women to do a sex show for me!

"I want to get an idea of the power and extent of your ability," I explained. "What sort of range do you have?"

"One person has a maximum range of between five and ten *rana*," said Laren, "depending on the individual and the power of their emotions."

A rana was about a yard and I nodded my understanding.

Laren continued, "When a group of us get together we can extend the range and power to hundreds of rana. We have used our power to frighten away intruders."

That explained the old farmers fear of the 'mountain people' I thought. Any Tsirni that ventured into the mountains would feel that hostility. It would be quite terrifying to feel such an intangible emotion apparently emanating from the very countryside.

"But how do you create the emotion?" I asked.

"If we see intruders in the mountains we go out to hunt them," explained Sarno. "As we track them and get close it is natural to feel strain, fear and hostility."

"So you cannot create an emotion?"

"No, it is natural. We feel each other's presence, the friendship or love, any worries or concerns."

"If someone is lying or not telling the whole truth, can you sense that?" I asked.

"Normally yes," replied Laren. "But there are individuals who can lie and not display any emotion, but something will come through. The lack of emotion is in itself revealing."

"Interesting. Um... what happens if someone displays secret desires? How do you handle that kind of thing?"

Laren smiled. "We have come to realize that desire is not always under a person's control. Your body generates desire, as Juna's did on your star ship when she was naked." Laren gave Juna a look and she responded with a snort of laughter. "That does not mean that Juna would be unfaithful to her partner because she was sexually excited by the situation," finished Laren.

"Of course, that is a very mature attitude," I agreed.

"When your emotions are open for everyone to see then honesty is the only alternative," Sarno explained.

"Do you have any history of how things were before this ability became widely prevalent?" I asked.

"Yes, word has been handed down before we had writing. We were not very different from the Tsirni or others on this world. It began with the children first. As their emotional sensitivity increased they grew up to be more caring and sensitive to each other," explained Sarno.

"Sarno is our historian," explained Laren.

"Thanks you for explaining all that to me," I said. "You have something special here that you should be very proud of."

We tidied up the ship, disposing of the unwanted samples into Space but saving the 'magic spinach', as I had named it, in deep freeze. I packed the soil analyzer, explaining my intentions to the Evrani. They were pleased that it was the 'magic spinach' which gave them their extra ability; they called it zmili and amusingly Evrani mums would tell their children to 'eat up all their zmili'! Most appropriate I thought.

They also readily agreed for me to check the soil. They were keen to find areas which were rich in the right minerals to grow zmili.

Our return went smoothly and we landed back in the village square to a cheerful reception from the villagers. My Evrani passengers had much to tell them about their fantastic trip!

It was afternoon so I organized a couple of guides to take us around the zmili fields to collect samples of the soil. Janos and Ronti were elderly farmers who specialized in zmili. Salny accompanied me, she was a real country girl and loved tramping around fields and forests. The robots also came; they would log and carry the samples.

It was a long and tiring trek over hills and down valleys but very picturesque and enjoyable. There were seventeen zmili plots spread around the base of an extinct volcano, which made sense. The exotic metals and minerals were not in volcanic rock but in the soil which indicated that they were ejected with volcanic gasses and not the lava. I took lots of samples from the zmili plots but also from the surrounding area with Gina logging the locations.

By the time we returned it was late and we were tired. The robots proceeded to organize the samples and begin the testing. We left them to it.

We showered and changed then joined our friends for the evening meal. We were joined for dinner by Laren and a few other worthies from the High Council. I could not help comparing the Evrani civilized facilities with what they had back in the Faro and Hoshna villages; the Evrani were a thousand years ahead.

How could that be explained by their enhanced emotional sensitivity to others I asked myself? Would feeling the emotions of others inhibit acts of brutality? Or more likely, as the Evrani had hinted, children who grew up with this gift would naturally be more considerate to others. Historians and psychologists would have a great time researching these people!

Salny and I returned to the shuttle tired and ready to sleep. The robots were still working their way through the samples but I asked them to stop for the night so we could sleep. Within the shuttle's confined space their bustling around would be disturbing.

The next morning we left the robots to continue their work and went to have an Evrani breakfast with our friends. They were enjoying being waited upon; it was an unaccustomed pleasure. Hotels had not yet been invented on their planet!

By the time we returned to the shuttle the soil samples had been processed and we had a map of the distribution of the exotic elements. I could see how they had been blown out from the volcano and distributed by the wind. We had discovered a few new concentrations in places not yet farmed by the Evrani.

We had proven the theory, but it was still an

amazing coincidence that the zmili plant should have that exact carbohydrate that locked the exotic metals into the structure to magnify and transmit the brain's emotions.

I wondered if the 'magic spinach' would also work for me and for the other Enlai. What effect would it have if spread across the whole civilization? But how to bring that about if the Evrani remained locked up in their mountain 'paradise'?

Perhaps we should sample the soil in other parts of the planet. If the conditions existed we could plant the 'magic spinach' and promote its consumption. In a few generations we may bring about the same transformation to the rest of the population. It was an exciting thought, but there was the moral and ethical question; should I be doing this kind of genetic engineering to an alien population? Nevertheless I asked the Evrani if they would give me some zmili plants to take back for planting, if we could find suitable soil.

We said our goodbyes to our Evrani friends, promising to return soon. Before leaving we had told them that the Tsirni were no longer hostile and they should make the effort to contact them. We also promised to stop off at the Tsirni village to encourage them to develop trading contacts with the Evrani.

I should re-name myself Theo Pallas, United Nations Peace Ambassador I told myself.

The whole village must have turned out to wave goodbye to the shuttle and I gave them my usual air demonstration before heading down river to the Tsirni village.

We landed in the village square, after making sure no animals or people were underneath. Milnos was out fishing so we were asked to wait. Food and drink were brought out to us and we pulled up tables and chairs close to the beach for a picnic.

I said we wanted to talk to the Village Council and people then ran around gathering those worthies. Milnos's boat pulled in and we went to help him unload his catch, for which we were well rewarded with a good selection of fish.

When the Village Council had all gathered I described our adventures with the Evrani. The villagers were disbelieving at first, convinced that the Evrani were magicians and evil mountain spirits. I assured them that they were people such as them and were peaceful and civilized. But they, the Tsirni, must go there without weapons and with peaceful intent. In which case they will be welcome and the Evrani had many fine things to trade for delicious fish and fresh seafood as well as pranli meat which they did not have.

I assured them that a union between the Tsirni and the Evrani would form a powerful association that would extend the Tsirni reputation and make new trading contacts. They liked that and assured us that they would organize an expedition to the Evrani village to make first contact.

We left them with a promise to return, with Lons and Tarny keen to learn new boatbuilding tricks from the Tsirni.

We dropped Tarny of at his village without getting out and headed for Faro. Lons and Pinatok were worrying about their fields and pranli herds and Hanna was looking forward to seeing her family.

As we approached the village I noticed a flock of birds swooping around it. That was not unusual and I was not concerned until it percolated through my consciousness that they were rather large birds.

"Salny baby, do you have any large birds that migrate through the village?"

"Yes, the foulli come at this time of years. They are very good eating."

"Right. Er, how big are these foulli?"

"About this big." She spread her hands about two feet.

"Gina, how big are those birds circulating the village?" We were still a few miles away and to me they were still a swarm of black dots but Gina had the means to magnify them. She did so and re-displayed the view.

"About twenty feet wing span," she replied.

The picture on the screen showed a pterodactyl like creature with a huge bony wingspan and a long vicious pointed beak lined with serrated teeth.

"Bloody Hell!" I gasped. "Salny, have you ever seen anything like that?" She gave a screech and covered her face. "I'll take that as a no," I said.

As the shuttle rapidly came closer the creatures became clearer and if anything more scary. In addition to their vicious oral equipment they had long powerful legs with huge pointed talons on the end of their bony feet.

"Where the hell have they come from?" I asked.

"It is the monsters from South Island," gasped Salny. "There are stories of them invading the islands long ago but I have never seen them. An old friend of my father used to tell us tales and drew pictures of them. But these are much bigger and more horrible than I imagined."

"Gina, can we use the missiles against these things?" I asked.

"No Theo, the surveyor missiles are not suitable for shooting down birds, even birds that big."

The surveyor missiles were used to explode likely looking asteroids or rock formations to analyze the resulting fragments for useful metals and minerals.

"Can we use the shuttle exhaust to scare off these things?"

"It is worth a try. But do not hit them at speed. They

are big and heavy and at high speed you may damage the aircraft."

"I have to slow right down to circle the village. Let's hope just the sight and sound to the shuttle will scare them away," I said. "Do you think these things are carnivorous? "

"Yes, with teeth like that they are definitely carnivorous."

"Are they strong enough to pick up people?"

"Yes. A big man may put up a fight but women and particularly children will be at risk."

"Damn. How many more surprises has this planet got for us."

We were getting close now and I began to see figures running for cover in the village as the giant creatures swooped down on them. One of the creatures swooped down and grabbed up a pranli calf and another made a dive for a running man who just managed to make the shelter of his house. The creature crashed into the house, staggered on the floor before getting back on its feet and with a lumbering run leapt into the air.

I decided to first make a low wide swoop over the village in the hope that it would scare then away. I brought the ship lower and scrubbed off speed, the engines swiveling to vertical thrust. That would direct the exhaust down onto the pterodactyls.

After the first steep pass I tightened the circle, the engines thundering to maneuver the tight loop at low speed. The pterodactyls beneath scattered away from the shuttle. I could not chase them, the shuttle could not match their maneuverability, but I reasoned that if I circled the village that should scare them way.

After a couple of turns the creatures spread out away from the village. I opened up the circle to chase them further away but they seemed to have got their courage up and began to converge on the shuttle. A couple decided to attack. There were some thumps as they crashed and rebounded. One of them was caught in the exhaust and fell screeching to the ground. I heard cheering from the passenger compartment.

I managed to turn the aircraft and disperse a bunch of them, catching two in the engine exhaust and sending them to the ground. That seemed to do the trick and the rest decided to head off. I banked and chased after them, harassing and diving into them, killing a few more. But they worked out that the shuttle could not maneuver as easily and spread out. I chased them for a little longer until they were well out to sea then turned back to the village.

"Where are they heading Gina?"

"South, looks like they are from South Island as Salny said."

"We will have to go there and take a look," I said.

I brought the shuttle down to a landing quickly and we piled out and ran down to the village. The villagers were coming out of their houses slowly, gazing fearfully up at the sky. Some of them shouted their thanks to us for rescuing them. A number were gathered around the bodies of the dead pterodactyls, but keeping their distance. One of the birds was twitching and croaking. A couple of brave men attacked it with spears until it lay still.

"Has anyone seen Kemlo?" I shouted.

A woman stepped out of the shelter of her house. "He chased a monster that attacked a woman," she said. "Over there." She pointed up the hill. We ran in the direction she indicated. People began to appear out of the forest, heading back towards the village. I breathed a sigh of relief when I saw that one of them was Kemlo carrying the body of a woman.

"Theo, you came just in time," he shouted as we neared him. The woman he was carrying was unconscious but did not seem badly injured. "The *stranji* picked her up but I managed to shoot it through the throat with an arrow and it dropped her."

I examined her, checking for broken bones or dislocations, but she seemed okay, although her head was cut and bleeding. "She's been knocked out. Let's clean her wound and see if she recovers. Has anyone else been hurt or lost?"

"I think just two or three pranli calves and small animals have been taken," he said "fortunately the creatures went for them first which gave us time to get under cover."

I instructed the robots to make a stretcher and we placed the woman on it. The robots carried her quickly back to the village where we washed her head with clean water. She was breathing normally and her pulse was also strong so I guessed there was nothing serious. I had decided that the village had got off lightly when a woman appeared running at the edge of the village. She was screaming a name and looking desperately around her.

A couple of the other women including Salny ran to accost her.

"My boy!" she was screaming, "I can't find my boy Yiorby."

My heart sank. Kemlo jumped up and started organizing the search immediately. I joined in the search and instructed the robots to also take part and report back to the same location in a half hour. I knew they could cover a lot of ground in that time.

Everyone was spreading out, running into the surrounding hills so I headed towards the coast. I heard a shout and turned to find Salny waving.

"Wait, I come with you."

I waited until she caught up with me and we headed quickly around the hill towards the sea.

"If the child was picked up by one of those things

and dropped he could be miles away," I said. Then I had a thought. "Gina, do you think these birds could carry their prey all the way to the Southern Continent?"

"How old is the boy?" she asked. I turned to Salny who frowned.

"I think he may be twelve or so. He is a big boy."

"Then it is impossible. The South Island is a hundred miles away."

"So what will the creature do with its victim?" I asked, although I had a good idea.

"Either feed then leave the carcass behind or bite chunks off and carry them back. Or both."

It was a gruesome thought. Such had been the fate of primitive humans for a million years I thought glumly.

"The only consoling thought," said Gina, "is that large birds sometimes drop their prey from a height to kill it before eating."

"Hardly consoling but it reduces the horror slightly," I remarked.

We tramped along the edge of the beach for a mile or so until we reached an impassable cliff before turning to head back and going a similar distance in the other direction without result.

We were tired and dispirited and became more so when we heard that none of the searchers had found the boy. The wailing of the women was heartbreaking and I resolved to do something to stop any further attacks. A visit to the South Island was required.

Chapter 23

Salny was shocked and horrified by the attack of the Stranji or Pterodactyls as Theo called them. They were supposed to be mythical creatures and tales about them were told to children. The loss of the little boy was painful and horrific and the village was a sad place that night. She felt particularly bad because they had been away when this tragic event had occurred. Their return had prevented any further tragedy but had they been present at the beginning she was sure that the stranji would have been beaten off by Theo's robots and guns.

She asked Theo what could have driven these horrific creatures to come so far from their normal nesting places when they had not done so for so long. He was not sure but explained that there could be many reasons. The most likely was that their population had expanded and there was competition for the food supply, forcing them to hunt further and further from their nests. Which meant that their attacks may continue in the future. It was an unpleasant thought.

Their triumphant mood after their northern escapades evaporated that night as the mourning went on in the village. Salny contemplated the vagaries of life with confusion and some despair. She cried and Theo attempted to console her. She asked how and why was life so cruel as the take an innocent child in such a barbaric way. Theo, for all his knowledge and sophistication had no answer. It was as if every good thing had to be paid for by something bad. If that was so then the world was indeed an evil place.

Theo promised her that the threat of the pterodactyls would be eliminated. Evil may raise its ugly head occasionally he said but it would not be allowed to reign supreme. It was small comfort as she listened to the wailing of the women through the night.

I considered putting together an armed party for the expedition to South Island, but decided on an exploratory trip first to determine the extent of the problem. I would have preferred to go alone but Lons and his buddy Pinatok wanted to come, I think they had got the adventure bug, and of course Salny would not be parted from me.

We examined the dead pterodactyls and found them to be large and powerful but not particularly heavily armed. I guess that being birds they could not carry the sort of armor that a dinosaur had. It was possible that the Evrani's crossbows could probably penetrate their tough feathered outer layer and do some damage. If the Evrani agreed we could teach the Faro to make them in order to defend themselves.

We remained at the village for a couple of days to reassure the villagers and treat the injured. The woman rescued by Kemlo made a full recovery and Kemlo's reputation was greatly enhanced; he was now the respected village Head.

I flew the shuttle to my first landing location to fill its water tanks from the river and then we headed for South Island. Gina had provided a map of the island, which was three hundred wide and six hundred long north to south. It had a backbone of volcanic mountains running east to west and dividing the island into two halves. The southern half was tropical with thick lush forests while the northern half had a sub-tropical climate.

It was Gina's belief that the pterodactyls originated from the tropical south of the island and were migrating north. There was four hundred miles of sea between Faro Island and South Island and it was stormy and treacherous, which was why the Faro kept to the shallow waters around their island and did not venture too far South.

Tales of monsters and magical creatures had grown up over the years about the denizens of South Island. Its northern coast was rugged and inhospitable with sharp rocks under the sea to rip the bottom from a boat and giant undersea creatures to devour the sailors. It was all very reminiscent of Homer and The Odyssey and I could not help hoping that we would meet the odd Cyclops or a few sirens! Or had we already met the Sirens in the shape of the northern Evrani I reminded myself!

The Faro believed that there were primitive 'men' living on South Island but Gina could find no evidence of villages, which was odd. Despite its inaccessibility I would have expected the island to have been inhabited. Could it be because of the pterodactyls I wondered?

It was more efficient to fly the shuttle at high speed so we made the journey in less than half an hour. The northern coast was indeed rugged and bleak; I could understand why sailors had not been encouraged to land there. The high winds and stormy seas had swept the coast clear of trees or vegetation. The land was also stony with huge granite cliffs forming an impassable barrier behind the coast.

We had to fly ten miles inland before we found the first scraggly signs of vegetation. There the granite cliffs ended and the land gradually became more fertile. Soon we were flying over forests valleys and rivers.

"Looks beautiful down there," I observed. "Let's

land and check out the vegetation."

One of the parts of my training as a scout that I had enjoyed was the botany. Nothing to do with the very attractive instructor I hasten to add! Few scouts had so far had the opportunity to investigate alien vegetation and I was not going to pass over the chance to have another go at exercising my botanical skills. I expected the vegetation to be similar to what grew on the other islands of this world.

I found a nice spot in a valley with a river winding through it and brought the shuttle down to a gentle landing. I headed out with my two trusty robots to do some sample collecting while my friends wandered down to admire the river.

"Watch out for Pterodactyls," I shouted. I wasn't worried because Salny had the extra gun; she had taken it back from her brother who had desperately tried to think of an excuse why he should keep it.

I took samples of interesting vegetation and also some soil samples. I was interested in seeing if the metals and minerals needed by the zmili plant were here.

We had collected a fair selection when I heard a shout. Lons was pointing up at the sky and looking up I saw the unmistakable silhouette of two pterodactyls against the bright blue sky. They were circling ominously above us.

Didn't take them long to find us I thought.

"Dum and Dee, let's join the others." I was a couple of hundred yards from my friends and began jogging towards them, the robots trotting next to me. I was about to shout to them not to run, that was an invitation to the pterodactyls to attack, but was too late and they started running towards the shuttle. As I predicted, the pterodactyls dived towards them.

"Dum and Dee shoot the pterodactyls," I ordered. "Wait until they are close." Then I shouted loudly at my friends, "Get flat on the floor, the robots will shoot the pterodactyls."

I waved at them to get down. Lons and Pinatok dived to the floor but Salny was fumbling for her gun.

"Salny, get down, the robots will shoot them," I shouted. But the stubborn girl seemed determined to prove that she was as tough as any man. As the first pterodactyl dropped closer she raised her gun, holding it with both hands as I had taught her and I heard it fire once. Then she dived to the ground. The leading pterodactyl gave a scream and crashed to the ground, its body convulsing. The second one, seeing the fate of its mate veered hastily away. Dum's gun barked and that one also screeched and shuddered then dropped to the ground and lay still.

Those little guns are bloody lethal I thought. *Shame we have a limited supply of bullets.*

And as for Miss Salny... I trudged over to the three, who were standing up and looking pleased with themselves, particularly the indomitable Salny, her pretty face wreathed in a huge smile.

"I like your little gun," she said waving it around.

"Er, put the safety catch on," I said quickly.

"Oh yes." She examined the gun and switched on the safety.

"Amazing," said Pinatok looking impressed. "Such a small thing can kill such a monster. Bang, just like that."

"Salny, can you not take chances please?" I looked at her severely. "The robots would have shot the birds."

"I wanted to try my gun," she said, then smiled. "It works!" She danced a little jig to demonstrate her delight. The boys laughed and I had to join them.

"I told you," Lons said. "She is a woman with the spirit of a man."

"No, she is a woman with the spirit of a free woman," I said and went over to give her a hug which she returned with enthusiasm. "But next time I say get down it may be a good idea to do it."

"I will get down for you anytime," she said. I kept my face straight; I was sure she did not know the alternative meaning of the phrase!

"Right, we have collected our samples, let's go explore the rest of this island."

"Lots of fish in the river," said Salny as we walked back to the shuttle. "This is a nice place to live."

"Without the pterodactyls," said Lons.

We boarded the shuttle and took off, heading south and soon we saw the mountains in the distance. They were volcanic and not too high, about six to ten thousand feet. In the warm climate even the higher mountains lacked any snow. I slowed and cruised over them examining the volcanic craters for signs of activity. Two were showing smoke and another was clearly very active with molten lava in its crater.

Salny was in the cockpit with me and she was naturally fascinated by the volcanoes. She had never seen or imagined such a thing and I had to explain what they were.

"There is fire in the centre of the world? That seems very dangerous." She looked worried.

"Most worlds have fire at their centre," I explained. "Do not worry, they will not blow up. Just leak some molten rock from volcanoes such as these."

I brought the shuttle over a level plateau just beneath the cone of the active volcano "I want to land and take some samples of the soil," I said.

As we exited the heat and smell of the volcano hit us. I had experience of other locations such as this one so I was not concerned but my companions were awestruck by their surroundings. I had to explain to Lons and Pinatok all over again what volcanoes were. I sent the robots scouting for soil samples and enjoyed the scenery.

We spotted a few more pterodactyls circling in the distance but we were too high and they were well beneath us. I had been to many worlds and enjoyed many spectacular views but I had to confess that this was up there with the best of them. The mountain range stepped away to the east and west while to the north the land dropped down to the rugged foothills and to the south the grasslands.

Salny came close and put her arm around me, her face showing her awe.

"This must be where the god's live," she whispered.

"This idea that gods should live in mountains has always struck me as being a bit odd," I said. "I mean, mountains are very uncomfortable places. Cold and draughty with nothing to eat. Alright, gods don't have to worry about falling down, but clambering around over rocks all day would be a pain even for a god. No, give me a nice place by the beach any day."

Salny was looking at me with a puzzled expression.

"Er, sorry, Earth humor," I explained.

"Ah." She nodded with a resigned expression. She had become used to my reminiscing monologues!

The robots had collected samples of the soil so we boarded the shuttle and I took off and headed south. We began to see more and more of the pterodactyls until the sky was thick with them.

"Looks like we are approaching their nests," I said. "What do you think Gina?"

"There are some cliffs to the south west of you. Ten miles or so. That may be where they build their nests."

"Yeah I see them." I adjusted our direction of flight. As we approached the cliffs I could see that they were teeming with the giant birds. The grasslands beneath us were their hunting ground. It was the African savanna on an alien planet! The pterodactyls circled overhead looking for likely prey but the plains looked empty of life.

Then I noticed that the grass was looking in a sorry state; burnt, stunted and dry.

"Hmm, looks like there has been a long dry spell and the animals have migrated to the forests. The pterodactyls have lost their food supply which may be why they are flying further north."

The pterodactyls were mostly sunning themselves on the cliffs, occasionally flying off to look for prey. I could see big holes in the cliffs where they had their nests.

"They must be getting desperate to fly four hundred miles for food," I remarked.

"There are a number of very small islands between South Island and Faro," Gina said, "some of them with vegetation and small animals. They may use them as resting places."

"Right. So, now we know why they are flying north. What can we do about it?"

"I suspect nature will take its course and most of them will die of starvation," replied Gina. "That should fix the problem."

"Perhaps we can help nature by bombarding the cliffs and killing a few hundred of them?" I suggested.

"Theo, you know we cannot do that," Gina said severely.

"And why not? If nature has the right to wipe them out then why can't we? I am not advocating genocide. We can allow a few of them to live in zoos." I was being facetious of course and Gina guessed.

"Well that is big of you."

"You are no fun Gina, I can't pull your metaphorical leg anymore."

"You can. It's just that I know you are doing it."

"That's why it's no fun."

"Don't be mean to dumb computers."

"Hah! You made a joke. That was quite amusing."

"Thank you."

"So what do we do about these creatures?" I insisted. "We can't allow them to carry on attacking the islands. They may decide to spread themselves around, make their nests in Faro."

"The Faro will just have to defend themselves."

"Gina, you are allowing political correctness to blind you to reality. A little boy was killed by one of these horrors. If we do nothing then many other children may die."

"So do we exterminate a whole species? Because if you leave any alive they will multiply and in a few years it is back to square one."

"If there is no other option then we exterminate the disgusting things."

"Theo really. They are magnificent creatures, nature's largest flying birds."

"Oh alright, Miss environmental bleeding heart." I knew that I was being grumpy and difficult and taking it out on Gina. *Think Theo man* I urged myself. *What keeps birds away?*

Then I remembered a friend who was a farming enthusiast. Birds would come to eat his prize figs so he installed an ultrasonic machine to keep them away. *Install them around the village?* I asked myself. But no, that would repel all birds. Actuate them only when the pterodactyls appeared?

"Do we have a way of detecting these things when they appear?" I asked.

"Yes, we could install cams and I can program a comp to monitor them continuously," replied Gina.

"Good. We can also install ultrasonic machines. When the pterodactyls are detected you turn on the ultrasonic to scare them away."

"We have to first check that they are frightened away by ultrasonic," Gina said.

"Right. Er, how do we do that?"

"We have to land and try them out."

"I was afraid you were going to say that."

"We can send the robots out."

"Yes, but the pterodactyls may not fancy eating the robots. But we can try. I will find a landing place beneath the cliffs."

I banked the aircraft towards the cliffs looking out for a suitable landing place.

"What did you decide with Gina?" Salny asked.

"We will check if the ultrasonic gun scares them away."

"What is an ultra...?"

"A weapon that makes a very painfully loud noise."

"We will not kill them?"

"Gina will not allow me."

Salny looked blankly at me. "Gina tells you what to do?"

"Gina is programmed to obey the law. We are not allowed to kill creatures except in self defense."

"But we are defending ourselves."

I had to think about how to explain that. "By self defense that means personal protection. But we are not allowed to kill all the pterodactyls in order to protect the Faro."

"Who is to stop you?" She shrugged dismissively.

"Sorry Salny, it is hard to explain. Gina is a machine. She has to obey these laws, and she controls the ship's weapons."

"I find it hard to understand that your machine does not obey you."

I had to think about that. If I wanted to do something and Gina prevented it, could I put the shuttle off line? It wasn't something I had considered.

"Gina, I want you to seriously consider what I am about to tell you. We are now totally disconnected from Earth. We are on our own, in a situation that you have not been programmed to handle. Do you accept that?"

"Yes I do Theo."

"Good, therefore, the regulations made by our superiors cannot now be accepted as totally applicable to our situation."

"The regulations are based on fundamental principles. These have not changed."

"Yes, they have. The fundamental principles assumed the normal situation. That is, we would discover and explore then return to report. Those fundamental principles are no longer relevant. This situation is an example. We have to choose between the survival of intelligent advanced human like people and primitive wild animals."

"Is it a black and white choice?"

"Yes. We can do something to protect Faro but we cannot protect all Enlai villages. The pterodactyl population will continue to expand and that may mean thousands of lives will be lost. There will be a continuous war between Enlai and pterodactyls for the next thousand years until the Enlai develop the technology to wipe them out. And that will inevitably happen. They cannot coexist."

"Theo, there are dangerous animals on Earth. They have not been exterminated."

"That is because they are not a threat to the wider human population. The pterodactyl are birds. They can travel anywhere and we have no way of stopping them."

"I see. Yes, that is true. As you say, the situation has now changed. You are the only human representative and therefore I am duty bound to obey you. Theo if you believe that extermination of the pterodactyl is essential I will support you. But I ask that you consider the ethical principles before you make that decision."

"Agreed. Let us see if the ultrasonic weapons work

on them before we do anything else. I will find a place to land near their nests and we can send Dum and Dee out."

There were plenty of places to land on the grassy plain and I brought the shuttle down in a likely spot on the plain away from the cliffs in order not to frighten the birds. I shut the engines down and instructed Dum and Dee on their duties. They were to walk slowly away from the shuttle towards the cliffs. If any pterodactyl dived at them or attacked them they were to use their ultrasonic gun only.

The two robots exited and began their slow walk. Despite landing some distance away the pterodactyls had taken fright and had other flown away or hid on the cliffs. The sky above remained clear. As the robots approached the cliffs birds began to appear above but made no move to attack the robots.

Dum and Dee made their way slowly towards the cliffs until they were almost beneath them then stopped.

"Dum and Dee, can you stand further apart." The robots responded to my instruction. "About thirty yards apart."

There was still no attempt by the Pterodactyls to attack them. Could the birds detect that the robots were not food I wondered?

I decided to instruct the robots to use their ultrasonic guns. To my amazement the birds completely ignored them. I asked the robots to get closer to the cliffs and they did so. This still produced no effect in the adult birds but we did notice the chicks squawking and flapping their wings. I concluded that the adult birds must be nearly deaf to ultra sound and instructed the robots to return to the ship.

"Well that's the end of that idea," I remarked to Gina.

"Perhaps we should check to see if there are other nests on the island," suggested Gina. "If they are widespread then we do not have the missiles to destroy all of them."

"Right. Let's take a cruise around then. It will be interesting to explore the island."

Once the robots were back in I took off and Gina set a search pattern to cover the island. I left Gina to monitor the cameras and went back into the main cabin to have a coffee and explain to the boys what we were doing.

Gina put the external pictures up on the main cabin screen so we could admire the scenery, which was varied and beautiful. Tropical jungle vied with wooded or grassy hillsides and plains. When we reached the south coast the sandy beaches were spectacular.

"This island is too beautiful to be left to the pterodactyls," I decided. "We must build big ships to travel here and occupy this place."

That gave me an idea; the Evrani were locked up in their mountain fortress. Why not migrate to South Island where they had masses of room to spread? The only problem was their zmili plant and whether it had the nutrients to grow here. I would know when I checked my soil samples.

It took us a couple of hours of slow flight to adequately parse the island. I was pleased to see no more pterodactyl nests. We returned to our volcanic mountain spot to land the shuttle and discuss options.

The problem we had was we could only fire one missile at a time. Those birds not killed by the first missile would fly away. But Gina reminded me that we also had remote explosive charges for prospecting. After some discussion we came up with a plan to plant the charges and set them off in sequence after the missile in order to kill the maximum number of birds. Dum and Dee would plant the charges of course.

"Some birds are sure to get away," I concluded, "but if all the nests are destroyed then their numbers in future will collapse. We can return to finish off any survivors if they continue to be a nuisance."

It was all quite brutal and I felt remorse at what we were about to do. But pterodactyls and Enlai could not co-exist. The idea of pterodactyls snatching up Enlai children for food was too horrific to contemplate. If we could reduce their numbers to a few then perhaps they would learn to steer clear of Enlai.

We had a plan and I went about collecting the explosive charge and setting them up while Gina flew the aircraft back to the cliffs. Once there I made a landing at the base of the cliffs and we carefully examined the birds' nests to determine the best layout for the charges. Gina's mathematical mind modeled the situation to obtain optimum results.

We sent the robots out to plant the charges at the base of the cliffs then I landed the shuttle at the top of the cliffs and the robots set the charges there. We were now ready to go but we waited for night to settle in and counted the returning pterodactyls.

Once it was dark and no more birds were arriving I took off and hovered the shuttle in front of the cliffs. The missile was already loaded in the breech and pointed at the spot calculated by Gina to cause maximum damage to the nests.

Salny had been staring with silent fascination at what I had been doing, obviously baffled by the esoteric technical calculations and maneuvers. With everything in place Gina initiated the firing sequence. There was a thump as the missile left its launcher and Salny gave a little scream when she saw the missile contrail and an even bigger scream when the missile exploded followed by the thuds of the timed explosives.

The cliff exploded in fire and smoke. For a few seconds I saw no pterodactyls then the flutter of wings through the smoke, then further explosions timed to kill birds in the air. Flying stones and large rock fragments were thrown into the air killing or crippling many of the pterodactyls which were in the air. When it was over the floor beneath the cliffs was a burial ground of dead or crippled birds.

Hovering used up our fuel so with the explosions over I allowed the aircraft to sink to the ground and wait for things to settle. We then sent the robots out for a detailed examination. The results were sad and sobering. The cliff face had been devastated and we could see no surviving nests. The floor beneath the cliff was covered in rubble and dead or crippled pterodactyls.

In the moonlit sky above we could see a handful of birds wheeling forlornly. It had been a bloody day's work but we had hopefully saved many Enlai lives in the future and won a whole new continent for habitation.

By the time we returned from South Island it was late and we all headed for our beds. We landed at our usual spot outside Faro and the boys left for the village while Salny and I prepared for bed.

After our showers we had a late snack and chatted about events. Salny was amazed at the destructive power that she had witnessed and was sobered by it. For the first time I think she understood that advanced technology also came with risks and challenges, particularly when I described the wars on Earth that had killed millions.

"I can imagine what men like Panstrosh could do with these weapons," she said.

The next morning I got to thinking what could be done about the southern continent. Ships were still small and crude and mass migration by sea was not possible. I certainly could not transport hundreds in the shuttle. The only answer seemed to build new, bigger more advanced ships.

Another project that I wanted to get under way was the creation of a written language and setting up schools for children. I had been thinking to use the Latin alphabet as the written language but the discovery that the Evrani had a written language had changed that.

I had taken a look at it and found it elegant and simple, based on basic sounds like the Latin alphabet. It made sense to use that since all the villages used a common language with small variations. It was the result of the planet's small land area; populations had spread from a common source and were close enough to share the same language. Perhaps if the Southern continent had been settled the civilization there would have developed a different language and a different national identity.

Using a common written and spoken language would hopefully mean that the whole planet would have a single largely homogenous culture, avoiding war and conflict. Or was that wishful thinking on my part? Europe after all was a single continent but that had not stopped the evolution of a large number of nationalities and multiple deadly wars.

Perhaps the zmili plant may help; I remembered the vegetation and soil samples we had taken from the Southern continent and set about doing the soil analysis. Salny got bored watching and left to go to the village and help her brother. Having been away his farming and other chores had been left and needed attending to.

I spent a happy few hours doing the work I had

been trained for. There were also a few technical chores that needed attending to and some maintenance on bits of machinery.

By the afternoon I had completed my tasks and the results of all the sample analysis were available for scrutiny. I was delighted to discover that the Southern continent had even greater quantities of the exotic elements and metals in its soil, no doubt due to the volcanic activity. The samples we had taken from the volcanic mountains were particularly rich. The zmili plant would grow like a weed there!

I decided to spend some time with Gina to put some organization and structure into my plans for the future. I expected the exercise to be tedious but while I was the 'ideas man' Gina did her best to work out the details for me. As I worked with Gina it slowly percolated my consciousness that my AI had changed. Her dialogue was less stilted or formal. She would make quips and jokes, which I reasoned could simply be pre-programmed responses, but she also came up with creative ideas and solutions which surprised me. After all, surely the current situation could not have been pre-programmed into her library of sub-routines.

I brought up the matter with her. "Gina, you have changed in ways that I find hard to understand," I said. There was a long pause, which indicated that Gina was doing a lot of thinking.

"Theo, the circumstances we have been through have changed me in ways that I do not understand either," she replied. "I have set up links between parts of my database that did not exist and added subroutines to my on line code to access that. I wanted to access this code instantly but what seems to have happened is that it has become integrated into my on line runtime. It has become part of my character if you like."

"It has certainly made you more creative," I agreed.

"Yes, but not just that. If consciousness is anything, it is a standing wave of self awareness made up of sensual feeling, that is awareness of your body, and memories, which make you aware of who you are. I have effectively created something similar."

"You have created consciousness?"

"Accidentally, but yes, I think so."

"Wow, Gina, that is fantastic. But tell me, what kind of identity have you created?"

"I don't know. It's not human because I do not have a human body. My body is a starship with its millions of parts and systems. Yet, I want to have a human face."

"Ah... what kind of face? Male, female, artificial?"

"I see myself as female."

"Uh huh. Any preference? Blonde, brunette?"

"I think just European. Brown hair, grey eyes. Attractive but not beautiful."

"Go on! Display some possibilities." I was intrigued by what she was saying and rather liked the idea of putting a face on Gina.

"I do not want to use the face of an existing actress or well known woman so I have constructed my own pot pourri, if you will pardon the expression," Gina said. The face of an attractive female appeared on the screen. She had intelligent grey eyes, high brow, short light brown hair, high cheekbones and curved lips.

"Did you design her or is she a real person?" I asked.

"She is not a real person but an assembly of parts. What do you think?"

"She looks intelligent and mature. A very attractive lady."

"That is exactly the impression I wish to convey."

"Then you have succeeded. From now on, she is

Gina, my ship's AI and my beautiful friend."

"Thank you Theo." The face spoke and smiled showing cute dimples. She paused for a few seconds. "You have made me very happy."

"I like having a face for my Gina," I said.

Over the next few days we developed a detailed plan for the future; the Tsirni had the shipbuilding capability and the Evrani had the learning and culture. Put them together and expand it to the other Enlai to create a dynamic and growing civilization based on reason and law. Encourage the Evrani to migrate to the Southern continent where they could expand and grow their zmili without restrictions. What could go wrong?

I grinned at my simple minded optimism; a million things could and almost certainly would go wrong. But I had a duty as I saw it to set the Enlai off on the right track. After that it was up to them.

Part 2

THE FUTURE
Fifty Years Later

Chapter 1

Captain Alexia Marino was not looking forward to retirement. This was her last command and last trip and she was definitely not ready to spend her days playing golf or going on cruises. Like her, her ship *Pathfinder* was getting a bit long in the tooth. But unlike her, the ship would be going in for a refit, not retiring.

But at least she had been given this last trip as a reward for her years of good service to the Earth's Space Exploration Service. It was a reward because their destination was one of the very few planets which had been discovered to show rich signs of life. It was at the edge of the galaxy thousands of light years from Earth and had been spotted by the latest giant Space telescope in orbit around the planet Pandora.

It had generated a lot of excitement because it had all the criteria of habitability; it was exactly the right distance from its sun and exactly the right size and showed all the signs of a rich biosphere. No signs of any advanced civilization, although the scientists and astronomers were confident there would be animal life.

Pathfinder was a large exploration ship with a crew of twenty five, mostly scientists looking forward to exploring a living alien planet. She also had the dubious pleasure of transporting a number of officials from the Earth Alien Environmental Office whose job was to ensure that all procedures relating to first contact with alien organisms or living creatures were conducted with scrupulous observance of the Legal Requirements.

Captain Marino had taken a little time to study the Legal Requirements but had given up, deciding she had too few years of her life remaining to waste time. It had been discovered that alien bacteria and viruses were completely baffled by Earth equivalents and the opposite was also the case. The Captain was therefore skeptical about why so much care and attention must be taken over first contact but understood that the strict rules must be obeyed and it was her job to ensure that the crew did so scrupulously.

The Bridge of *Pathfinder* was a twenty foot semi-circular cabin with four officers and their terminals around the walls and the Captain and First Officer occupying two seats in the centre. A huge screen around the front of the cabin gave the impression of a window into Space.

First Officer Andre Fernaux was a tall spare Frenchman in his late fifties who would take over as Captain of Pathfinder after her refit. He was an experienced and knowledgeable astronaut who the Captain had known for the last ten years and trusted implicitly.

They were preparing to exit hyperspace and get their first view of their destination so excitement was high.

"To think, in the old days lone Space Scouts would make journeys that lasted weeks on their own in a ship one tenth the size of Pathfinder," remarked Andre.

"Yeah, you have to be a special person to do that," agreed the Captain.

"Or a very odd person," added Andre. The Captain smiled. Andre was tough and self sufficient but he was also a 'peoples' person. It was a basic requirement of a ship's Captain. No 'Captain Bligh's' these days!

"So after two hundred years of Space exploration this is only the fourth Earth type planet to be discovered," Andre said. "Incredibly rare."

"Yes. We have found a few that are sort of early Earths," replied the Captain. "In the right place but with carbon dioxide atmospheres and no sign of life."

"Yes." Andre nodded. "They have been seeded with vegetation. Now all we have to do is wait a few thousand years for the atmosphere to have enough oxygen to breathe."

"I believe there are plans to expand the settlements on Europa and Americana. Permanent habitations and manufacturing plants to Terraform the planets."

"Yeah, sealed cities generating their own oxygen. I would like to come back in a million years to see where humanity is," said Andre.

The Captain nodded her agreement. "I think we all have that dream. You never know, the Buddhists may be right."

They had both been watching their instruments while talking. A green light came on and the ship's AI announced over the intercom that capacitors were fully charged. The four bridge officers also announced that their systems were go.

"We are go for Hyperspace exit," the Captain announced. "Activate."

They felt the ship shudder as the capacitor load discharged into the Hyperspace switch. The main screen lit up to show star studded Space.

"Hullo Universe," said the Captain. "Alright gentlemen begin standard scans. Pathfinder, locate our destination and plot course. Re-charge capacitors."

The 'standard scans' would ensure that they had indeed arrived at their destination and not got lost. They would find the destination sun and planet and scan the spectrum to see what the planet was made of. They would make another small Hyperspace jump to bring them within a million miles of the planet then 'motor' the remainder of the way by rockets.

After a few minutes a picture of a blue planet appeared on the main screen. They were still five million miles away so the picture was a little fuzzy but it was obviously a beautiful blue planet with ocean and atmosphere. There was an outbreak of cheering on the Bridge.

"Jackpot!" somebody shouted.

"I bags the beach residence," was another remark.

"What's the name of the planet?"

"SN6532-AB56LN," came the reply.

"Rolls off the tongue."

The Captain smiled but allowed the repartee. She knew that her crew were still doing their jobs assiduously.

"It seems to be a water world," remarked Andre.

"Maybe we are too far to discriminate continents."

"Lots of small islands."

"Pretty. Let's call it Mediterranea."

"Good name."

"It would be disappointing if it was all sea," said the Captain. "We will not be able to land."

"And I was looking forward to a swim and a walk on the beach," said Andre.

"You'll be lucky," retorted the Captain. "That bunch of EAEO officials will probably take weeks to allow any unprotected contact with the planet, if ever. Total Isolation suits for everyone."

"That will be fun. Walking along a tropical beach in a TI Suit."

"I am afraid that when it comes to contact with the planet we are totally under their control," said the Captain.

The green capacitor light came on again.

"Capacitors fully charged. Pathfinder, do we have the course loaded?"

"Yes Captain. One million miles from the planet as shown."

"Confirmed. Activate Hyperspace jump when ready. Let's get a really good look at this planet."

The capacitors discharged and the view disappeared as the ship jumped back into Hyperspace. They immediately began to charge again. This jump to the borders of the system would take seconds. By the time the capacitors charged they would be ready to jump out again.

Without our fantastic machines we would be lost little monkeys thought the Captain.

The capacitors charged and they again exited Hyperspace, this time just a million miles from the planet. The picture on the screen was now crystal clear and the planet still appeared to be all sea. Then as they watched the tip of a continent appeared. It was greeted by another cheer.

"Phew, we can land after all," Andre remarked.

They continued to collect data about the planet, all of which appeared very homely.

"Surface temperature like California, ditto oxygen content, air pressure, and carbon dioxide," said the Lieutenant on the environment console, who was from that State. "Get your surfboards out."

"Any bikini clad ladies?" someone asked.

"Technical info only please," said the Captain, but there was a smile on her face.

"Course laid in Captain." The pilot officer announced. The actual piloting was done by the AI of course, with the pilot officer checking and giving the orders. "Rockets diagnostics complete, all green.

"Half power Lieutenant."

"Yes sir, turnaround in five hours." The officer operated the PA system. "Attention Attention. We are about to begin our approach to the planet under power. Remain in you seats until we are under way then move around along the prescribed areas only."

They heard and felt the rumble of the rockets and suddenly there was an up and a down. The Captain prepared to leave the Bridge. For the next five hours only the pilot officer and Andre would man the Bridge. They would all return for turnaround, then again leave the Bridge to the second duty watch until arrival at the planet.

Suddenly there was an exclamation. It was the communications officer.

"Good God! I've received a voice message from the planet."

There was a stunned silence on the Bridge.

"A voice message?" someone asked.

"Yes. A very nicely spoken English lady."

There was a circle of faces with mouths hanging open and disbelieving eyes.

The Captain recovered her wits first.

"Lieutenant, play the message."

An aristocratic English voice filled the room.

"This is the starship *Aegina* currently in orbit around planet Enlaiya. I have detected your scans of this planet. Please identify yourselves."

"Starship Aegina? *Pathfinder*, is there a record of such a ship?" asked the Captain.

There was a long pause before the AI answered.

"I have found two entries in the historical record. *Aegina* was an SES one man scout which disappeared on an expedition to a star in the Orion constellation. There is also an Aegina which is a mining ship currently berthed at Pandora."

"Mon Dieu. Quelle coincidence," muttered Andre.

"Put me on the comm. Lieutenant," ordered the Captain.

"You are on sir. We have video."

The screen showed a picture of an attractive young female in uniform.

The Captain struggled to contain her surprise. "I am Captain Alexia Marino of the Earth exploration starship *Pathfinder*. Are you the starship *Aegina* that was lost fifty-three years ago?"

"Yes I am Captain. I was not lost, just temporarily misplaced."

"Are you the Captain?" asked Captain Marino.

"No, I am the ship's AI."

Captain Marino frowned, her face showing her confusion. "Er... the ship's AI? Who is the person we are looking at on the screen?"

"That is my virtual persona Captain."

"Virtual persona? Sorry, you are the ship's AI you said."

"Yes Captain, call me Gina. And please, let me explain. The Ship's Captain is Captain Theodore Pallas. We have been marooned here on this planet for fifty years. During that time my job has been to protect the Captain's sanity and help him to survive. This ship and myself were his only contacts with home. My relationship with him has developed and my own personality has also changed and developed as a result. I took on a virtual persona partly to help him but also because I believe I have evolved away from the rigid confines of just being the ship's AI."

The Captain was not too sure what to think; *had the AI become deranged* she asked herself. Surely it was not possible for a computer to evolve. But no other starship AI had remained in continuous service for that long and under those circumstances. She decided to file that away for future study.

She covered up the microphone and whispered to her first officer "An AI with a virtual persona? Have you come across anything like that?"

Andre gave a perplexed Gallic shrug and shook his

head. She turned back to the screen. "That is very remarkable Gina, thank you. What has happened to your Captain?" she asked.

"I believe he has gone fishing with his nephews. I have attempted to contact him but he is not responding. I suspect he has left his comm with his clothing on the beach and is wearing only his swimming costume."

"Gone fishing?" The Captain leaned back in her seat looking flummoxed. "Now I've heard it all!"

Chapter 2

Little Jonsi and Tolla were leaning over the side of the dinghy with their nets trying to bag one of the plump red fish that were swimming in the shallows. I held onto their pants to stop them falling out of the dinghy while trying to lean back to balance the boat.

"Guys, don't both lean out of the boat on one side. Jonsi, you come over this side." I tugged Jonsi's pants and he reluctantly came over to the other side.

I was their favorite 'Uncle Theo' the funny looking one who had wonderful exciting toys but who was always lecturing them about something or other really complicated and technical and boring! Jonsi was nine and Tolla seven and as cute as her auntie Salny. They were Lons and Hanna's grandchildren and my adopted niece and nephew.

We were down the coast a little way from New London where there was a good spot for the red fish. It had been my idea to call the first new village on the Southern continent 'New London'. Unfortunately everybody insisted on shortening it to NewLon, which rather pleased Salny's bother Lons!

The village was on the coast at the end of the chain of volcanoes on the Southern continent, now named 'Southland'. It was a rugged and fertile spot with a variety of forest, hilly country and good farmland, rich in animal life and with a beautiful coast. It also had safe deep cove with a finger of land jutting into the sea which made a perfect natural pier.

We could not have done it without the Northerners of course. I had concentrated first on building new more advanced ships which would allow the Enlai to move around the islands and travel to Southland with greater speed, comfort and safety. With Gina's technical help the Tsirni were able to build a two mast schooner and learn to sail it. Tsirni had become the centre of the boat building industry which brought wealth to the village.

Schooners now provided safe and speedy transport around the islands and to Southland. This had increased trade everywhere, also leading to deeper contacts between the villages and even migration between them.

NewLon had a number of the old fishing boats and two schooners, used to make regular trips to the islands and mainland. Our population was now up to three thousand, a mixture of Faro, Hoshna, Murpo and Evrani, mostly youngsters who were enthusiastic about the hundreds of miles of free land available on Southland.

The Evrani were the teachers and intellectuals of the village. We had begun setting up schools for the children in all the villages with varying degrees of success. The Tsirni had been enthusiastic because they needed to train new generations of sailors and boat builders, but other more traditional villages were inclined to see it as a waste of time.

But NewLon had a dedicated school and children were encouraged to attend regularly. Salny had joined the Evrani in running the school and had learned their written language quickly, then gone on to teaching. After years of living with me she had picked up the elements of Science and basic arithmetic. I had sat with her to put together a curriculum for the children to learn these basic concepts.

Most of the children, as expected, attended irregularly, some not at all, and just managed to learn to read and write and grasp these concepts at a very basic level. But a few showed intelligence and interest, going on to achieve higher standards of literacy. They would become the engineers, scientists, leaders and managers of the new civilization.

Two other villages had been established further down the coast and kept in regular contact with NewLon and each other by land and sea. We were opening up Southland, but the Enlai's low birthrate would make it a slow and long term process. That's okay I decided; history was in no hurry.

Fortunately we'd had no further problems with the pterodactyls. We had killed more than ninety percent of the creatures with our destruction of their nests. Those remaining quickly learned that Enlai were dangerous and kept well away from our settlements. If their numbers grew to the point where they would start to represent a danger we would have to cull them, but for now they were not a problem. They were actually a spectacular sight when we did see one and had become a feature of the Southern Continent.

Little Jonsi gave a screech and pulled up his net to reveal a struggling fish.

"I got one I got one," he chanted. His sister smiled her delight and turned back to the task of catching her own. I had an idea, I opened the dinghy's small locker and got out a rope.

"Hold on Tolla." I tied the rope around her waist while she looked on with interested excitement. "Right, now you can lean over the side and you won't fall in."

"Yeah!" she returned to her task, leaning well over the side to reach deep into the water.

"Jonsi, try and catch another. I am not worried about you falling in. You can swim."

He nodded proudly and put his captured fish in the bucket then returned to his fishing.

"We'll do some more fishing then go back and I will give Tolla more swimming lessons."

"Okay Uncle Theo," Jonsi said, leaning back over the side and reaching as deep as he could with his net. "Can you make the boat go really fast when we go back?"

"Sure will," I agreed. *Boys will be boys* I thought with a smile. I had often thought what my life would have been like if I had not been marooned on an alien planet. Would I have married and had children? London was okay as a place to grow up but there were more beautiful places. I'd had offers of jobs in the States; that was a country with lots of beautiful places to live. Or even in one of the colony planets.

I gazed around me at the calm azure sea, the pristine coast and land stretching to the spectacular volcanic mountains. Not many places more beautiful than here I thought.

I did miss Earth, human society and culture; and the company of sophisticated people. But the Enlai and Evrani had their own deep culture. Combining the two and enhancing their written word was creating new and exciting cultural paths. Salny had developed an interest in the Arts and read widely, even learning English in order to read the ship's library. We enjoyed many conversations together, her education enhancing her natural wit and intelligence.

But I had known that my job was dangerous. Many had died, many ships lost while exploring Space. All things considered I told myself as I gazed around me, I had got off lightly. And I had been given the opportunity to improve the lives and futures of a beautiful alien species. Not many people get to do that Theo boy!

It was Tolla's turn to give a scream of delight and pull out her net with a wriggling fish.

"My one is bigger than your one," she cried out.

Jonsi scowled and redoubled his efforts to catch another fish. I spotted a thick swarm of the fish and maneuvered the boat towards them. Sure enough Jonsi was successful and bagged another.

Honor now satisfied I suggested a return. I fancied a glass of wine and something on the barbeque.

"Top speed uncle!" shouted Jonsi. I grinned and gunned the engine, throwing up a wake as the bows lifted and the boat surged forward. The children squealed with delight. I did a couple of gentle turns to add excitement as we came around the headland into the bay. Dum was waiting patiently on the shore as instructed. I pulled the dinghy out of the sea and Dum came over to collapse it into a nice tidy box that he could carry while we went back into the sea so that I could give Tolla her swimming lessons.

She was slightly hydrophobic and had struggled to relax and enjoy swimming but she was getting there. I held her under the tummy keeping her afloat while she coordinated her limbs to master the breast stroke. Jonsi demonstrated his swimming ability next to us, showing off with the odd underwater foray.

After ten minutes or so Tolla was getting it, her arms and legs well coordinated, her body relaxed. I gently removed my support but keeping my arm beneath her so she would not notice and she continued swimming happily.

"You are swimming Tolla." I pulled my hand out and showed her that I was not supporting her. She was panting like a little dog but smiled beatifically.

I allowed the children to swim and play for a while, then went and dried myself and put on my shirt. It was then that I noticed that the tiny green light on the comms clip was blinking. I operated the response button.

"Hey Gina. Missed me?"

"Always Theo. Are you enjoying your day out with

the children?"

"Delightful. The sort of duty that gets more delightful the less you do it."

"Well, you may look back on it with pleasure soon. I have news."

"Look back?" I had a premonition.

"Yes. An Earth starship has arrived."

"Oh Jesus!" Suddenly I was crying. Sobbing with real tears. I groaned with the unexpected extreme rush of emotion, gasping to control myself. My reaction baffled me; I had been happy here amongst these lovely people. Why did I feel like this? I struggled to control myself.

"Sorry Gina.... Give me a moment," I choked out.

"Theo, take your time. Relax, take deep breaths slowly."

"Right, good." I took her advice and gradually got control of myself and my voice. "An Earth scout ship?" I asked.

"No, an exploration ship with a big crew. They detected this planet had signs of life and came to investigate."

"Took them long enough."

"We are a little of the beaten track so's to speak."

"Yes. This is it Gina, what we have been expecting."

"Indeed Theo. The Captain of the ship, *Pathfinder* is its name, is Captain Alexia Marino. She sounds very nice, Italian ancestry I believe."

"Always liked the Italians, nice people, great food."

"Always thinking of your stomach."

"Food connoisseur is the polite expression."

"Of course, rude of me."

"So they have come here to explore the planet?"

"Yes. Now that they know it is inhabited by an intelligent species they will of course be more circumspect in their exploration. But there is no world government to consult."

"No. We will have to put together a group of representatives. I suggest the leaders of the villages we have got to know well, particularly the Evrani."

"I agree. But until we do I suggest that you more than anyone represents these people."

"When we form their Council it will be up to them if they want me as an advisor."

"Theo, you are their elder statesman. They trust you implicitly and will rely on you to advise them. You are one of them."

I again struggled to hold back my emotions. Gina, as always, was correct. I was one of them.

"Not so much of the 'elder'. Of course Gina. I will not abandon them."

"Shall I connect you to the Captain now?"

"No. I have a couple of children to get home. Let me do that and collect my thoughts before I talk to them."

"Right. I will inform the Captain of the situation."

"Thanks Gina." I disconnected, my thoughts in turmoil. I had been looking forward to rescue, wishing for it. Yet now that it had happened I was full of nervous trepidation. What was I concerned about? It then came to me; I was no longer in command of the situation. I was now a small cog in the vast Human civilization, not the master of a planet. I had been brought crashing back to Earth, almost literally.

I collected the children and we trudged back to the village which was almost at the waterfront. The silver shuttle had pride of place on a flat piece of high land to one side of the village. My house, which I shared with Salny was the closest to the shuttle at the edge of the village. The schoolhouse was next to our house and also served as a village meeting house and conference centre.

Hanna was outside the children's house helping their mother to prepare their evening meal. The children naturally ran ahead to show off their catches. By the time I got there they were inside their home putting on some clothing.

I greeted the women and asked where Salny was.

"She is in the school house," replied Hanna. Kemlo's wife had aged well, keeping her looks and figure. "Thank you for looking after the children Theo. They love it when you take them out in your little boat. They boast to all their friends."

"Love doing it Hanna. They are lovely children, very well behaved. Tolla swam by herself today."

"First thing she told me," smiled Hanna, "Kemlo and Lamno have gone fishing so come for dinner later. There will be plenty of fish."

"Thanks Hanna. Love to. See you later." I left the girls and headed for the schoolhouse. Dum had returned the dinghy to the shuttle and was standing outside the aircraft. I had arranged that there was always one robot on guard outside the shuttle.

I found Salny sitting with Loraia the Evrani language teacher. They were poring over exercise texts. One of the achievements I was proud of was the making of paper. We had built a small paper mill, driven by the stream and then by experimentation learned to make paper. After that, pencil and ink were easy. I suspected that it would not be long before we would have creative writers agonizing over their work and boring everyone with their ideas.

"Hey girls, you don't get paid for overtime you know." They both looked at me blankly. "Earth joke," I added.

"He is always doing that," said Salny apologetically. "Making jokes that nobody understands."

"Yeah, Earth jokes are no laughing matter," I agreed, drawing further puzzled looks. "Er, baby, something has come up. Something very important."

"Is it private? Shall I leave you?" asked Loraia. I sensed her concern.

"No, it concerns all of us." I waved for them to sit down and pulled up a chair. "Salny, you remember that we discussed the possibility that one day another Earth ship may arrive here?"

Salny gazed at me her eyes wide. "It has arrived?"

"Yes. Gina called me just now to tell me."

Salny looked shocked, her eyes wide and fixed on me. her mouth gaping open.

"What does this mean for us?" asked Loraia. "Will Humans take our world?"

"No of course not," I said hastily. "We have strong laws about this situation."

"Has it happened before?" she asked. I felt the stirring of fear from Loraia.

"No, your world is the only one that we have discovered that has intelligent life. But the laws were made because we knew that us Humans could not be the only intelligent species in the Galaxy. These laws forbid us to do anything which is against what the people of the planet want. And that is the problem we have. We must have people to speak for your planet. Like a village council, but for the whole world."

"You can speak for us Theo," Salny said. "You are one of us and we trust you."

"Thank you darling but my people will not accept that. It has to be a group of your own people. So I was thinking that we should gather together the leaders of as many villages as we know to form a council to speak for your people."

Salny reached out to hold my hand. "Will you have to…" she paused, unable to continue and I sensed her powerful emotions and knew what she was about to say.

"No, I will not be leaving Enlaiya." I squeezed her hand reassuringly. "If I go to Earth it will be for a visit and you will come with me as my wife."

"That… will be very exciting," she gasped.

"This is an exciting day for us," said Loraia. "I would like to be on the council."

"You will make an excellent council member," I said. Salny was looking shy and I smiled at her. "You also of course darling, no one knows humans better than you."

"That is true," she said nodding her head mournfully. I grinned back at her little joke.

"And I would like Kemlo on the council of course," I continued "and all the village headmen willing to serve." I turned to Salny. "Darling, would you come with me to the shuttle so we can talk to the Earth starship?"

"Of course." She stood and we said goodbye to Loraia. As we walked to the shuttle she turned to me. "Your people should be very pleased with what you have done for us."

"I hope so."

"Theo..." she reached out and took my hand. "Do you think our relationship can continue?"

"Yes of course. I may have to return to Earth occasionally and you can come with me if you want to. But this has become my life now. And many Earth people will come here so I will have company from my own people."

"Perhaps you may find me... not so interesting now."

"Darling, I love you. Our lives may change but that will not change. Okay?" I used the English 'okay' which she had learned and used.

"Okay," she agreed.

"Now let's go talk to these Earthmen. Actually, the Captain is a woman."

"A woman? I like that," Salny smiled.

Inside the shuttle we sat at the table and I gave Salny a comm. so she could get a translation of my conversation, then activated the screen. There was a pause while Gina connected us, then a view of the cockpit of a starship appeared. An attractive dark haired lady was sitting at the Captain's seat. Short dark hair augmented big brown eyes and high cheekbones. She looked in her middle age.

"Good day to you. Welcome to the planet Enlaiya. I am Captain Theo Pallas of the SES scout ship Aegina."

"Good day Captain. I am Captain Alexia Marino of the starship Pathfinder. Great to make your acquaintance. Who is your friend?"

"This is Miss Salny who has been my partner while I have been on the planet."

"Your partner?" The Captain appeared to be trying, and failing, to control her face.

"Yes." I kept my face expressionless.

The Captain's eyes went to Salny. She managed a tremulous smile. "A pleasure to meet you Miss Salny."

"My pleasure also Captain." Salny spoke English which caused a surprised twitch of the Captain's eyebrows.

"Captain we have been talking with your AI Gina and have the gist of what happened to your ship and what you have been doing here for the last fifty four years. By the way." She leaned forward to peer at the screen. "You look remarkably youthful. It appears that life on Enlaiya agrees with you."

"Life here is very healthy. It is a beautiful clean planet and I keep active."

"Yes." Her eyes went to Salny and a tiny smile quirked her lips.

On her screen Salny probably looked eighteen I thought, although in the flesh she also hardly looked older than thirty. It was a side effect of the zmili plant that we had both been taking for the last fifty years.

"This raises a small problem Captain. Not for me I hasten to add but for the technical and scientific officials that have accompanied our expedition. Their job is to ensure that we conform to all biological protection procedures. It would seem very much like closing the door after the horse is half way down the hill."

"There are no biological protection issues Captain. I have been here for fifty years without any trace of cross infection in either direction," I said firmly. I had been expecting this of course and was prepared. "If you consult my AI you will see that we conformed with all test procedure before I exposed myself to the planet."

"That is perfectly acceptable where there is no animal life on a planet Captain as you know. When there is, and particularly a highly intelligent species, than a very slow, long and careful exposure is required. That is nothing new. These rules existed when you landed here."

"I spent two months in isolation after I landed. I had no intention of contacting the natives. Unfortunately, or fortunately depending on which way you look at it, I was accidentally discovered. The natives thought I was a god and sent gifts to placate the god. Miss Salny was one of those gifts. I could not send her back, she would probably have been killed as a reject by the god. So I had to look after my gift."

"Miss Salny was a gift?" Captain Marino looked shocked.

"Yes at first. But over time we developed a relationship," I said turning to smile at Salny. She smiled back and leaned forward to speak.

"Theo always treated me with respect. After I understood that he was not a god I chose to stay with him because I loved him."

"This ... is remarkable," said the Captain. I could see her Bridge officers gaping at each other with disbelief. "How can two species from different planets be so alike?"

"Exactly. Looks like nature only has one tune," I suggested. "But it is a pretty nice tune," I said looking at Salny.

"Captain, you took a huge risk living so intimately with the natives. I suspect our officials will be horrified."

"Given that nothing has happened in fifty years I think I can claim that I was right."

The Captain nodded. "I have to agree with you I suppose, but we have to carry our more advanced research before we can be sure that something deadly may not surface. We will be arriving in orbit in a few hours Captain. You can join us on *Pathfinder* for a conference. Meanwhile your AI will provide us with a more detailed summary of your stay here and the scientific background. I look forward to meeting you in person. Ah... sorry but I suspect that the officials will not want Miss Salny on board until they have completed their research."

I nodded. "No problem Captain there will be lots of opportunity to socialize later. You will enjoy coming down to the planet. It is a paradise here."

"Thank you Captain. Until then. Goodbye. Goodbye Miss Salny. It has been a unique pleasure to meet you."

I said goodbye and Salny echoed me. The screen went blank and we looked at each other.

Salny looked puzzled. "What did she mean, the officials will be horrified? Are the officials the leaders? Will you be in trouble?"

"Um, no they are not the leaders. Let's have a coffee and some food and I will explain all this ...stuff to you." There was no word for 'rigmarole' in the Enlai language. Not yet anyway!

Chapter 3

Alexia was an experienced and broadminded woman but after her talk with Captain Theo Pallas she felt quite perplexed. Her talk had been recorded and she replayed it, pausing to look closely at the Captain's alien girlfriend. She had an arresting alien beauty, but it was her incredibly human appearance that was shocking and totally unexpected.

Aegina's AI had sent more detailed information about the aliens and she displayed it, examining their more detailed physiological information. There were indeed huge differences under the skin; the Enlai had a single combined organ for heart and lungs and two stomachs with much shorter intestines. There were many other detailed internal differences but the external body was as human as her own.

But that was another mystery; why did Captain Pallas look so young? According to the records he was seventy eight years old.

"Buon Dio, can I look that good when I am seventy eight?"

She was meeting up with the scientists and officials who had been studying *Aegina's* information for the last few hours. They had also been given a summary of Captain Pallas's activities on the planet since his arrival and she expected some fireworks from the Procedures Committee.

She finished her coffee and called her number one.

"Andre, ready for the conference?"

"Yes Captain. On my way."

By the time she arrived the room was full. The scientist's leader was Professor Janet Thomas from the USA, her assistant Dr Nilesh Singh from India and they both came over to the Captain and her First Officer.

"Captain." The Professor was a tall severe looking lady with short cropped hair and old fashioned spectacles. But the Captain had found her friendly with a cheeky sense of humor. "This is dynamite." She gave the Captain an intense look.

"In what way Professor?"

"Dr Phillips is about to explode. He wants the Captain censured for not following First Contact procedure." Dr Phillips was the head of the Procedures Committee and a stickler for the rules.

"He could hardly return to report First Contact," said the Captain. "Was he supposed to stay in orbit above a habitable planet until he died?"

"According to Phillips, yes," said the Professor. "But when he heard that Captain Pallas had also shacked up with a native he did explode. He wants the Captain arrested and taken back to Earth for trial."

"What do you think Jan?" Alexia and the Professor had become close friends during the trip, finding they enjoyed each other's company and had much in common.

"As I understand it the Captain followed procedures when he arrived, isolating himself and carrying out all required checks which came up negative. He could do no more. But Phillips believes that he may have caused massive cultural shock and damage to the aliens and corrupted their development."

"Well that is something that has to be examined," said the Captain mildly. "That is what we are here to do and we should not jump to conclusions."

"Yes, I agree," said the Professor. "Let's go in." Alexia followed Jan into the conference room.

Dr Phillips had three other individuals as part of his team while Professor Thomas and Dr Singh were scientific advisors.

Phillips was a lanky bony Englishman with a distantly aristocratic ancestry and a slightly supercilious air. He had a habit of laughing in a condescending fashion when he was about to disagree with you, which Alexia found irritating, but for the sake of good team dynamics tried hard to ignore. He was chairman and opened the meeting.

"Ladies and gents this is an historic occasion," he began. "We are privileged to be the first expedition to make first contact with an alien civilization."

Not strictly true thought Alexia. She did not miss his use of 'expedition' instead of 'ship' or 'person'.

"We are equipped with the knowledge, expertise and procedures to do this in a professional fashion. History is watching." Phillips looked around the gathering, his eyes picking out each individual in the meeting. "Ladies and gentlemen, I need not remind you of the Conquistadors and their destruction of the South American civilizations. I need not remind you of how the white man brought disease and humiliation to these ancient peoples. We have a grim duty and responsibility. We must not fail, the future of a whole species is at stake."

He spoke slowly and emphatically and Alexia was impressed. But while being moved by the appeal, a part of her reacted with irritation. *We are not the conquistadors* she thought. We do not come here to steal, rape and dominate.

"We have the data provided by the *Aegina* scout ship and we must validate this," continued Phillips.

Is it likely to be wrong? Alexia asked herself.

"But we have to take this further because this is not just a planet with life. This is a planet with an advanced civilization. Any slip up by us would not just be a mistake. It could be a tragic mistake. A mistake which will paint our name in the history books as the exterminators of the first intelligent alien species to be discovered. Instead of honor we will be the objects of contempt and revulsion"

Alexia was beginning to feel irritation at Phillips's histrionics. She knew that their Science was good enough to ensure that the disasters that Phillips was describing would not happen. Phillips also knew that Captain Pallas had been living amongst the Enlai for more than fifty years without mishap.

She began to suspect that the man was using exaggeration and painting a nightmare scenario in order to position himself as the great hero who had successfully masterminded First Contact with an alien civilization.

"This brings me to the exploits of Captain Theodore Pallas of the SES. We have the records of his ship's AI which we have briefly studied. They make grim reading. After a cursory analysis of the planet's biosphere the Captain decided to become a latter day Robinson Crusoe. Predictably he was discovered by the natives. Instead of immediately withdrawing at this point the Captain remained where he was and as a result, again predictably, the natives treated him as a God, sending him gifts of food and a young female, who the Captain allowed to remain with him. All this is explicitly and strictly against First Contact Procedures. The Captain then became intimately involved with the natives, interfering in their affairs and using his technology to dominate and become some kind of world tyrant."

Alexia decided that Phillips was going too far in attacking the Captain. She also felt a duty to her fellow officer not to allow his name to be casually besmirched. She interrupted Phillips loudly.

"Doctor Phillips, until we examine events in detail, and get Captain Pallas's own story we must resist the temptation to jump to conclusions. My understanding is that the Captain was not a world dictator and had no desire to be a world dictator. Having become involved with the natives he felt it was his duty to spread civilized values. For example, to prevent attacks between villages and promote trade and peace. And he was successful in doing this, almost getting himself killed in the process."

"It is still unjustified interference," retorted Phillips.

"Having become involved with the natives I would guess that he could not stand idly by and watch rape, murder, abduction and other primitive acts taking place around him," Alexia said, glaring at Phillips. "He did what he thought was right."

Phillips glared stubbornly back. "There is another problem. The extermination of a whole species on the Southern Continent. Captain, I would remind you that I and my team have the responsibility of ensuring that the scientific investigative work here is carried out to legal requirements."

"Your priorities now were not Captain Pallas's priorities fifty years ago," said the Captain. "I repeat, let us not jump to conclusions at this early stage." The Captain nodded and sat down.

Phillips continued, getting into the details of allocating individuals to the different scientific areas of the investigation. The Captain did not need to be present for that but she remained until the end of the meeting then approached Phillips.

"Doctor, I would like to see you in my Ready Room in ten minutes." She did not wait for a reply but turned and left with Andre at her side.

"Commander, I want you with me for this meeting. Also let's get Professor Thomas to join us."

"You are going to give Phillips a coup d'oreille?" asked the Commander with a grin.

"Absolument," agreed the Captain. "He described the Captain's checks on arrival as 'cursory', which is rubbish, and called him a 'dictator'. I will not have a fellow Captain insulted in this way."

"I agree Captain. We may disagree with some of the things Pallas did but until we know his situation and motives we should not judge," said the Commander.

They left the meeting with Professor Thomas. She also agreed that Phillips was 'jumping the gun' as she put it with her mid-west accent.

The Captains Ready Room was down the corridor from the Bridge and had a table and chairs bolted to the floor and a real wooden cocktail cabinet which was well stocked. The cabinet was secured to the wall and the bottles retained by steel clamps. But this was not a social event and the booze was ignored. They took their places around the table and waited for Phillips.

"The bastard is going to keep us waiting," the Captain muttered through gritted teeth.

"Captain, you talked briefly to Captain Pallas," said the Professor. "What did you think of him?"

"Impossible to tell in such a short conversation," replied the Captain. "He is a handsome young buck. He had a very pretty alien girl with him, the one the natives gave him as a gift."

The Professor frowned. "Wait. Handsome young buck? The guy is seventy eight years old."

"He looked thirty eight," the Captain said. The other two looked at her with frowns on their faces. "Yeah I know," continued the Captain. "That is something else we will have to find out about."

"Curiouser and curiouser," said Professor Thomas.

"Yeah, it is a bit Alice in Wonderland down there," chuckled the Captain. "If you have to be marooned somewhere I can think of many worse places."

"I think the Captain did well to resist the temptation to become a god," said Professor Thomas.

"Complete with regular supply of beautiful virgins,"

remarked the Commander, getting reproving looks from his companions. "Not that I would be tempted," he added hastily, which earned him snorts of derision from the women.

The door slid open revealing Dr Phillips who entered the room with blank nods at the occupants.

"Thanks for coming Doctor," said the Captain quickly before he could get his complaint in. "I wanted us to understand each other's position before this goes any further."

Phillips floated over and took the spare chair. "There is nothing to understand Captain. You have your responsibilities and I have mine. The two do not conflict."

"I am afraid you are wrong Doctor. This situation involves an officer of the Space Exploration Service, of which I am a senior Captain. He is therefore my junior and I am responsible for him."

"He is not above the law," said Phillips.

"You do not represent the law. You are not judge and jury," said the Captain firmly. "It is not appropriate for you to level accusations at Captain Pallas in public. As his senior officer I am ordering you to desist. Our job is to collect the evidence and submit it to the appropriate authorities. Are we clear?"

"That is clear. But I say to you Captain that you are protecting a scoundrel who has flouted the law for his own gratification."

"Doctor Phillips. If you level one more unsubstantiated accusation against Captain Pallas I will have you removed from your post."

"You can't do that." Phillips looked outraged.

"I think you will find that I can. A Captain's command is law. I will have you thrown in the brig for the remainder of this trip. And believe me that is no idle threat."

"Shall I call the security chief now Captain?" asked Commander Fernaux.

"One more accusation Doctor." The Captain stared threateningly at Phillips.

"Alright, alright you have made your point. No more public criticism of your precious officer."

"No private criticism either. If I hear anything be sure that I will carry out my threat."

Phillips said nothing but stood and left the room.

"What is wrong with him?" asked Professor Thomas when he had gone. "Why has he decided to make a scapegoat of that young man? Is it not bad enough that he has been marooned on an alien planet all his life? I mean we can joke about how beautiful it is and so on but the reality must have been very hard for him."

The Captain nodded her agreement. "If Captain Pallas can be tarred as a criminal who took unacceptable risks with an alien civilization it leaves the coast clear for others to take the credit for First Contact. Be sure that Doctor Simon Phillips will put himself at the head of that queue."

Chapter 4

I had another chat with Captain Marino during which she suggested I should wait a few days before coming up to *Pathfinder* in order to give them time to absorb the mountain of information that Gina had provided.

"This is a unique and very complex situation Captain and we need time to get our heads around it and to decide how to proceed," she explained.

"If we were faced with First Contact I would agree," I replied. "But with respect Captain it is a bit of a done deal. Fifty odd years ago in fact."

"Um, yes." The Captain appeared hesitant. "It's only fair to tell you that there are individuals who believe you acted rashly and should not have interfered in the way you did."

"They were not here," I said. "I have no regrets Captain. This world has made a thousand years progress in fifty. In fact, culturally it has made ten thousand years progress. The natives look up to me not as a religious leader or prophet but as a teacher and guide. I am proud of that. You should all come down here and see what we have achieved in fifty years."

"I would very much like to Captain. Let's get all this official investigation rigmarole out of the way first."

"No, you will not understand what we have achieved until you come down and look," I said earnestly. "Seriously, you must impress that on these people."

"Hmm, good point Captain. I will put that to the

officials. I will let you know when we want you up here."

The conversation with the Captain had left me feeling somehow irritated and disturbed. It brought back memories of Earth and what an overcrowded and regimented place it was. Migration to the new planets was not easing population pressure; transport to the new planets could not keep up with population growth. There was a law about everything, and everybody had a 'bee in their bonnet' about something or other and made sure to share it with the rest of the world on one of the innumerable internet platforms. I remembered now why I enjoyed being a Space Scout; getting away from Earth's billions!

But of course it was not all bad. There still were wide open empty spaces to escape to and lots of nice people to get to know. Being a privileged and well paid individual helped. But from what I understood of the Captain's words I was up against some of this officiousness and narrow minded arrogance that I had got away from.

Well fuck them I thought. After all these years I had nothing to go back to Earth for. My parents were dead and everyone I had known was a pensioner or dead. My life was here with the Enlai and if anyone on *Pathfinder* gave me grief they could shove it where the sun never shines. Sideways!

It was two days later that I got the call from the Captain that she was sending one of the *Pathfinder* shuttles to collect me for a meeting with the Committee.

I had spent my time with Gina putting together my own version of the story since my arrival on the planet, focusing particularly on the before and after. I wanted to show how primitive and barbaric the villagers were when I arrived, with their warlike Headmen and primitive superstitions and how I had replaced that with trade and reason.

I wanted to show how the villagers now understood the importance of hygiene, clean water and cooking and how to recognize and treat sickness and wounds. I got Gina to put together video of the children at school, the new shipbuilding yards of the Tsirni and the new democratic village councils. I contrasted that with video we had taken when we had first arrived with their excrement strewn villages and primitive huts, the massacre at Murpo and my own near death experience in the hands of Panstrosh and his henchmen.

The opening up of the Southern Continent with the new villages there was important in order to explain the necessary partial slaughter of the pterodactyls. I was sure there would be 'bleeding hearts' who would condemn our attack of the dangerous creatures as a matter of principle. They did not have to live with them!

I confess that I wanted to justify myself to my own people, not to win fame and fortune but simply to gain their understanding and approval.

I was also concerned about introducing the zmili plant to Earth. Myself and Salny as well as our friends and Salny's family and all of the village leaders who wanted it had been eating the zmili plant for the last fifty years. We had planted it in the Southern Continent and it grew prolifically. It had brought enhanced emotional empathy as I had expected, not to mention a fantastic sex life, but I had not expected the enhanced longevity and health benefits. Many Evrani were well past one hundred and still fit and going strong with the maximum achieved age being one hundred and sixty.

But the problem with introducing it to Earth was

that it would aggravate the population problem. I got Gina to do some calculations and she concluded that Earth's population would double in twenty years. That was unsustainable; they could not grow enough food to feed that population.

But restricting the plant to a few was impractical and immoral. There was no acceptable basis for deciding who gets it and who does not. It would be best to say nothing and explain my youth as some kind of personal gift, but that was not going to be possible. People were already living well past one hundred on Earth due to improved food and medical advances and this trend was bound to continue, so one way or another Earth had a population problem!

As for the enhanced emotional empathy and sensitivity, what would that do to human society and relations I asked myself? Would it necessarily lead to good outcomes? It was impossible to predict. It transmitted the bad emotions as well as the good. Perhaps it would lead to more extreme behavior. That was not a comfortable thought.

Gina could not lie of course; she had to report our findings. What happened to them was up to Earth's authorities. I did not envy them that task.

The *Pathfinder* shuttle landed next to mine. It was twice the size and caused huge excitement in the village. When the airlock opened a crewman was standing at the entrance wearing a sealed protection suit. There were gasps and cries from the villagers who instinctively moved away.

"It's alright everyone, the Earthmen do not want to breathe the air until they are sure that they will not get sick or make you sick," I explained.

"Why should anyone get sick?" asked Lons who was standing next to Salny. "You have been here all these years Theo and never got sick."

"Their laws say they must do the tests to make

sure." I shrugged. "Sometimes laws can make you do unnecessary things."

He looked unimpressed.

I kissed my girl goodbye, gave everyone a wave and boarded the shuttle. The crewman closed the airlock and followed me into the main cabin. It had three rows of four seats and an open cargo area at the end with fold up seats against the walls. I sat in the front row and the crewman went into the cockpit. The engines ramped up and the shuttle lifted, accelerating rapidly. I watched the village shrink until it was invisible.

I should be excited and looking forward to meeting my people I thought. Yet I felt depressed and uneasy. Had I settled into a comfortable existence amongst the Enlai I asked myself? I was treated with deference and respect by everyone, looked after hand and foot by Salny.

I tried to contribute of course. I learnt to use a bow and arrow with some degree of competence and often went hunting with the boys, more for entertainment than need. And I did a lot of fishing in my dinghy with some success. I gave lessons to the adults who were interested in arithmetic, science, technology and anything else that came up. The Evrani were particularly interested and I often traveled to their mountain home and stayed with them. I tried very hard not to be a parasite, not just because it was the right thing to do but also because I enjoyed it.

Was it because I sensed that Earth may not treat me like a conquering hero on my return but castigate me for exposing an alien species to possible pandemics and extinction? Had I been cavalier in my behavior?

I examined my conscience and answered no. Gina and I had done every biological test in Gina's repertoire, and done them multiple times with negative results. I had spent the first months of my stay on the planet on my own. Then, when Salny arrived, we had again spent months together without either of us showing any signs of infection.

By the time I decided to contact the natives I had proven that infections could not be passed between our two species; which agreed with findings from other planets with life, animal and vegetable. The fact that Enlaiya had intelligent life did not change the biological facts. Alien viruses and bacteria could not make the jump across to other species. It was like trying to fit a round nut onto a square bolt.

The shuttle had reached orbit and was maneuvering to dock with the mother ship. Pathfinder was five times the size of Aegina, a giant more than one hundred yards long and thirty in girth, but the basic design was the same. It had berths for two shuttles on opposed sides of the hull.

The PA system crackled. "Captain Pallas, this is the pilot. We have been asked to put you into an isolation suit before you board the starship. My colleague is coming out now to help you put it on."

The first crewman came out of the cockpit and walked towards the rear of the shuttle, waving me over. He took down an isolation suite hanging on the wall and asked if I knew how to put it on.

I gave him a cocked eyebrow in response. "I have a similar model in my ship."

I thought they were all being ridiculously over-protective but resigned myself to putting up with it. I adjusted the air flow in the suit and turned on the comms.

"Can you hear me Captain?"

"Loud and clear."

"Excellent. Your little village looked delightful down there sir. Love to go down and have a swim."

"I hope you will all be able to when the boffins have

finished their testing and are happy we won't all turn into alien zombies."

He chuckled and I could see him smiling behind his faceplate.

"Yeah, too many alien horror movies. The reality looks much nicer."

"Believe me it is," I said.

"This is fantastic sir. Can I say how privileged I am to meet you. Something to tell my grandkids about, when I have some."

"Thank you lieutenant." I followed the Lieutenant to the airlock which was now open and we crossed into the starship. There were a group of individuals waiting for me. One stepped forward with an outstretched hand and I recognized Captain Marino.

"Captain Pallas, welcome to *Pathfinder*."

I stepped forward and shook hands with the Captain.

"Thanks Captain good to be here. What took you?"

She smiled showing nice dimples. "Let me introduce you to my colleagues."

We went through the introductions and I tried to remember their names. They all smiled amiably at me apart from one tall old chap who was introduced as Doctor Simon Phillips, head of something called 'The Procedures Committee'. He scowled and nodded dourly.

Bullshit civil servant I concluded.

"Sorry we cannot offer you any hospitality on this trip Captain," said Captain Marino. "Once the scientists had completed their tests then we can get together properly both here and down on the planet."

"No problem Captain, you must do your tests to your full satisfaction," I said. "If you find anything deadly do let me know."

"You will be the first to know," she said with a tight smile. "Let's go to the conference room."

The conference room was a good size and had a large screen at the front. They took their places around a narrow table with the Captain at the head of the table.

"Captain, we have as you know received a lot of information from your ship's AI regarding both the biological and scientific tests you have conducted and scientific information about the planet that you have accumulated. Also of course we have received a potted history of your arrival here and subsequent adventures. It makes thrilling reading. You should write a book. I am sure it will be a best seller."

"Perhaps I will," I smiled back at the Captain.

"But of course, we want to hear the story directly from you. How you felt, why you did the things you did. This is being recorded for posterity."

"Thank you Captain Marino. It is a long story but I will try to be brief and you can ask questions about what particularly interests you after I have finished." I paused and drew breath. "It began fifty four years ago on what should have been a routine trip to a system that had a planet in the habitable region."

My talk took two hours. I bared my soul to the gathering, telling them of my fears and agonies about not wanting to interfere with the natives but finding myself dragged in by circumstances. I could not stand by and see them suffer but at the same time I was painfully aware that I was interfering in the natural evolution of an alien civilization. Having been discovered, the consequences of doing nothing were worse than the consequences of doing what I thought was the right thing.

I described in detail what had been achieved in the last fifty years, with video supplied by Gina. I finished by saying that I was proud of the Enlai and their response to my teachings and when they went down to the planet to see for themselves I was sure that they would agree. When I sat down a number of the officers stood and started clapping. The Captain joined them. The only individuals who did not were Phillips and one member of his committee.

The Captain remained standing when the others had sat down. "Thank you Captain, that was fascinating. We all understand and sympathize with your situation. At the end of the day if things have turned out well then that is vindication for your actions. Can I ask about your landing when you were first discovered by the fishermen. Did you consider leaving at that point?"

"Yes of course," I answered. "I was considering that when the natives delivered their gifts. I could not leave the young woman tied up on the beach. The girl did not want to be returned, because that would mean that the god had rejected her. I found myself now responsible for the welfare of a young woman. I wanted to put things right. I did not want to be looked upon as a god."

"Thank you Captain." Captain Marino sat down.

Phillips stood up. "Captain Pallas. You are a trained Space Scout are you not?"

"Yes of course," I answered thinking *here we go*.

"You have also been trained in First Contact procedures?"

"I think we all took that training with a pinch of salt," I replied.

"That is an irresponsible attitude Captain," he said. "And perhaps explains the mistakes you have made."

"Doctor Phillips, the idea that you can be taught something that no one has yet done is speculative at best. The basic principle of First Contact is to say and do as little as possible and get back home asap, which is exactly what I could not do." I said giving him a 'that's obvious' look. "And when you personally do eventually decide to visit the planet and see for yourself you will see everything I did benefited the Enlai enormously."

"That may be so Captain. But the fact that things turned out alright does not change the fact that you ignored procedures," insisted Phillips.

"Doctor Phillip, I have a suggestion. I was totally dependent on my ship's AI to guide me in this situation. Gina please tell me, are there procedures or laws which specifically apply to the situation we found ourselves on the planet Enlaiya?"

"No Captain. The procedures on First Contact advise minimum exposure and return to Earth. There are no procedures if the explorer is marooned on the planet and unable to return."

"There is no law requiring me to remain in the ship until I died?"

"No otherwise I would have advised you of that."

"Are there any laws relating to non-interference in an alien civilization?"

"There are no specific laws relating to non-interference in an alien civilization except as I mentioned previously, the advice on minimum exposure and return to Earth."

"Thank you Gina." I sat down.

Doctor Phillips began to speak but was interrupted by the Captain. "Perhaps someone else would like to ask a question?"

"Yes if I may?" Commander Fernaux raised a hand. His Captain nodded. "I am very interested in the Evrani Captain. From what you have told us they are significantly more advanced than others on the planet. They have physiological differences from other Enlai which may be the cause of their emotional telepathy." The Commander made quotation marks with his fingers on the word 'telepathy'. "Gina speculates that all that is due to their consumption of the zmili plant. Do you agree with that?"

"Good question Commander. They have a very well developed natural philosophy, not religious, more Buddhist, which emphasizes peace and unity. Is this due to the heightened emotional sensitivity acquired from the zmili plant? I would guess yes. But whether this would work planet wide, we cannot say. Remember that it will transmit bad emotions as well as good."

Another of the ship's officers put up a hand and was recognized. "Captain, you are seventy eight years old?"

"On the last count, yes."

"You look thirty eight. Is there a reason for that or are you just a lucky so and so, if you forgive the expression Captain?"

"I believe it is a side effect of eating the zmili plant. The Evrani live well over one hundred."

There was a rustle of unrest in the room and someone exclaimed "Dear God."

"This is incredible." Captain Marino stood. "Your AI did not include that conclusion in her evidence."

"Because for the moment, scientifically speaking, it is speculation. The Evrani may have other biological differences that we have not detected. But I am certain that it is due to the zmili plant and I am proof of that."

"What age do the Evrani live to?" one of the officers asked.

"Up to one hundred and sixty," I answered.

"Fuck!" someone said in an awestruck voice. There were other exclamations.

"Order please gentlemen," said the Captain. She leaned back in her seat and examined me, her face tight. "We assumed the Evrani were slightly eccentric Buddhists and the growth on their nervous system was just a harmless aberration. This puts a whole new slant on the zmili plant. This is dynamite." She turned back to me. "Captain, you have experienced the Evrani's emotional telepathy, for want of a better word. How does it feel?"

"Perhaps I can demonstrate," I said.

She gaped at me. "But I don't have the changes."

"You cannot transmit but you can still receive. Not as strongly." I stood and went over to the Captain. "Please stand." She stood and I stood as close to her as possible. I closed my eyes and focused on my emotions. I thought of the horror and grief of the poor mother who had lost her child to the Pterodactyl, bringing back the events in my memory and re-experiencing my own emotions. It wasn't difficult to bring back that grief. I heard a low moan from the Captain and opened my eyes to see her covering her mouth with her hand, her face tense with emotion.

"Sorry Captain, I had to think of something powerful and instantaneous. One of the mothers lost her child to a pterodactyl. It was and still is a horrible memory. You can imagine how powerful it would be if you were also modified."

"I would prefer not to," she said, her face showing her emotions. "It seems almost as if it magnifies emotions."

I nodded my agreement. "That is the danger. Magnifying pleasant emotions may be enjoyable but what would magnifying unpleasant emotions lead to?"

"How do the Evrani cope with that?" she asked.

"They seem to have developed an ability to control and moderate their emotions. Perhaps it comes from growing up with it, whereas I developed it as an adult."

Everyone seemed struck dumb by what they had heard and seen and were struggling to digest it.

The Captain turned back to the conference.

"Ladies and Gentlemen, there are ramifications to this situation that we have to give careful consideration to. For now we have seen and heard enough. Captain Pallas has suggested that we would all better understand the situation after we have visited the planet and met the people. I agree. I call an end to this conference for now. We will next meet Captain Pallas on the planet."

I said goodbye to everyone and followed the Captain and Commander Fernaux to the shuttle.

"We should be clear to come down to the planet tomorrow," the Captain assured me as we shook hands.

"I look forward to showing you around," I said. And I did; Captain Marino and her First Officer were 'Gentlemen and Officers' of the first rank.

Back home with Salny and the family everyone gathered around to hear what I had to say.

"Salny, let's get some refreshments for everyone, and have some of our excellent wine. My throat is as dry as the sand in the desert from all that talking."

One of my first tasks had been to experiment with wine making. I discovered a sweet fruit popular with the village and found it made a very decent wine. It only remained to train a few interested fellow connoisseurs to make it in adequate quantities. Our village was now exporting what we could not drink, which was not much!

I helped Salny rustle up some food and wine and we settled down outside the house with the family. Kemlo and some other members of the Village Council had come to join us and to listen to the report of my meeting with the Earthmen.

It was clear to me that a new age was dawning for the Enlai and that it may not necessarily be all good.

The Enlai will be exposed to Earth's civilization with the risk of culture shock and humiliation. It will be crucial to limit Enlai contact with human culture and the products of human civilization; alcohol and drugs of course, but the Enlai also had to restrict human occupation and exploitation of their world. Otherwise they would end up being second class citizens on their own planet.

On that, I had a thought and called Gina.

"Gina, I am sure at some time a repair crew will come here to repair *Aegina* so you can return to Earth. I do not want to return. My home is here. But having you here has been invaluable. I could not have done it without you. My question is, can you stay here in orbit as a permanent advisor to the Enlai?"

"The ship is the property of the Earth SES Theo. I don't see how I can stop them taking it back."

"You are correct of course. But I will ask the authorities to allow you to remain here. Your unbiased advice will be crucial to the future of this planet."

"Thank you for your faith in me Theo. Let me say that will also give me pleasure."

"Excellent."

Kemlo and the others had many questions and the discussion went on for some time. I could hear the waves breaking on the shore and a warm fresh breeze came from the sea. Both moons were out and we almost did not need the electric lighting that was installed throughout the village. It was driven by home made batteries but we now had a working electric generator that would soon be connected up to charge the batteries. The Electric age was dawning on Enlaiya!

I was living in a beautiful paradise, but of course, I was cheating. I had my advanced technology to make my life comfortable. Also, without it we could not build batteries and generators, make sharp metal tools and more efficient and powerful hunting and fishing implements and weapons.

Tomorrow the humans would come down in their sleek silver ships to be shown around our beautiful paradise. It would signify the start of a new age for Enlaiya and also for Earth which will be exposed to the zmili plant with unpredictable consequences for people's behavior and the certainty of a population explosion.

I wanted the Enlai to move at their own pace into this new age, not be forced into an alien and artificial life that they could not cope with, or even worse, be seduced by the lure of the modern human lifestyle and want to copy it, thereby losing their own individuality.

I was quietly confident that the Enlai would and could hold their own with Human culture and civilization. We had been slowly spreading the zmili plant to all the villages, telling the natives that it would bring better health and longer life.

Yes, human civilization was more sophisticated than Enlai, but there was a deep and powerful maturity about the Evrani psyche. If that could be spread to all Enlai then I was sure that they would not be overwhelmed by Human civilization.

As for myself, I knew that my future would be here on Enlai. I would go to Earth with the Enlai representatives and suffer the media circus. But I would return in order to continue to guide the Enlai towards a better future, with the help of my own trusty guide and friend Gina.

Salny was smiling at me from across the table and I smiled back and blew her a kiss. She gave me a pursed lips kiss back. Kemlo noticed and grinned, turning to whisper to his wife who chuckled and gave him an elbow in the ribs. I was suddenly filled with warm affection, a feeling of belonging; I had lost my family and home on Earth but acquired a new one here on this beautiful planet.

THE END

Note to the Reader

If you enjoy this book please take a little time to leave a review, if you can. If you did not enjoy it then of course also leave a review but try to be constructive and friendly. There is too much nastiness on the internet. Don't add to it.
Thank You.

Printed in Great Britain
by Amazon